Andrey Platonov
THE RETURN
and Other Stories

Translated from the Russian by
Robert and Elizabeth Chandler
and Angela Livingstone

THE HARVILL PRESS
LONDON

First published in Great Britain in 1999 by The Harvill Press

4 6 8 9 7 5 3

Introduction © Robert Chandler, 1999
"Note on Translating Platonov" and "Note on the Peasant Hut"
© Anglea Livingstone, 1999
Translation © Robert and Elizabeth Chandler and Angela Livingstone, 1999

The Harvill Press
Random House, 20 Vauxhall Bridge Road
London SW1V 2SA

Addresses for companies within The Random House Group Limited can be found at:
www.randomhouse.co.uk/offices.htm

The Random House Group Limited supports The Forest Stewardship
Council (FSC®), the leading international forest certification organisation.
Our books carrying the FSC label are printed on FSC® certified paper.
FSC is the only forest certification scheme endorsed by the leading
environmental organisations, including Greenpeace. Our
paper procurement policy can be found at
www.randomhouse.co.uk/environment

Printed and bound in Great Britain by Clays Ltd, St Ives PLC

Random House UK Ltd Reg. No. 954009
www.randomhouse.co.uk/harvill

ISBN 1 86046 516 1

Designed and typeset in Adobe Caslon by Libanus Press, Marlborough, Wiltshire

CONTENTS

ACKNOWLEDGEMENTS

"The Motherland of Electricity" *Izbrannye proizvedeniya* (Khudozhestvennaya Literatura, Moscow, 1978)

"The Epifan Locks" *Vzyskanie pogibshikh* (Shkola Press, Moscow, 1995)

"Rubbish Wind" *Vzyskanie pogibshikh* (Shkola Press, Moscow, 1995)

"Lobskaya Hill" in: *Novoe literaturnoe obozrenie* No. 9 (1994) An earlier version of this English translation appeared first in *Grand Street*, No. 63 (1998) pp. 138–145

"The River Potudan" *Vzyskanie pogibshikh* (Shkola Press, Moscow, 1995)

"The Cow" *Vsya zhizn* (Patriot Press, Moscow, 1991)

"The Seventh Man" *Vsya zhizn* (Patriot Press, Moscow, 1991) An earlier version of this English translation appeared in *Partisan Review* (Fall, 1998)

"Nikita" *Vzyskanie pogibshikh* (Shkola Press, Moscow, 1995) An earlier version of this English translation appeared in *Glas, No.* 16, (1998), pp. 23–35

"The Return" *Vzyskanie pogibshikh* (Shkola Press, Moscow, 1995)

"Two Crumbs" in: "Kostyor", No. 6 (1968)

INTRODUCTION

Andrey Platonov's father, Platon Klimentov, was a metal worker and a self-taught inventor. It was in homage to him and to the Greek philosopher alike that Andrey, as a young writer, adopted the pseudonym *Platonov*. The eldest of eleven children, Andrey began work at the age of fifteen, also as a metal-worker and assistant engine-driver. A passionate, even fanatical believer in the new world to be constructed by Science and Socialism, he began publishing poems and articles in the Voronezh press in 1918, at the same time as beginning his studies in the electrical science department of the railway polytechnic. Whether he took part in active fighting during the Civil War is not entirely clear; we know that at one point he was attached to the Red Army as a journalist and sent to Novokhopersk, where he witnessed six changes of power in the course of a month.

Shocked by the terrible drought and famine of 1921, Platonov abandoned literature for work in land reclamation. His reasons would have been understood by Tolstoy: "being someone technically qualified," he wrote, "I was unable to continue to engage in contemplative work such as literature."[1] The first of the stories in this volume, "The Motherland of Electricity", is clearly based on his own experiences during the following years. Two sides of the young Platonov – the visionary poet and the practical engineer – are embodied in the two main characters: Zharyonov, the village-soviet chairman who speaks and writes letters in verse, and the engineer-narrator. The heart of this compassionate and humorous story lies in the conversation between the old peasant woman and the narrator. He tells her there is no point in praying to God for rain. She agrees, surprisingly, and continues:

> You're right – we cross ourselves in vain! What haven't I
> prayed about? I've prayed for my husband, I've prayed for

my children – and not one of them's been spared, they're all dead now. If I keep going, my dear, it's from habit – do you think I choose to live? My heart doesn't ask me, it breathes by itself, and my hand's just the same – it makes the sign of the cross by itself: God's our curse. [. . .] Don't think it's just God we bow down to – we're frightened by the wind and by the ice beneath our feet, and by downpours, by drought, by our neighbours, by passers-by, and we cross ourselves before all of them! Do you think we pray out of love? There isn't anything left of us to love with!

After parting from this old woman the narrator says wryly: "I decided to dedicate my life to her, because in youth it always seems that there is a great deal of life and that there will be enough of it to help every old woman."

* * *

"The Motherland of Electricity", written in 1926,[2] contains all the elements of the mature Platonov except tragedy. The next story, "The Epifan Locks", is unremittingly doom-laden; the hero is aware, almost from the first pages, of impending disaster, but can do nothing to avert it. Platonov's change of tone most probably reflects a crisis he underwent during the years 1926–27. Repeated problems with the security organs and with his colleagues in Tambov, where he was director of the land-reclamation bureau, appear to have set off some profound disillusion, perhaps to have reawoken doubts that Platonov had suppressed since witnessing the violence of the Civil War. In any case Platonov left Tambov and returned to Moscow to pursue a vocation as a writer. And it was during the next four years that he was to write much of his most important and subversive work.

"The Epifan Locks" is about an English engineer, Bertrand Perry, who is commissioned by Peter the Great to build an ambitious system of locks and canals. He is sentenced to death when the project fails; eventually – though this is not spelled out – he is strangled by a sadistic homosexual of an executioner. This complex story can perhaps best be understood in the light of a prescient article Platonov was to write several years later, "About Socialist Tragedy".[3] In this article Platonov insists, heretically, that neither socialism nor technology can alter the fundamentally tragic nature of life. At the same time, apparently contradicting himself, he insists that socialism *must* resolve the tragic encounter between man and nature.

> [Nature] is not great and is not abundant.[4] Or her disposition is so severe that she has never yielded her greatness and her abundance to anyone. This is a good thing; otherwise [. . .] we would long ago have got drunk on nature, we would have looted, squandered and devoured her to the bone. [. . .] The tragic encounter between man, armed with machine and heart, and the dialectic of nature must in our country be resolved through Socialism. But it must be understood that this task is an extremely serious one. Ancient life on the "surface" of nature was able to obtain what was essential to it from the waste products and excretions of elemental forces and substances. But we climb inside the world, and in return the world crushes us with an equivalent strength.[5]

"The Epifan Locks" is in some respects as autobiographical as "The Motherland of Electricity". Platonov had himself been in charge of projects not so very different from Perry's; by early 1926 he had apparently been responsible for the digging of 763 ponds and 331 wells, in addition to draining 2,400 acres of swamp land. [6] And he had himself received death-threats from colleagues during his months in Tambov; we can only guess at the reasons for this hostility – did Platonov upset the locals by being excessively zealous? – but it is clear that Platonov felt as alien and endangered there as Bertrand Perry in Epifan. Nor is the story any less relevant to the concerns of 1920s Russia for being set in the eighteenth century. Platonov was keenly aware of similarities between his own time and that of Peter the Great. He had even written newspaper articles about the possibility of improving communications in Central Russia through a programme of canal-building very similar to that abandoned by Peter.[7] But, as so often with Platonov, there is a gulf between the rationalist, positivist, utopian tone of the journalism and the deeper perspectives revealed by his fiction.

"The Epifan Locks" describes an arrogant attempt to force both nature herself, and the life of the people, into a different channel, to cajole nature and the people to yield more than they wish. At one level the story can be read as a warning: grand schemes thought up by ambitious rulers will fail unless they take into account the practical wisdom of the people. One of the finest sections of the story describes the tortuous journey from Petersburg to Epifan; it is as if Petersburg and Epifan represent different worlds, between which one can move only with difficulty. The work Perry does in Petersburg is clearly of a high calibre, and Platonov explicitly points out that he avoids "the reefs and shoals of theory"; nevertheless Perry is aghast when he first sees the Don: "In Saint Petersburg, on plans, [Peter's venture] had seemed clear and practicable, but now, in their noon passage towards the Don, it seemed devilish, arduous and overwhelming."

A second failure of communication is between Perry's reason and his feelings. While still in Petersburg, Perry learns that his fiancée has married another man. In his speechless fury he bites so tightly on his pipe that his gums start to bleed; metaphorically he castrates himself. This pipe appears to foreshadow a later pipe[8] with which the engineers – inadvertently, but with catastrophic results – pierce through the clay bed of Lake Ivan. Perry's "arithmetical reason" is defeated by both internal and external nature. The phrase "arithmetical reason" points to the significance of Perry's first names:[9] Bertrand – evidently after Bertrand Russell, the philosopher and mathematician; and Ramsay – after Ramsay MacDonald, England's first Labour Prime Minister. These two figures, both of whom had written critically on the Soviet Union, are seen by Platonov as representative of an exclusively intellectual understanding of the world and the inadequacies this entails.

A third failure of communication, or failed marriage, is between Perry and his fiancée in Newcastle. Perry's brother returns from Russia to his own fiancée, one of the German engineers marries a Russian, but Perry himself is unable to get close to a woman. His only intense relationships are with Peter the Great, by whom he is "charmed" while still in England, and with his homosexual executioner, into whose arms he falls at the very end of the story. A word used many times in the story is "abundant"; the opening paragraphs, in particular, vividly evoke the abundance of the natural world in Russia. Perry's own life and work, however, are sterile.

These various themes are brought together in a complex literary joke which may well have served as the original inspiration for the story.[10] A number of words are repeated almost obsessively throughout the story, but no image occurs so frequently as that of windows. This image not only serves, paradoxically, to heighten the general sense of claustrophobia, but is also a clear allusion to two of the most celebrated lines of Russian literature, words put by Pushkin into the mouth of Peter the Great: "Here we are destined by Nature to cut a window through into Europe." Perry hopes to become Peter's companion in his project of bringing enlightenment to Russia, but proves unable to let in any light, to open any window except the "well-window" at the bottom of Lake Ivan. It is while they are cleaning out this spring, to provide more water for the canals, that Perry's subordinates pierce through the bed of Lake Ivan and destroy the project's last window of hope. After he has been arrested, Perry experiences an unexplained moment of enlightenment – or *epiphany* – as he gazes from his prison window at the "lawless" stars. This epiphany is clearly linked, through a number of exact verbal repetitions, to a brutal enforcement in the last page of an untranslatable rhyme that has been lurking all along in the sub-text of the original. The most obvious rhyme for

Evropa, the Russian for "Europe", is *zhopa*, meaning "arse": in an unpublished poem Pushkin himself used this rhyme. Perry's punishment for his failure to open windows, to let in light, is to be sodomised, to have a window "cut through" into his arse.

The complexities and heretical aspects of "The Locks of Epifan" seem to have gone largely unnoticed at the time. The story furnished the title of Platonov's first volume, published in 1927, and received high praise from the influential Maxim Gorky. Platonov was to publish two more volumes of stories in the next two years, but was then to fall out of favour. The "lyrico-satirical"[11] long novel, *Chevengur*, about an attempt to establish a "City of the Sun", a Communist utopia in the steppe, was completed in 1927, but remained unpublished in Russia for sixty years. *The Foundation Pit*, a bleak fable about Stalin's drive towards collectivisation and industrialisation, was completed in 1930, but was also first published only during the years of *perestroika*. Both these works embody the painful conflict between Platonov's early utopianism and his awareness of the violence and suffering inflicted on Russia in the name of the construction of a new world. Other, slightly less subversive, stories were published, but then subjected to vicious criticism, apparently instigated by Stalin himself.

* * *

"Rubbish Wind", written in 1934, had to wait only thirty-two years for publication. This denunciation of Nazi Germany is perhaps the most horrifying of all Platonov's works. There are passages where I found myself having to read each sentence twice, so shocked that I thought I must have misunderstood something. The description of Lichtenberg's life in a rubbish-pit anticipates Samuel Beckett; his self-mutilation in an attempt to feed a dying woman is equally reminiscent of folk tale. All this, unsurprisingly, was too heady a brew for Soviet publishers – and for Maxim Gorky, to whom Platonov turned for support. Gorky replied: " . . . I have read your story – and it stunned me. You write strongly and vividly, but this, in the given instance, only underlines the unreality of the story's content, a content which borders on black delirium. I think it improbable that your story can be printed anywhere."[12] Gorky's response is interesting. He appears to have wished to protect himself from this story – whose power he clearly felt – by insisting on its unreality. The content does indeed "border on black delirium"; what Gorky chooses not to see is that this does not make the story any less real. Platonov has created an unforgettable image for "the black delirium" which, during the thirties, gripped both Germany and the Soviet Union. He has also created a work of art that is filled with a surprising beauty and vitality. Firstly, the intensity of Platonov's rage is itself life-giving. Secondly, the story presents us with an unforgettable image of the persistence of love amid a desolate world; in the final scene the hero is about to die, he looks more like an animal than a human being, and yet he acts with Christ-like love.

* * *

In 1920, Platonov attended the first All-Russian Congress of Proletarian Writers. In reply to a point in a questionnaire – "What literary movements do you belong to or sympathise with?" – Platonov wrote: "None, I have my own." This self-assessment is equally apt with regard to his political views. Much has been made of the idealistic and enthusiastic welcome given by Platonov to the Revolution. Nikolay Fyodorov, however, a nineteenth-century Christian philosopher greatly admired by Tolstoy, Dostoevsky and many other writers, seems always to have meant more to Platonov than Marx did. Platonov welcomed the Revolution in the hope that it might realise some of Fyodorov's utopian ideas. Many of Fyodorov's ideas – his vision of a breaking-down of the division between physical and intellectual work, his emphasis on the importance of remembering our dead forefathers, his extraordinary belief that humanity's most important scientific endeavour is to gather together, molecule by molecule if necessary, the remains of *all* the dead and then resurrect them – remained important to Platonov throughout his life. Even if he ceased to take these ideas literally, Platonov never ceased to argue with them or be inspired by them.

Platonov may never have been an orthodox Communist,[13] but it is still more mistaken to look on him as an anti-Communist. If *The Foundation Pit* and parts of *Chevengur* read like indictments of Soviet society, it would appear that Platonov delivered these indictments almost in spite of himself. In one of his letters to Maxim Gorky he expresses bewilderment that editors should say that *Chevengur* might be "understood as counter-revolutionary". [14] And, as he himself wrote in a draft ending to *The Foundation Pit*, "The author may have been mistaken in representing the death of Soviet society through the death of the little girl, but this mistake was occasioned only by excessive anxiety with regard to something loved, something whose loss is equivalent to the destruction not only of the entire past, but of the future as well."

It seems that Platonov took to heart the criticisms of his work in the late twenties and early thirties, that he genuinely tried to write in a more acceptable manner. It is not that he acted cynically, rather that he longed to be accepted by a world that, at some level, he still believed in. The remaining stories in this volume are examples of Platonov's attempts to simplify his style, to tone down his social criticism and to make his writing more accessible to the Soviet reader. None of this makes them in any way inferior to the earlier stories. The language is less distorted, less extraordinary, but it is in many ways more subtle. The unfinished draft of "Lobskaya Hill", first published in Russia only in 1994, is as perfectly written as anything in Platonov's oeuvre. A comment on these stories by Joseph Brodsky is suggestive: "[Platonov's] case could be regarded as that of Joyce in reverse: he produced his *Portrait of the Artist* and *Dubliners* after *Finnegans Wake* and *Ulysses*".[15] The fact that Platonov remained a great writer was not, however, of any help in his battles with the authorities. A volume of stories entitled *The River Potudan* was indeed published in 1937, but this was followed by the usual frenzy of criticism, and by the arrest of Platonov's fifteen-year-old son.

* * *

"The River Potudan " has been described by Mikhail Heller, the author of the first full-length study of Platonov, as "one of Platonov's finest works, one of the finest stories about love in Russian literature".[16] Platonov appears at this time, the height of Stalin's purges, to have sought salvation through a personal religion of love. In a letter to his wife he wrote: " . . . How good it is not only to love, but to believe in you as in God (with a capital letter), to have in you a personal religion of my own. [. . .] In the worship of the beloved lies the highest and most enduring love."[17] If I now add that the heroines of two other of Platonov's love stories are called "Aphrodite" and "Fro" (clearly intended as short for Aphrodite), and that the heroines of "The River Potudan" and "The Return" are both called "Lyubov" (the Russian for Love) or "Lyuba", the reader may imagine that Platonov has turned to writing stories for some Soviet equivalent of Mills & Boon. In fact the tone of "The River Potudan" is almost unremittingly bleak. The hero, Nikita, is impotent, apparently because he is afraid of hurting his beloved wife. His guilt and shame lead him to leave her. He spends several months as a down-and-out, mute and mindless, barely human; news of his wife's attempt to drown herself then leads him to return to her. The marriage is finally consummated, though without rapture and in the shadow of the fact that Lyuba may well be fatally ill. The mood of the final scene is finely balanced between triumph and tragedy. Both Nikita and Lyuba are unremarkable people, living ordinary lives, but there is a strangely epic quality to the story. Nikita, like Platonov himself, is a utopian idealist who finds it difficult to accept the world as it is. By normal standards he is anything but heroic; Platonov's achievement in this story is to reveal the depth of inarticulate heroism required of Nikita before he can accept love and the world.

The central themes of this story are reinforced through a number of remarkably subtle puns which we have been unable to reproduce in translation. One cluster of these puns centres around the word *pol*, meaning "sex" or "floor"; Nikita scrubs the floor to distract himself from his anxieties about sex. Another related word is *polye*, meaning field; the little animal that appears in Nikita's nightmare on the second page is both a "field" animal and a "sexual" animal. A still more important cluster of puns includes *utopaya*, meaning "drowning", *utopiya* meaning "utopia" and *(za)topit*, meaning "to heat" or "to kindle". The motif of drowning appears a number of times; Nikita has to be dissuaded by Lyuba from lying too long on top of the ice, he contemplates drowning himself in despair at his impotence, and Lyuba nearly succeeds in drowning herself. This pun, so unforced that it can easily pass unnoticed, suggests that all we can do in Utopia is drown there, that utopian longings are linked to the death wish, that they incapacitate us for the real world. And one of Nikita's defences against this potentially overwhelming force is to kindle the stove. *Potudan* itself is the name of a real river in the Voronezh region, but the word suggests "over there" or "over in the beyond". Nikita longs to escape to another world, a world where it is possible to love without occasioning hurt. It is intimated that this longing may be the result of some trauma undergone in the Civil War. When Nikita is feverish, his father asks, slightly surprisingly, if he was wounded anywhere in the war; Eric Naiman[18] has suggested that Nikita's answer, "nowhere", could be read as a calque from the Greek *ou-topos*, meaning *no-place*, from which the word *utopia* is itself derived. According to this reading Nikita's utopianism might itself be a war-wound; some trauma has made Nikita wish to escape the real world, and this has the effect of rendering him impotent. But, as we have seen, the story ends on a note of muted triumph. Once again, this reading is confirmed by word-play. Spelt backwards – and there are other instances of metathesis both in the titles of Platonov's works and in the names of his characters – "Potudan" reads *nad-utop*, which is close to the Russian for *above utopia*; Nikita is the first of Platonov's heroes to conquer his utopian longings rather than be drowned by them.

* * *

Between 1936 and 1946 Platonov wrote a number of fine stories about children. These were mostly published at the time and received at least some praise from contemporary critics. More recently, however, they have been somewhat neglected; critics tend to dismiss them as attempts on Platonov's part to placate the authorities by finding uncontroversial subject-matter. Many of these stories, however, are in fact extremely subtle. "Nikita" is so simple that it can be taken for a "children's story" rather than a story about a child; in its quiet way, however, it is as powerful an evocation of isolation and terror as "Rubbish Wind". A product of Platonov's most mature period, it also presents a rare example of a successful resolution to a problem that is central to his earlier work: the lack of any real connection between father and son and the son's resulting alienation from the realm of meaningful work.

"The Cow" is a wry meditation on the title of an essay the hero has to write at school: "How I will live and work in order to be of service to our Motherland." Platonov, as I have said, had always wanted to find a place for himself in Soviet society; more than that, he longed to be of service to it. According to an OGPU dossier,[19] Platonov said after being criticised for his story "For Future Use": "I don't care what others say. I wrote that story for one person (for comrade Stalin), he read the tale and in essence has given me his reply".[20] The same dossier goes on to say that Platonov argued that publication of his works would, for the following somewhat surprising reason, be in the Party's interests: "After all, there is no writer who has such an approach to the inmost secrets of souls and objects as I have. A good half of my work helps the Party to see all the mould covering certain things better than the Workers' and Peasants' Inspectorate." And in a letter to Gorky in

1933 Platonov had asked, "Can I be a Soviet writer, or is that objectively impossible?"[21] "The Cow" is a more autobiographical story than one might first think. Vasya, the little boy, represents the young Platonov, sharing his love of steam-engines[22] and his desire to know the world; less obviously, the cow, inconsolable in her grief for her dead calf, must represent the older Platonov, whose own son, at the time the story was written,[23] was probably either dead or in a labour-camp. The conclusion of "The Cow" perhaps implies that true service to the motherland entails giving up everything for her sake and then being killed.

* * *

During the war years the Soviet authorities were, for once, more preoccupied with real, external enemies than with imaginary, internal ones. Censorship was eased; disgraced writers like Akhmatova and Platonov were again able to publish. Like his friend, Vasily Grossman, Platonov was a successful war correspondent. He was also the only non-Jewish writer to agree to collaborate with Grossman and Ehrenburg on their "Black Book", their documentary history of the Holocaust.[24] Platonov also published no less than four books of stories. Many of these war stories, however, seem closer to propaganda than to art – though it is possible that this impression arises at least partly from the fact that the only available texts are bowdlerised.[25] "The Seventh Man", however, needs no apologies; in it the theme of war allows Platonov to explore many of his most deeply personal obsessions – the debt owed to the dead by the living, the nature of the boundary between life and death, the survival of love in an apparently loveless world – with originality and wit.

* * *

The publication of "The Return" in 1946 led to a furious campaign against Platonov, and to his being unable to publish original work during the remaining six years of his life. This story of a soldier's troubled homecoming after the end of the Second World War is free of political implications. After the war, however, during the period of Stalin's greatest triumph, the only acceptable mode in which to treat such a theme was the optimistic and the heroic. And Platonov's hero, once again, is far from heroic. The central theme, as in "The River Potudan", is the hero's struggle to accept the real world and its imperfections. On his return, Ivanov is upset first by his twelve-year-old son, who is reluctant to yield his dominant position in the household, and then by the news that his wife, Lyuba, has been unfaithful. After only one night at home he decides to abandon his family and return to Masha, a young woman with whom he has had some kind of affair during his journey home. Ivanov goes to the station and catches the train that is to take him to Masha; after the train has begun to move, however, he sees his children running after him, senses his true feelings and jumps off to return to his family. In descending from a train, Ivanov is following the example of a number of Platonov's earlier heroes; just as they renounced their belief in the political Utopia to which the train of Revolution was to carry them, so Ivanov renounces his hopes of a personal revolution, a fresh start with an attractive young woman considerably younger than himself. Like Nikita in "The Potudan River" – though his difficulties have been of a different nature – Ivanov is finally able to accept the love he is offered rather than destroy it for failing to meet his ideals.

Even in Russia Platonov is still often seen as a "rough diamond", a self-taught writer with an original vision who wrote brilliantly but awkwardly, eschewing niceties of style. It is only gradually that readers are coming to realise that he is an extraordinarily accomplished and sophisticated craftsman. I have already discussed the dexterity of his word-play. His skill with narrative construction is also of the first order. The apparently simple narrative of "The Return" possibly represents the acme of this skill. Firstly, the story is delicately symmetrical. The story both begins and ends with the hero getting on or off a train: in the first pages Ivanov gets onto a train after a long delay, meaning to travel to his own home but instead going to Masha's; in the last pages he hurries onto a train, meaning to travel straight to Masha's, but instead getting off and returning to his own home. And there are two important kisses, both of which become objects of discussion: while they are waiting for the train Ivanov asks Masha to allow him to kiss her "carefully" and "on the surface"; and when he gets home, Ivanov learns that Lyuba has earlier allowed herself to be kissed by Semyon. Secondly, and more importantly, the architecture of the story is extremely complex: without the least show of artifice, the story of Ivanov's return frames a second story, which frames a third story, which in turn frames a fourth.

These framed stories are at least partly responsible for Ivanov's change of heart; it is after listening to Petya's story, about another soldier who comes home to an unfaithful wife, that Ivanov first begins to admit to himself that he too might be less than perfect. The story Petya tells is about Uncle Khariton, an honest man who works at the bread-shop and who enjoys telling customers the story of how he salvaged his self-esteem and his marriage, both almost shattered by the discovery of his own wife's infidelity, through telling her an imaginary story about his sexual conquests. A story within a story within a story within a story, all of them capturing the texture of real life with extraordinary vividness. And this is in no way merely an adroit game. Platonov was always a deeply moral artist; it was probably his hope that, just as Uncle Khariton's story enabled him to overcome a crisis in his marriage, and just as Petya's story helped his parents to overcome a crisis in their marriage, so "The Return" would help his own readers to return more easily to their own peace-time lives.

"The Return", in short, is about the fear of exclusion, and the way in which telling stories can help people to live with this fear. Every character at one point or another in the story feels they have been excluded. In the first pages Platonov states that both Ivanov and Masha felt "orphaned" without the Army. Ivanov, we may imagine, intends his relationship with Masha to be "careful" and "on the surface". In the end, however, he hurts Masha, and without realising it. On his return, after excluding Masha from his life, Ivanov embraces his wife for too long, frightening his five-year-old daughter. Then, once again, it is his own turn to feel excluded: Petya seems to have usurped his own role around the house, and Lyuba appears to have been unfaithful. Little is said of Petya's feelings as he eavesdrops at night on the parental quarrel, but he too eventually breaks down – after going too far in his criticisms of his parents and then being rejected by his father. This series of rejections and exclusions culminates in Ivanov's departure. Unable to bear the pain of relationship, Ivanov imagines it will be easier to abandon everything than to accept his and his family's inadequacies. And then, at the last moment, as we have seen, Ivanov chooses to leave the train, to follow Uncle Khariton's example and accept his loving, if imperfect, wife.

One last point about "The Return". It was written in 1945 and is set, evidently, in the same year. Similarly, *The Foundation Pit* was written in 1929–30, also contemporaneously with the events it represents. And "Rubbish Wind" was written in late 1934, within a year of Hitler coming to power. I know of few writers, if any, who have been able to respond so immediately, and at the same time profoundly, to events around them. Platonov would probably always have called himself a socialist; his later writing is deeply realistic; he was also one of the few major Soviet writers of working-class origin; it is both ironic and entirely unsurprising that Platonov, who could have been hailed as the greatest practitioner of Socialist Realism, has in fact been the Soviet writer who has had to wait longest for publication and recognition, both in Russia and elsewhere. "The Return" is the finest example of Platonov's later, more classical manner; in it he has given voice to what are likely to have been the feelings of millions of people. Had the Soviet Union been a saner place, this story might have won Platonov acceptance into the family to which he so desperately wished to belong; it is ironic that in the event it marked his final exclusion from Soviet society.

* * *

Platonov had few friends in the literary world. His one influential supporter during his last fifteen years, somewhat surprisingly, was Sholokhov. It was Sholokhov who was responsible for Platonov's son being released, in early 1941, from the camps. It was also Sholokhov's patronage that made possible the publication of the only books Platonov was able to bring out after the war – two volumes of vigorous, witty adaptations of traditional folk tales. These stories may have resulted from a chance commission, but they also represent a return by Platonov to his social and artistic roots: there is a folkloric element in much of Platonov's work, and his surrealism has little in common with that of the hyper-intellectual French movement. Our final story, "Two Crumbs", also bears the influence of folk tale. His last published work, it appeared in a children's newspaper, *Pioneer Pravda*, in 1947, and was attacked – almost unbelievably – for its pacifism. Like Tolstoy, Platonov moved in his last decade towards an ever-greater simplicity; this story shows that he was able to attain this simplicity while remaining true to the uniqueness of his vision.

Platonov died in 1951, of tuberculosis contracted while nursing his son, who had himself contracted tuberculosis in the camps and who died of it after his release. To this day unpublished works continue to surface in Russian journals: the short novel, *Happy Moscow*, one of Platonov's greatest masterpieces, was published in Russia in 1991, and a play, *Noah's Ark*, in 1993. Many of Platonov's works, including *Chevengur*, are still available only in unreliable texts. Russian scholars are collaborating on the compilation of a definitive edition of his works, but this enormous project will not be completed until well into the next millennium.

Robert Chandler

A NOTE ON THE TEXT

Angela Livingstone made the first draft of "The River Potudan" and "The Return", while Robert and Elizabeth Chandler made the first draft of the remaining stories. These drafts were then revised and rewritten many, many times by all three of us. We are grateful to many other friends and colleagues who answered questions or offered criticisms. We are especially grateful to Nadezhda Bourova and Eric Naiman, both of whom have checked these translations against the originals and whose help has been truly indispensable. We have also received valuable comments from Valentina Coe and Mark Miller, as well as from Susan Biver, Philip Bullock, Elizabeth Cook, Sheila Gleeson, Igor Golomstock, Nick Leera, Nigel Manson and Geoffrey Smith. Translating Platonov is probably beyond the abilities of any single individual. These translations should be regarded as the product of collective labour.

Definitive texts of Platonov's works have yet to appear. The existing texts tend to differ from one another, sometimes in important respects. The volume *Vzyskanie pogibshikh* (Moscow, 1995, Shkola Press), almost certainly contains the most reliable texts so far, and we have followed them consistently except with "Rubbish Wind" where we have incorporated one particularly fine paragraph from earlier editions that is omitted in this volume. A number of the stories we have chosen, however, were not included in *Vzyskanie pogibshikh*. "The Cow" and "The Seventh Man" were translated from the volume *Vsya zhizn* (Moscow, Patriot, 1991), though we have also incorporated some sentences from earlier editions of "The Cow". "The Motherland of Electricity" was translated from *Izbrannye proizvedeniya* (Moscow, Khudozhestvennaya Literatura, 1978). The Russian text of "Lobskaya Hill" was first published only in 1994, in the journal *Novoe literaturnoe obozrenie*, No. 9 . And "Two Crumbs" was translated from the text published in *Kostyor*, 1968, No.6.

R.C and A.L.

THE RETURN
and Other Stories

THE MOTHERLAND OF ELECTRICITY

IT WAS THE HOT DRY SUMMER OF 1921, MY YOUTH WAS passing by. In winter I was studying at the polytechnic, in the electro-technical section; in summer I worked in the machine room of the town electricity station. The work made me very tired, because the station had no reserve power and the single turbo generator had been running non-stop, night and day, for over a year; the machine demanded such precise, tender and careful attention that all the energy of my life was expended on it. In the evenings I passed the young people strolling along the summer streets, and made my way home like a man half asleep. My mother gave me some boiled potatoes and, while I ate, I took off my work jacket and my bast shoes, so that little clothing would remain on me after supper and I would be able to lie down to sleep straight away.

In the middle of the summer, one July evening when I had come home from work as usual and gone to sleep as deeply and darkly as if all my inner light had been extinguished for ever, I was woken by my mother.

The chairman of the Provincial Executive Committee, Ivan Mironovich Chunyaev, had sent me a note with the night watchman, asking me to come to his flat immediately. Chunyaev had once been a fireman on a locomotive, he had worked with my father and that was how he knew me.

By midnight I was at Chunyaev's. He was haunted by the task of the struggle against ruin, and, fearing for the whole people, he was profoundly troubled by the turbid heat of this dry summer when not a drop of living moisture had fallen from the sky and all nature smelt of dust and death, as if a hungry tomb already lay gaping open for the people. That year even the flowers had no more smell than metal filings, and deep fissures had formed in the fields, in the body of the earth, like the gaps between the ribs of a thin skeleton.

"Tell me, do you know what electricity is?" Chunyaev asked me. "Is it a rainbow?"

"It's lightning," I said.

"Ah, lightning!" pronounced Chunyaev. "That's what it is! A storm and a downpour . . . All right then! And you're right, lightning really is what we need, that's true . . . We've reached such a state of ruination, dear brother, that it's lightning we need, lightning and nothing else. That would really hot things up! Here, read what people are writing to me."

Chunyaev handed me a memorandum that was lying on his desk. The Verchovka village soviet had written to him as follows:

To the Chairman of the Provincial Executive Committee, Comrade Chunyaev, and the entire Presidium. Comrades and citizens, don't waste a tear, amidst a world so poor and drear. Our power of science now rises like a tower; our thoughtful power will soon wipe out this Babylon of lizards and of drought. We're not the ones who made God's world so blighted, but we'll fix it up good and proper. And life will be splendid and mighty, with hens' eggs for every pauper! A Communist's mind never dozes; no man can deflect his hand. He applies true diagnosis and the pressure of science to our land. Our hearts are warlike, vast, so do not cry, you who are poor of belly, this deathly thing will soon pass by and we shall all eat pie with jelly. We can hear the beat of the machine, the light of electricity can now be seen, but we need help to make things even better in the village of Verchovka, because our machine used to belong to the Whites, it came into the world as a foreign interventionist and its nature makes it reluctant to aid us. But my fateful heart does not sorrow, my tear burns in my brain and thinks only of the universal tomorrow.

p.p. the Chairman of the Soviet (he has gone out for a brief period on counterattack against all the bandit parasites and he will not return to his home until victory) – Secretary Stepan Zharyonov.

Secretary Zharyonov was evidently a poet, but Chunyaev and I were practical, working men. And through the poetry and enthusiasm of the secretary we were able to see the truth and reality of Verchovka, a distant village we did not know. We saw a light in the gloomy dark of a destitute and barren space – the light of man on an earth that had suffocated and died; we saw wires hung on old wattle fencing; and our hope for the future world of communism, a hope essential to us in the difficult existence we led day after day, a hope which alone made us human – this hope of ours turned into electrical power, even if the only light it had lit as yet was in some far-off little huts made of straw.

"You go and give them a hand," said Chunyaev. "You've been studying and eating our bread long enough. I'll sort things out with the town electricity station, they'll let you go . . ."

The next day I set out in the morning towards the village of Verchovka. My mother boiled up some potatoes and put some salt and a little bread into a bag, and I set off south down the cart tracks and walked for three days, because I had no map and there turned out to be three Verchovkas – Upper, Old and Not-so-Poor. But Chief Secretary Comrade Zharyonov thought, of course, that his Verchovka was the only Verchovka and that it was famous, like Moscow, throughout the whole world, and so he did not give a second name to his village, which in fact turned out to be the one known as Not-so-Poor, to distinguish it from the other Verchovkas.

Avoiding the other two Verchovkas, where there were no electricity stations, I reached Not-so-Poor Verchovka in the afternoon of the third day of my journey. When I first saw the village, I stopped; there was a lot of dust to one side of the track and I could make out a crowd of people processing along the bald, dry earth. I waited for them to draw closer, and then saw a priest, his assistants, three women with icons and about twenty worshippers. The earth here sloped down towards an old, dried-up gully, where the wind and the spring waters deposited the thin dust they gathered from the broad upland fields.

The procession had come down from the high ground and was now moving through the dust of the valley, making its way towards the track.

In front walked an exhausted priest; his skin was black and thick grey hair grew all over him. He was singing something in the hot silence of nature and swinging his censer at the wild, silent vegetation he met on his way. Sometimes he would stop and lift his head to the sky in an appeal to the blind radiance of the sun, and then bitterness and despair could be seen on his face, together with teardrops or drops of sweat. The people accompanying him gazed into space and crossed themselves, went down on their knees in the ashy dust and prostrated themselves on the poor earth, frightened by the endlessness of the world and by the weakness of their home-made icon gods, which were being carried by old tear-stained women on bellies that would never bear children again. Two children – a boy and a girl –, barefoot and wearing only shirts, were walking behind the church crowd and looking at the adults with the

6

interest of study; the children were neither crying nor making the sign of the cross, they were frightened and silent.

Near the track was a large pit from which clay had once been obtained. The procession came to a stop beside this pit, the icons were propped up with the countenances of the saints towards the sun, and the people climbed into the pit and lay down for a rest in the shade beneath the clay wall. The priest took off his cassock and turned out to be wearing trousers – which made the two children burst into laughter.

The large icon, now supported by a lump of clay, depicted the Virgin Mary, a solitary young woman, with no god in her arms. I looked hard at this painting and thought about it, while the women worshippers sat down in the shade and began to busy themselves with work of their own – searching through one another's hair.

A pale, weak sky surrounded Mary's head on the icon; the one hand that could be seen was huge and sinewy and did not match the dark beauty of her face, her fine nose or large eyes – which did not seem like those of a worker, since such eyes tire too quickly. The expression of these eyes interested me: they looked out without meaning or faith, and they were so densely filled with the force of sorrow that her whole gaze had darkened to the point of seeming impenetrable, numb and merciless. It was impossible to make out any tenderness, deep hope or sense of loss in the eyes of the painted Mother of God, even though her usual son was not now sitting in her arms; her mouth was wrinkled and creased – a sign of Mary's acquaintance with the passions, troubles and spites of ordinary life; she was simply an unbelieving working woman who lived by her own labours and received no favours from any god. And the peasants, when they looked at this painting, perhaps also secretly understood the truth of their common

7

sense awareness of the world's stupidity and the need for action.

Beside the icon sat a withered old woman, no taller than a child, who was looking at me inattentively through dark eyes; her face and hands were covered in wrinkles that were like the fixed convulsions of suffering; and in her gaze could be seen a keen mind that had undergone such trials in her life that in all likelihood the old woman's knowledge was no less in scope than the entirety of economic science and she herself could have been a respected academician.

I asked her: "Granny, why go around praying? There isn't any God, and there won't be any rain."

"I dare say," the old woman agreed. "Happen you're right!"

"Then why make the sign of the cross?" I went on.

"You're right – we cross ourselves in vain! What haven't I prayed about? I've prayed for my husband, I've prayed for my children – and not one of them's been spared, they're all dead now. If I keep going, my dear, it's from habit – do you think I choose to live? My heart doesn't ask me, it breathes by itself, and my hand's just the same – it makes the sign of the cross by itself. God's our curse . . . Ay, ay, ay, what a calamity – we've ploughed and we've sowed, and all that's come up is thistles!"

I fell silent for a moment in distress. "It's better, Granny, not to pray to anybody. Nature doesn't listen to words or prayers, the only thing she fears is reason and work."

"Reason!" the old woman uttered with clear awareness. "I've seen so many years that's all there is of me – just reason and bone! Worries and work took the flesh off me long ago – there's not much left in me to die, everything's died already, little by little. Look at me!"

The old woman resignedly took her scarf off her head and I saw her bald skull which had cracked into its component bones, now ready to fall apart and commit to the irretrievable dust of the earth a charily accumulated, patient mind which had learned about the world through labour and hardships.

"Come winter I'll be going and humbling myself before my neighbour too," said the old woman, "and I'll be weeping on rich men's doorsteps. Maybe I'll get enough millet to last till summer, and then I'll have to pay it back if it kills me – one and a half sacks for each sack, and four days' labour, and another five sacks worth of bowing and scraping . . . Don't think it's just God we bow down to – we're frightened by the wind and by the ice beneath our feet, and by downpours, by drought, by our neighbours, by passers-by, and we cross ourselves before all of them! Do you think we pray out of love? There's nothing left of us to love with!"

I walked away from the old woman, filled with sorrow and thought. The people began to gather together again after their rest, and the procession of those who had been praying for rain set off back towards the village. The only person left was the old woman who had been talking to me.

The old woman wanted to rest a little longer and in any case she could never have kept up on her little childish legs, not now the others were walking fast and purposefully and even the priest was striding along in trousers.

Seeing her condition, I picked the old woman up as if she were a girl of eight and carried her in my arms towards the village, conscious of all the eternal value of this aged labourer.

The old woman got down from my arms beside one of the huts. I said goodbye to her, kissed her on the face and decided to dedicate my life to her, because in youth it always seems there is a great deal of life and that there will be enough of it to help every old woman.

Verchovka turned out to be quite a small village – not more than thirty homes, yet few of the structures were in good repair.

The huts looked decrepit and the lower beams of their frames were already rotting in the earth. Military imperialism, which had passed over the whole world, had turned everything in sight – everything that had been procured, built up and cherished by generations of labourers – into something resembling a cemetery.

A boy, whom I afterwards lost sight of, willingly accompanied me to the electricity station. It was in operation half a verst away from the village – on the road, beside the communal pond.

An English twin-cylinder motor cycle, made by "Indian", its wheels half buried in the earth, was roaring powerfully as it drove a small dynamo attached to it by a belt; the dynamo was mounted on two small logs and was shaking from the speed with which it was turning. A middle-aged man was sitting in the side car and smoking a cigarette. Close by was a tall post, and on top of it burned an electric bulb, lighting up the day. Round about stood some carts; the horses had been unharnessed and were eating their fodder, while the men sat on these carts, observing with pleasure the action of the high-speed engine; some of the thinner peasants were giving open expression to their joy, walking up to the mechanism and stroking it as if it were some creature they loved, smiling meantime with as much pride as if they were playing a part in this enterprise, even though they were not from the village.

The electricity station mechanic, who was sitting in the motor-cycle side car, was paying no attention to the reality around him; he was intently imagining the element of fire that raged in the cylinders, listening like a musician, with a passionate look on his face, to the melody of the whirlwind of gas that burst out into the atmosphere.

I loudly asked the mechanic why he was working to no

avail, just for the sake of a light on a post, wasting fuel and wearing out the machine.

"I'm not working to no avail," said the mechanic indifferently. He then climbed out of the side car and held his palm against a bearing on the dynamo, beside the large home-made wooden pulley that drove it. "No," the mechanic went on, "in the evening we work, but now we're just trying out the machine, turning it over so the parts can all shake down and get used to one another. Anyway we need to show off a bit to the passers-by – you could call it propaganda. Let people have something to gaze at!"

There was good sense in the mechanic's words about giving the assembly a trial run, since the motor cycle engine was an old machine that had endured the roads of the war, and some of the factory parts had probably been replaced by parts made by hand in the local blacksmith's, and it was necessary to try these out and get them bedded in.

I silently studied the layout of the electricity station, paying no more attention to the thoughtful mechanic. Beneath the seat of the motor cycle I read the number of the machine, E-0-401, and – beneath it – a small inscription in English which read, when translated: "The 77th Royal British Colonial Division".

The wires from the electricity station to the village ran underground, in an insulated cable; in the evening, no doubt, the windows of the village huts shone triumphantly, defending the revolution from darkness.

The mechanic came up to me and held out a tobacco pouch.

"Have a smoke, it'll do you good," he said to me. "What are you staring at? I suppose you've worked on a threshing machine and reckon you know all about engines?"

"No, I've never worked on a threshing machine," I answered. I then asked the rural engineer, "What do you use for fuel?"

"Grain alcohol, of course," said the mechanic with a sigh.

"We make extra strong liquor, and then we light up the village with it."

"And for oil?" I inquired further.

"Whatever I can get hold of," the man answered. "I filter it through a rag and dribble it on."

"Shame to burn up good grain in an engine," I said. "Is it worth it?"

"It is a shame," the mechanic agreed. "But what's to be done? It's the only fuel we've got."

"And whose grain is it you turn into fuel?"

"Whose do you think?" said the mechanic. "It belongs to society, to the people. We built up a store from self-taxation – so we've got that, and then there's one or two other sources."

I expressed surprise: how was it the peasants were so willing to feed last year's harvest to a machine when this summer there would be no grain because of the drought?

"You don't know our people," the mechanic said slowly, listening all the time to the work of the engine; we had now moved some way away from it and were standing beside the tethering post. "Just because there's nothing to eat, you think people don't need to read? The landowner left us a fine library here in Verchovka. Now the peasants read books in the evenings – some read out loud, some read to themselves, and some are still learning . . . And we give them light in their huts – so we've got light and we've got reading. Until people have some other joy, let them have light and reading."

"If you didn't fuel the machine with grain, things would be better still," I said. "Then you'd have bread, light and reading."

The mechanic looked at me and gave me a reserved but polite smile.

"Don't you worry about the grain: it's dead anyway, you can't eat the stuff . . . We had a kulak here, Vanka Chuev – he and all his family went off with the Whites, and he buried his grain in a distant field. So Comrade Zharyonov and I searched all year for the grain but, by the time we found it, it had gone mouldy and died – it was too rotten to eat, no use for seed, but good enough to make a harmful chemistry like alcohol from. And there was plenty of it, nearly four hundred poods![1] And we haven't so much as touched the self-taxation and mutual-help store: that's twenty poods, the same as before. Our chairman won't let you have a crumb from it, not till you're swollen from hunger. And that's the only way – otherwise . . ."

The mechanic then stopped speaking and rushed to the electricity station, because the belt had jumped off the dynamo pulley.

I turned round and made my way back to Verchovka. On the outskirts of the village a stove pipe was steadily pouring out smoke, and I went to have a look at this hut that was being heated so fiercely on a summer's day. Judging by the yard and the gates, the owner had either died or else had abandoned the hut. The gates were quite overgrown, and the yard had been taken over by tough, pestilent weeds, the kind that carry on through heat, winds, and downpours of rain, and always survive.

Inside the hut was a stove, and inside the stove someone had installed a home-made still. The stove was fuelled by rhizomes, and on a small stool beside the spout of the apparatus, in the light from the flame, sat a gay, blissful old man, with a mug in his right hand and a bit of salted potato in his left hand: the old man must have been waiting for the next discharge of mindless liquid in order to check whether it was fit to be burnt in the engine or whether it was still too weak. The elderly taster's stomach and guts were an instrument for testing the fuel.

I went out into the yard to find the electricity cable, since there was nothing to be seen on the street. The main cable went through the yards; the insulator hooks had been fixed into the walls of sheds or the trunks of the occasional willows, or else had simply been screwed into poles made from fencing stakes nailed one on top of another, and the smaller cables branched out from these hooks to the outbuildings and the living areas of the huts. In this part of the world, where there was no forest, it had been impossible to find posts for the construction of a normal street grid. And, from both an economic and a technical point of view, something like this was the only possible solution to the problem of electricity transmission.

I was worried, however, that the overhead cables might have been hung incorrectly and that this might cause a fire, so I made my way through the yards, climbing over the poles and wattle fences between neighbouring properties and checking from outside how the main cables had been hung and fastened. The tension of the line was good, and nowhere did the cables pass close to straw, or to any frail and combustible substances that might begin to smoulder as a result of being heated by live copper.

After putting my mind at rest as regards fire, I found a cool secluded spot in the shade of a barn and fell asleep there to get some rest.

But I was forced to wake up before I had had the rest I needed – someone was kicking me and attempting to rouse me.

"No time to rest, no time for us to snooze, not till sorrow's been suppressed and the dead raised from their tombs!" an unknown man pronounced above me.

I came to in horror; like delirium, the late heat of the sun filled all nature. A man with a kind face, wrinkled with animated fervour, was bending over me and greeting me in rhyme as a brother in the bright life. From this I guessed that he was the village-soviet secretary who had written the memorandum to the Provincial Executive Committee.

"Rise up, rise up at once from sleep, and rage amid the gaping deep – thus fearless Bolsheviks do yell as they bring down the walls of Hell!"

My own mind, however, was full not of poetry but of resolve. I got up and talked to the secretary about the motor-cycle electricity station and the need to get hold of a pump from somewhere.

"The wind is wild, and my thoughts jump," answered the secretary, "I cannot think about . . . what comes next?" he asked suddenly.

"Your pump!" I prompted him.

"About your pump! . . . Let's go to my estate," the secretary continued in the inspiration of his heart. "And you can leisurely relate if grave or wedding-bed's your goal and what it is that eats your soul . . ."

In the village soviet I gave the secretary a precise outline of my plan to irrigate the dry earth with water and so put an end to the people's processions for rain.

"I read beneath your youthful brow," exclaimed the secretary. "And in response," he continued, pointing towards his chest, "my war-like heart now thunders out its vow!"

"Do you have any communal vegetable land, without too many owners?" I asked.

The secretary immediately and without hesitation informed me: "We do have some such land. It used to be for cows. But now it's owned by widows and the spouse . . . what's the word?" He lost the thread, but then went on, "by the families of Red Army soldiers wounded in the war! One hundred acres of it. Ploughed, sown and harvested by our new power – the village soviet! It's where the village used to stand, it's waste ground now, but still the soil is full of good manure, and wheat shoots up like chimney smoke into a winter sky. But now there's not a single ear of grain, not even sun can help us without rain!"

I realized there might not be enough motor-cycle power to water a hundred acres, but I decided all the same to irrigate at least a part of this land that belonged to the very poorest peasants – the widows and Red Army soldiers.

On hearing this plan of mine, the secretary was unable to find any more words and burst into tears there and then.

"It's because of a coincidence of circumstances," he explained after a while, not using verse.

During the next two days the secretary and I, together with the mechanic from the motor-cycle electricity station, worked at installing the motor cycle in a new place – beside the Yazva, a shallow little river which was slowly flowing somewhere or other in a swoon of heat. This was the boundary of the land that was worked with communal horses by the village soviet and that belonged to the widows and Red Army soldiers. In spite of the fertility of this low-lying ground, nothing was growing there now except a few beds of potatoes and, beyond them, some insubstantial spikes of millet; but the plants were all exhausted, they were smothered by the deathly dust of torrid whirlwinds and had dropped down, in order to return into the darkness of ashes and contract back into the now dead seeds from which they had first sprung.

Cow parsley was growing patiently in these same fields, together with burdock, the pale flowers of "golden-lips" that were like the face of a man with an expression of madness, and the other weeds that take over the earth when the dry elements hold sway.

I tried the soil. It was like ash that had burnt up in the sun; the first storm wind would be able to lift all the dust of fruitfulness and scatter it in space till not a trace was left.

After installing the motor cycle, the secretary and I started to think about a pump. We looked through the sheds of the prosperous peasants, who had pillaged the landlords with especial greed and composure, and we found lots of good things there, even some paintings by Picasso and some marble bidets for women, but no pumps.[2]

After thinking for a while, I took from the motor cycle the thick iron name plate bearing the number of the English interventionist military unit, and cut two blades out of it in the smithy. Next, on the secretary's orders, the iron roof was removed from the building of the village soviet, and the iron was then used to make the five remaining blades, as well as housings for the pump, suction pipes and gutters for conveying the water onto the field.

The electricity-station mechanic and I worked on the motor cycle for another three days, until we had fixed all seven blades to the spokes of the rear wheel and installed the wheel in the housing. And in this way we constructed a centrifugal pump from a motor-cycle wheel and organized a water tower instead of an electricity station; this pump, however, would not be a hindrance to other work – when the earth no longer needed water, the engine could go back to turning the dynamo and giving light to the huts.

After five days of exhausting labour without the necessary tools and materials, amid the disarray of the fields, the mechanic and I started up the motor-cycle engine, and water began to flow onto the land of the widows and Red Army soldiers. The flow, however, was weak – about a hundred buckets an hour – and it was essential to distribute water to all the plots, which would require zeal on the part of the people. Some water, moreover, was being lost as a result of the poor jointing of our home-made gutters, which was an additional grief. Not that the secretary himself was grieved: "So what if science can only yield a drop for free – with the muscle of the masses we'll wring out a whole sea!"

The next day the secretary and twenty women, together with four elderly poor peasant men,[3] tried to direct the water deep into the fields with their spades, but the flow dried up not far from the water tower. From the crevices of the earth, frightened by the moisture, there emerged lizards, spiders, dry segmented worms of some unknown breed, and hard little insects that might have been made from bronze – it was they, evidently, who would inherit the earth if rain clouds failed to gather in the atmosphere and people became extinct.

Widows and poor peasant women surrounded us and began to harangue us about the lack of water and the feeble power of the machine. We heard them out with shame, but without fear, and the secretary then pronounced a concluding word of consolation. He looked into the hazy, oppressive sky of the crazed summer, his face radiant amid the silence of a terrible, blinding nature and said: "Everything's withered, gone to spoil – same with the grass as with the soil! But we shall live with might and main, since man has been vouchsafed a brain. And that is why we each must bear every trouble, every care – we weren't born stones or iron, or cattle, and we won't die until we've won the battle."

Secretary Stepan Zharyonov was tired out from heat and suffering; but his face had become different – clear and thoughtful – although it had lost none of the kindness of its folds. And he said in prose to the widows, who were looking at him with surprise and smiles of compassion, "Get digging, women, make that ditch longer. This machine is an interventionist, it was on the side of the Whites, it doesn't want to pour water into the gardens of the proletariat."

With the avidity of passionate thought the mechanic observed the strained work of the engine; it was doing fewer revolutions and was panting heavily from being overloaded. I ran my hands over all the body of the engine – it was overheating badly and was in distress; the powerful liquor was exploding in the cylinders with harsh fury, but the poor quality oil was unable to hold to the points of friction and coat them with a tender, soothing film. The engine was shaking in its frame, and a thin indistinct voice from within the mechanism sounded like a warning of mortal danger.

I understood the engine and put an end to its dry, angry action. We removed the housing from the wheel which served as a centrifugal pump, reduced the number of blades on the wheel from seven to four, and replaced the housing. I wanted to lessen the load on the engine; it would maintain a better speed and then four blades would do more work than seven.

By now it was evening and everyone had gone off to rest; only Comrade Zharyonov and I remained, sitting on the bank of a river whose trickle was getting weaker and weaker. I was in no hurry to get the engine going again; I wanted to think up something else to help it revolve more freely.

The sun set in a fierce and scorching space, leaving on the earth only darkness and anxious people, now wilting in their huts with difficult feeling in their hearts and no defence against disaster and death. After a while the secretary's children came up to him, a little boy and a girl, the ones I had seen in the church procession. They had grown dark from hunger and abandonment and they threw themselves at their father, happy to have found him and to know they would be spending the night together with him in the terrible, stifling darkness; they no longer asked for bread, glad that at least they had a father – a father who loved them and who also had nothing to eat. The father pressed the weak bodies of his children against him and began looking in his pockets for something to feed them with, but all he found was rubbish and memoranda from the local executive committee. Then the secretary decided to comfort the children with his warmth; he embraced them both in his huge arms, drawing them against his warm belly, and all three of them fell asleep on the dark earth. Probably the mother of these children was dead and the two orphans lived along with their father.

I realized what I should do: roll some hemp fibres into a wick, put one end into a cask of water and wrap the rest of the wick round the engine cylinders – then the water would be drawn up the wick, and the engine would feel the coolness and furnish extra power. I found some tow in the side car – in the tool box – and by midnight I had completed the work. After that I went back to the sleeping family of Stepan Zharyonov and did not know what to do – whether to pump some water, so as to guarantee these children something to eat at least by autumn, or to wait, since the children would be woken by the noise of the engine and would immediately start feeling the torment of hunger.

I sat in thought by the river, which was quietly flowing into the distance, and I looked up at the concentration of stars in the sky, that future field of humanity's activity, that deathless sucking emptiness filled with anxious and diminutive matter beating away in the rhythm of its unknown fate – and began to think about electricity, something that always brought me pleasure.

Soon, however, my attention was brought back to the village – there had been a resounding explosion from some cask there, followed by a hissing of steam, and then silence. The secretary woke up, lifted his sleeping head, uttered the lines: "Inside my brain the babe is crying again" – and went back to sleep.

Seeing that the family were so deeply asleep they had not been woken by the explosion, I started the engine. Onto the black earth flowed a thick stream of water from the mouth of the force pipe. The engine was doing an adequate number of revolutions, was not overheating and no longer sang in an agonized voice of exhaustion from the depths of its harsh being.

I walked quietly round the engine that was now vibrating in tension, and observed with satisfaction the calm flow of night through the world; let time pass by – it was not now passing in vain: the engine was reliably pumping water onto the dry fields of the poor peasants.

I used a bucket to measure the supply of water per minute – it turned out that the pump was now supplying about two hundred buckets an hour, twice as much as before. In my pocket I found a piece of dry bread from the town and I began to eat it, trying to finish it up quickly. Without admitting it to myself I was afraid the chief clerk's children might suddenly wake up and would then be sure to ask me for food . . . Chewing the last crumbs, I bent down over them – the children were breathing unevenly and restlessly, in a sad sleep which had subdued the ache of hunger inside them. Only their father lay there with a happy face that was as welcoming as ever; he was in command of his body and of all the tormenting forces of nature, the magic tension of genius continually bringing joy to a heart that had faith in the mighty future of proletarian humanity.

Something evidently caused the consciousness of the chief clerk to overflow. He unexpectedly opened his eyes, saw that I was chewing something and immediately said, as if he had not been sleeping: "Now is the time to chew good bread, not just to suffer life and dread."

I swallowed the rest of my food in alarm and began to think.

Out of the darkness of the river valley two people came towards the engine – the mechanic, now rested, and a tall old woman whom I did not know.

"Go on," said the old woman, "go and lift my husband up – he's not moving, he's lying on the ground and his heart isn't knocking inside him . . . It was for you bastards he kept brewing that liquid . . ."

I turned calmly to the motor cycle mechanic, learning to keep my composure in the thick of events. The mechanic explained that this old woman was the wife of the old man who had spent days on end brewing extra strong liquor to fuel the engine. In the absence of any apparatus to measure the proof of the alcohol, the old man had usually taken a mug in one hand, something salty – perhaps some potato – in the other hand, and then held his mug to the boiler outflow pipe until it began to drip. This time, however, the old man had been slow to evaluate the quality of the fuel; he had closed the tap on the pipe, put more wood on the fire and had fallen asleep still holding his emptied mug and a piece of potato; the pressure had increased, the boiler had blown up, and the force of the explosion had thrown the little old man out of the liquor hut, together with the door and the two window frames. Now the old man was on the ground, slowly returning to his senses; tomorrow he would start to repair the exploded installation.

"What do you want then?" I asked the old woman. "It was an accident – it's not our doing."

"Some kind of benefit," said the cross old woman.

"All right, I'll make a note."

I took out my note book and wrote: "Send the old woman some millet from town."

As soon as she saw that I was making a note, the old woman believed me and calmed down.

I gave the mechanic verbal instructions on how to look after the engine and pump, stood for a while beside Chief Secretary Zharyonov who was sleeping on the earth with his children, and then set off on foot through the warm night to my home, to my mother. I was walking alone in a dark field, young, poor and at peace. One of my tasks in life had been completed.

THE EPIFAN LOCKS

for M. A. Kashintsevaya

WHAT INTELLIGENCE THERE IS IN THE WONDERS of nature, my dear brother Bertrand! How abundant the hidden treasure of these spaces, more than can be sensed by the noblest of hearts or grasped by the most powerful understanding! Can you behold, if but through the eyes of your imagination, the dwelling place of your brother in the depths of the Asian continent? I am conscious this is beyond the grasp of your mind. I am conscious your gaze is bewitched by the many sounds of Europe and the many people of my dear Newcastle, where there is always a multitude of sailors and solace for an educated eye.

My longing for my homeland concentrates the more intensely within me, the sorrow of living the life of a hermit troubles me all the more.

The Russes are gentle of humour, obedient and patient in long and heavy labours, but wild and dark in their ignorance. My lips have joined together from never uttering enlightened speech. At the sites of my constructions I give only agreed signals to the peasant foremen, who then voice my commands to the men.

Nature in these parts is abundant: ship-timber pleasingly lines all the rivers, and even the plains are covered almost entirely by forest. Fierce beasts go about their lives on equal terms with man, and the Russes living in villages suffer great disturbance on their account.

However there is corn and red meat here in plenty,

and the abundant food has increased my girth, in spite of my heart's sorrow for Newcastle.

This letter is less detailed than the previous one. The merchants setting out for Azov, Caffa[1] and Constantinople have already overhauled their ships and are preparing for departure. It is with them I send this dispatch, that it may reach Newcastle the sooner. And the merchants are pressed for time, for the Don may dry up and will then no longer bear vessels of burden. But my request is not great, and to whom but you should I turn?

Tsar Peter is a most powerful man, although he is loud and disorderly to no purpose. His understanding is the image of his country: secretly abundant, but of a wildness made manifest by its beasts and forests.

Nevertheless he is unreservedly well-disposed towards foreign ship-builders, and treats them with an ardent generosity.

At the mouth of the Voronezh river I devised a two-chamber sluice with a bulkhead, which has made it possible to repair ships on dry land without occasioning great damage. I built, too, a large bulkhead and a sluice with a set of draw doors sufficient to let off the water. Then I built another sluice with a pair of great gates for the passage of ships, so they can be held at any time in a space closed by a bulkhead and the water can be let off from this space when the ships enter.

Sixteen months passed in the performance of this work. And another task followed in its train. Satisfied with my labours, Tsar Peter ordered me to build another sluice, upstream, so as to render the Voronezh river navigable, as far as the city, to ships of eighty cannon. I completed this undertaking in ten months, and nothing will befall my constructions so long as the world endures. This in spite of the instability of the ground around the sluice and the forceful springs. The German pumps proved feeble for these springs and, because of their abundance, our labours stood still for six weeks. Thereupon we built an engine that would discharge twelve barrels of water in one minute, which engine laboured day and night for eight months, after which we trod dry-shod to the bottom of the foundation pit.

After such tedious labours Tsar Peter kissed me and handed me a thousand roubles in silver – a not inconsiderable sum. He also informed me that not even Leonardo da Vinci, the inventor of sluices, would have constructed better.

The kernel of my thought, my dear Bertrand, is that I wish to call you to Russia. There is great generosity here to engineers, and Peter is himself eager to instigate works of engineering. I have heard from him in person that there is need for a canal to be built between the Don and the Oka, two mighty rivers of this land.

The Tsar wishes to create a continuous waterway linking the Baltic to the Black and Caspian Seas, so as to surmount the vast spaces of the continent and attain India, the kingdoms of the Mediterranean, and Europe. This project has indeed been conceived by the Tsar. But the inspiration arises from the merchant and trading class, nearly all of whom do their business in Moscow and the adjoining towns; while the riches of the country are situated in the heart of the continent, from which there is no issue unless by uniting the great rivers by means of canals and then voyaging to Saint Petersburg from as far as the Persians, and from Athens to Moscow, and furthermore to the Urals, Lake Ladoga, the Kalmyk steppes and beyond.

But for work of this scope Tsar Peter is in sore need of engineers. For a canal between the Don and the Oka is no small enterprise, requiring great diligence and still greater knowledge.

Therefore I promised Tsar Peter that I would summon from Newcastle my brother Bertrand; I myself am tired, and I love my betrothed and long for her. For four years I have lived as a savage, and my heart has withered and my intelligence dims.

Write presently of your decision in regard to this matter; for my part I advise you to come. It will be hard for you here, but after five years you will return to Newcastle a wealthy man, to live out your days in peace and plenty, in your home town. To labour for such an end is no sorrow.

Pass on my love and my yearning to my beloved Anna, and within a short period of time I shall return. Tell her that I am nourished now only by the blood aching for her in my heart, and may she wait till I come. And then farewell and look tenderly on the sweet sea, on joyful Newcastle and on the whole of our dear England.

Your brother and friend, engineer William Perry, the eighth day of the month of August 1708.

2

In the Spring of 1709, on the first ship of the year to sail there, Bertrand Perry arrived in Saint Petersburg.

He had made the voyage from Newcastle on the *Mary*, an old ship that had many times seen the ports of Australia and South Africa.

Captain Sutherland shook Perry by the hand and wished him a good journey into this terrible country and a swift return to his own hearth. Bertrand thanked him and stepped onto land – into a foreign city, into a vast country where there awaited him difficult work, solitude, and perhaps an early death.

Bertrand was in his thirty-fourth year, but his sullen, sorrowful face and his grey temples made him seem forty-five.

He was met in the port by an envoy of the Russian Tsar and the consul of the King of England.

After exchanging dull words, they parted: the Tsar's envoy went home to eat buckwheat kasha, the English consul went to his office, and Bertrand to the lodgings set aside for him near the naval stores and armoury.

Bertrand's rooms were clean, empty and secluded, but their very silence and comfort instilled melancholy. A desolate wind from the sea was beating against the Venetian window, and the cold from this window spoke still more dispiritingly of solitude.

On a low, solid table lay a packet under seal. Bertrand opened it and read:

By command of the Sovereign and Autocrat of all the Russias, the College of Sciences has pleasure in requesting Mister Bertrand Ramsay Perry, the English naval engineer, to attend the College of Sciences (Department of Waters and Canals) at its special establishment on Obvodnoy Prospekt.

The Sovereign is himself overseeing the movement of the project to join the Don and Oka rivers – by way of Lake Ivan, the River Shat and the River Upa. It is necessary therefore to complete the drafts speedily.

For this purpose you should present yourself to the College of Sciences with all celerity, first allowing yourself, however, to rest from your voyage until your sentiments and your entire corporeal body are recovered.

By order of the President,
Chief Regulator and Jurisprudent of the College of Sciences
– Heinrich Wortmann.

Bertrand lay down with the letter on the broad German sofa and unexpectedly fell asleep.

He was woken by a storm, which thundered alarmingly at the window. Out on the street, in darkness and desolation, moist thick snow was falling restlessly. Bertrand lit the lamp and sat down at the table opposite the fearsome window. But there was nothing for him to do, and he became lost in thought.

Hours had passed, and the earth had long ago been met by slow night. Sometimes Bertrand forgot himself; turning round sharply, he expected to see his room in Newcastle and its view, through the window, of a warm and crowded port, with the dim band of Europe on the horizon.[2]

But the wind, the night and snow on the street, the silence and chill of his rooms, reminded Bertrand that his lodgings lay on another latitude.

And his fantasy was overwhelmed in an instant by that which, in his consciousness, he had so long rejected.

Mary Carborund, his twenty-year-old betrothed, was probably now walking the green streets of Newcastle with a sprig of lilac pinned to her blouse. Someone else, perhaps, had taken her by the arm and was whispering persuasively of false love – and this would remain forever unknown to Bertrand. His voyage here had taken two weeks – who knows what might not have happened in Mary's mad, fantastical heart?

And was it possible for a woman to wait five or ten years for a husband, cultivating within her a love for an invisible image?

Hardly. Otherwise the entire world would long ago have turned honourable.

And yet, with a trustworthy love behind him, any man could go on foot even as far as the moon!

Bertrand filled his pipe with Indian tobacco.

"But Mary was right! What does she want with a merchant, or an ordinary sailor, for a husband? She is dear to me, and a girl of great wit . . ."

Bertrand's thoughts were moving at speed, but they were taking orderly turns and keeping to a clear rhythm.

"You're incontrovertibly right, little Mary. I can even remember the way you smelt of grass. I remember you saying, 'I need a husband like Alexander the Wanderer, like headstrong Tamburlaine or indomitable Attila. And if he's to be a sailor, then one like Amerigo Vespucci!' You know many things, Mary, you're a wise girl! And you're truly right: if your husband is to be dearer to you than life, then he must be more interesting and more rare than life! Otherwise you will grow weary, and your unhappiness will be your undoing."

Bertrand furiously spat out a wad of tobacco and said: "Yes, Mary, your young mind is too sharp! And it may be I do not deserve such a wife. Yet how good it is to caress such an impetuous little head! And what joy to me that beneath my wife's tresses dwells an ardent brain . . . But wait and see . . . For this have I come to this most sad Palmyra! William's letter counts for nothing in my destiny, though it helped my heart in its decision."

Stiff with cold, Bertrand began to prepare himself for sleep. While he imagined Mary and conversed with her in his mind, a blizzard had begun to rage over Saint Petersburg; checked by the buildings, it was freezing the rooms.

Wrapped in a blanket over which he had thrown a naval

greatcoat made from the toughest, most hard-wearing of cloths, Bertrand dozed, and a delicate, living sorrow streamed, never ceasing, never listening to his reason, throughout his dry, vigorous frame.

There was a strange, sudden sound outside, like the crack of a ship's planking when she hits ice; Bertrand opened his eyes and listened, but the sound had taken his mind off his suffering and so, without fully coming to, he fell asleep.

3

The following day, at the College of Sciences, Bertrand acquainted himself with Peter's design. The project was only just begun.

The Tsar's wish, in short, was that a continuous waterway be constructed between the Don and the Oka, linking Moscow and the Don region to the provinces of the Volga. This could be achieved only through the devising of great locks and canals, and it was to project these that Bertrand had been called from Britain.

Bertrand passed the next week in studying the survey documents on the basis of which these works would be projected. The documents proved methodical and had been drawn up by knowledgeable persons: a French engineer, Major-General Trouzesson, and a Polish technician, Captain Cickievski.

Bertrand was pleased, since good surveys made possible a speedy beginning to the construction works. Secretly, even in Newcastle, Bertrand had been charmed by Peter, and he desired to be his companion in the civilizing of a wild and mysterious country. And then even Mary would wish to have him as her husband.

Alexander the Great had made conquests, and Vespucci discoveries, but today was the age of construction work – the blood-stained warrior and the exhausted traveller had yielded to the intelligent engineer.

Bertrand laboured hard but cheerfully – the grief of separation from his betrothed was partly extinguished by work.

He lived in the same rooms: he visited neither the admiralty nor the civilian assemblies and he avoided acquaintance with the ladies and their husbands, though several society women themselves sought out the company of the solitary Englishman. Bertrand conducted the work as if navigating a ship – with caution, good sense and speed, avoiding the reefs and shoals of theory.

By the beginning of July the works had been projected and fair copies of the plans drawn up. The documents were all presented to the Tsar, who approved them and ordered Bertrand a recompense of one thousand and five hundred roubles in silver; henceforth he was to be paid a salary of one thousand roubles each month, and was appointed Chief Master and Engineer of all the sluices and canals that were to unite the Don and the Oka.

At the same time Peter issued instructions to the governors and deputies through whose provinces the locks and canals were to be built, ordering them to offer full assistance to the Chief Engineer as touching all his requirements. Bertrand was granted the privileges of a general, and made answerable only to the Commander-in-Chief and to the Tsar.

After the official conversation was over, Peter rose and addressed Bertrand directly: "Master Perry! I know your brother William. He is a ship-builder and engineer of enviable talent, gloriously able to control the power of water through artificial constructions. But to you, beyond compare with him, is entrusted a great labour of the mind by which we intend to unite for ever the chief rivers of our empire into a single aqueous body, thereby rendering great help to peaceful commerce, as well as to every military enterprise. It is our fast intention, by means of these works, to begin an intercourse, through the Volga and the Caspian, with the kingdoms of ancient Asia and thus, as far as we may, betroth the whole world to educated Europe. And through all this world-wide trade we shall both profit a little ourselves, and turn the hand of the people to ways of foreign artistry.

"And for these reasons I charge you to set to work forthwith – let there be a waterway!

"Should obstacles be offered you, inform me promptly by messenger – my punishment will be swift and keen. Here is my hand – your warranty! Command resolutely and conduct the work wisely – I know how to show thanks. I am also able to flog whosoever squanders the Sovereign's wealth or opposes the Tsar's will!"

At this point, with a speed out of proportion to the massiveness of his body, Peter went up to Bertrand and shook his hand.

Peter then turned and retired to his chambers, hawking and wheezing as he went.

The Tsar's speech was translated for Bertrand, and it pleased him.

Bertrand Perry's project encompassed the following stages: the construction of thirty-three locks from limestone and granite; the digging of a linking canal from the village of Lyubovka on the Shat river to the village of Bobrikov on the Don, a distance of twenty-three versts;[3] the dredging and deepening of the Don so as to render it navigable from the village of Bobrikov to the village of Gai, a distance of one hundred and ten versts; in addition, a rampart and earthwork dikes were to be raised around Lake Ivan, the source of the Don, and along the entire length of the canal.

All in all, two hundred and twenty-five versts of waterway were to be established, one extremity lying in the Oka, the other comprising a canal of one hundred and ten versts along the course of the Don. The canal was to be built to a width of twelve sazhens[4] and a depth of two arshins.[5]

Bertrand intended to supervise the project from Epifan, in the province of Tula, since this town lay at the centre of the prospective works. He was to be accompanied by five German engineers and ten clerks from the Service of Administration.

The day of departure was to be 18 July. On this day, at ten o'clock in the morning, coaches would draw up outside Bertrand's lodgings to convey him, by a remote and wearisome route, to the unremarkable spot of Epifan.

4

As long as the soul endureth, so long shall it know grief.

Perry and the five Germans met together for a substantial meal, intending to stuff themselves with food sufficient for a day and a night.

And they did indeed cram their bellies, readying themselves for a long contemplation of the then ailing spaces of Russia.

Already Perry was laying his packs of tobacco into his travelling case – his last act before any journey. Already the Germans were completing their letters to their families, and the youngest of them, Karl Bergen, had burst out weeping, his heart weighed down by unbearable longing for a wife who was young and still beloved.

And at this point the door shook from the brusque knocks of an official hand – the knocks of an envoy come either to make an arrest or to announce the clemency of a crazed sovereign.

It was a messenger from the Service of Posts.

He asked to be directed to Bertrand Perry, the English

engineer. And five German hands, marked with freckles and birthmarks, pointed to the Englishman.

The messenger thrust one leg forward awkwardly, and respectfully handed Perry a packet with five seals.

"Sir, be so good as to accept this missive from the realm of England!"

Perry moved away from the Germans towards the window, and opened the packet:

Newcastle, June 28

My good Bertrand!

You are not expecting this news. It is hard for me to cause you distress; love for you has probably not yet left me. But a new feeling already burns me. And my poor mind must strain to capture your dear image, which once my heart so sorrowfully adored.

But you are naive and cruel: in order to amass gold you have sailed away to a distant land; for the sake of wild glory you have destroyed my love, and my youth that expected tenderness. I am a woman. Without you I am weak, like a twig, and I have given my life to another.

Do you, my good Bert, remember Thomas Race? It is he who is now my husband. You are distressed, but you must grant he is a fine man and truly devoted to me! Once I refused him and preferred you. But you sailed away, and for a long time he consoled me in my terror and in my yearning love for you.

Do not be sad, Bert! I am so sorry for you! Did you believe I truly needed Alexander of Macedon for a husband? No, I need a man who is faithful, whom I love, and no matter if he loads coal in the docks or sails as a simple sailor – so long as he sings songs about me to all the oceans. That is what a woman needs – bear this in mind, my foolish Bertrand!

It is already two weeks since I was wedded to Thomas. He is most happy, as am I myself. I believe a child is stirring beneath my heart. See how quickly! Because Thomas is my beloved and will not leave me, while you have gone in search of colonies. Take your colonies then, as I have taken Thomas!

Goodbye! Do not be sad; and if ever you are in Newcastle, visit us – we shall be glad. And if you die, Thomas and I shall weep for you.

Mary Carborund-Race

Perry, all reason forgotten, read the letter three times from beginning to end. He then glanced at the huge window: a pity to smash it – the glass had been bought from Germans for gold. As for breaking the table, no heavy object lay to hand. He could punch a German in the face – but they were creatures without defence and one of them was weeping already. Fury raged within him, but Perry hesitated with his arithmetical reason, and his savagery found an outlet by itself.

"Herr Perry, something is wrong with your mouth," said the Germans.

"What do you mean?" asked Perry, now growing weak and sensing sorrow.

"Wipe your mouth, Herr Perry!"

With difficulty Perry pulled out his pipe from between teeth that had bitten into it. But, in gripping the pipe, these teeth had been so forced into their sockets that his gums had torn, and bitter blood now flowed from them.

"What has happened, Herr? Some sorrow at home?"

"No. It's over, my friends . . ."

35

"What is over, Herr? Tell us, please!"

"The blood is over, and the gums will heal. Let's start out for Epifan!"

5

The wayfarers moved slowly along the Ambassadors' Road, which leads to Kazan through Moscow, joining on the far side of Moscow with the Kalmiuss Sakma – the route the Tartars had once taken, along the right bank of the Don, into Muscovy. It was onto this road that the travellers were to turn, so as to continue along the Idovsk and Ordobazar high roads, and then smaller roads, to their future dwelling place – Epifan.

The head wind knocked out from Perry's chest not only his breath, but also his grief.

He looked with adoration at this nature that was so rich, yet so restrained and miserly. He was passing through lands where the soil was rich with minerals, yet what it bore was far from luxuriant: thin, elegant birches and the sorrowing, tuneful aspen.

Even in summer, the space was so resonant it seemed not a living body but an abstract spirit.

Now and again a little church would uncover itself in the forest – poor and wooden, its architecture bearing marks of the Byzantine. Just outside Tver, in one village church, Perry even glimpsed the spirit of the Gothic, despite the glum Protestant poverty of the building. And the warm breath of his homeland breathed upon Perry – the chary, practical reason of the faith of his fathers, a faith that understood the vanity of everything that is not of the earth.

The huge peat-bogs beneath the forests enticed Perry, and he sensed on his lips the taste of the improbable wealth hidden in these dark soils.

Karl Bergen, the German who in Saint Petersburg had wept

over a letter, was thinking the same thoughts. Alert and animated in the fresh air, he forgot his young wife for a while and said to Perry, swallowing his saliva: "England – Schachtmeister.[6] Russland – Torfmeister.[7] Am I right, Herr Perry?"

"Yes, yes, you're right," said Perry. And he turned away, noticing the terrible height of the sky above the continent – a height impossible above the sea or above the narrow island of Britain.

The travellers ate infrequently but plentifully at villages on the way. Perry drank entire jugfuls of kvass, which he found most palatable, and beneficial to a traveller's digestion.

After passing through Moscow, the engineers long remembered the music of its bells and the silence of the empty torture-towers at the corners of the Kremlin. Perry was especially delighted by the cathedral of Basil the Blessed – that terrible effort by the soul of a rude artist to comprehend the delicacy and, at the same time, the rounded magnificence of a world given to man as a gift.

Sometimes spacious steppes spread out before them, expanses of feather-grass without even a trace of a road.

"Where is the Ambassadors' Road?" the Germans asked the coachmen.

"There!" said the coachmen, pointing into round space.

"But there's not a thing to be seen!" exclaimed the Germans, staring at the ground ahead.

"It's a bearing – not a beaten road! It's like this all the way to Kazan!" the coachmen explained, as best as they could, to the foreigners.

"Ach!" laughed the Germans. "That is famous!"

"It is indeed!" the coachmen solemnly agreed. "There's more space like this, and you can see further! Steppe and sky – tears of joy in the eye!"

"Truly remarkable!" said the Germans in wonder.

"Of course!" said the drivers, and smirked into their beards, lest anyone take offence.

Beyond Ryazan, a sullen and incommodious little town, people lived far apart. Life here was cautious and withdrawn. It was the Tartars who had bequeathed this fear: anxious eyes watching every traveller, secrecy of character, and well bolted store-rooms where people hid their modest goods.

Bertrand Perry gazed in surprise at the occasional fortifications, with small churches in the middle. The inhabitants lived in little huts heaped up around these makeshift kremlins. And it was evident that these were new settlers. Previously, when the Tartars raided these parts, making forays over the grassy steppelands, the people had huddled inside earthen ramparts and wooden walls. And these stronghold-dwellers had, for the main part, been not even useful tillers of the soil, but soldiers committed there by princes. But now the settlements were growing, and there was the roar of fairs every autumn – no matter that the Tsar was at war now with the Swedes, now with the Turks, and that this was impoverishing the country.

Soon the travellers would turn onto the Kalmiuss Sakma, the Tartar path along the bank of the Don and into Muscovy.

One day, at noon, the driver cracked his whip in the air without need and let out a wild whistle. The horses tore forward.

"The Don!" shouted Karl Bergen, thrusting his head out of the carriage.

Perry stopped the carriages and climbed down. On the far horizon, almost in the sky, like a silver vision, shone a clear-cut, living line, like snow on a mountain.

"The Don!" thought Perry, suddenly aghast at Peter's venture: so great did the earth now seem, so splendid the vastness of nature across which he was to build this waterway for ships. In Saint Petersburg, on plans, this venture had appeared clear and practicable, but now, in their noon passage towards the Don, it looked devilish, arduous and overwhelming.

Perry had seen oceans, but these dry and inert lands that lay before him were no less mysterious, grand and magnificent.

"On to the Sakma!" shouted the lead coachman. "Hit it at a slant! To be sure to reach the Idovsk high-road by nightfall!"

The oat-fed horses, sympathizing with the impatient people, tore ahead at full gallop.

"Stop!" the leading coachman suddenly shouted. He raised the handle of his whip as a sign to the coachmen behind him.

"What's happened?" asked the Germans.

"We've forgotten the guard," said the coachman.

"How?" asked the Germans, calming down.

"When we halted, he went down into a little hollow to answer a call of nature. I looked round – and there was no one on our tail-board."

"Holy bearded burgomaster!" the second coachman said thoughtfully.

"Ah, there he is, the bald-pate – clutching his breeches and haring across the steppe!" said the guilty coachman, his mind now at rest.

And the travellers set off again, heading South, towards the Idovsk and Ordobazar high-roads, and then down the small roads of Epifan.

6

Once in Epifan, they started work straight away.

A language he barely knew, together with a strange people and the despair in his heart, plunged Perry into a dark hold of loneliness.

And all the energy of his soul was expended in work alone; sometimes he would rage without reason, and his subordinates dubbed him "the chain-gang master".

The governor of Epifan had conscribed all the peasants in the province: some hewed stone and transported it to the locks; some dug the canal; others, in water up to their bellies, dredged the River Shat.

"Well, Mary!" Bertrand would mutter, wandering at night around his room in Epifan. "This sorrow won't get the better of me! While there's moisture in my heart, I shall escape! I'll finish the canal, the Tsar will give me a deal of money – and then to India. Oh Mary, I feel sorry for you!"

And, in a confusion of anguish, oppressive thoughts, and the excessive strengths of his own body, Perry would fall heavily and dementedly asleep, pining and calling out in his dreams like a child.

Towards autumn Peter himself came to Epifan. He was displeased with the work.

"You're cultivating sorrow in a locked chest," said the Tsar, "instead of hastening the good of the fatherland!" The works were indeed going slowly, for all Perry's severities. The peasants hid from their duties, and some hotheads fled to places unknown.

Brazen locals handed Peter petitions, alleging corruption on the part of the authorities. Peter ordered an inquiry, which discovered that governor Protasyev had, on payment of considerable bribes, exempted State peasants from their obligations, and furthermore had amassed a million roubles through diverse book-keeping wiles and demands for funds from the Exchequer.

Peter ordered Protasyev to be whipped, then sent him to Moscow for a further investigation, but he died there ahead of time, from sorrow and shame.

Soon after Peter's departure, before this disgrace was forgotten, another calamity befell the works at Epifan.

Karl Bergen was directing the work at Lake Ivan, putting up an earth bank around the lake to raise the water to a navigable depth. In September Perry received from him the following report:

"Those men not from these parts, especially the officials from Moscow and the artificers from the Baltic, are nearly all, by the will of God, lying sick. Great affliction flourishes among them, and they fall ill, and for the main part die of fever and swell up. The common people from these parts are long-suffering, but should the work become harder or more pressed, in bog water turning cold with the autumn, they will be ripe for rebellion. I shall conclude by saying that, should this continue, we may end without foremen and without artificers. And so I await speedy instructions from the Chief Engineer."

Perry already knew that the German technicians and the artificers from the Baltic were not only falling sick and dying in the bogs of the Shat and the Upa, but were also running away by secret paths to their motherland, taking with them considerable moneys.

Perry was afraid of the Spring floods, which threatened to destroy constructions still incomplete and defenceless. He desired to secure them, so the flood waters would inflict no especial damage.

But this was hard to achieve; the technical clerks were dying and running away, and the peasants grew still more turbulent, whole villages failing to go out to work. Alone, Bergen could never control such villainies, neither could he cure bog fever.

To cut out at least one evil, Perry promulgated a decree at all the construction sites and throughout all the neighbouring provinces: "It is forbidden, upon pain of death, to allow passage to any foreign artificers working on the canals or sluices; let no one transport them in carts, or sell or lend horses to them."

Beneath the decree Perry appended the signature of Peter – to induce fear and obedience. Let the Tsar censure him afterwards; it was impossible to ride to Voronezh, where Peter was equipping a fleet for the Sea of Azov, and lose two months of time in obtaining his signature.

Not even this, however, brought the artificers to heel.

Perry then grasped that he had been mistaken to conduct the works at such a forced pace and to press so many labourers, clerks and artificers into them at once. He would have done better to begin more quietly and so enable the artificers and the peasants to grow accustomed to the work and find their footing.

At last, in October, work came to a stop. The German engineers made every effort to guard the constructions and stores of materials, but in this too they failed. Therefore the Germans missed no opportunity to send Perry reports, begging to be released from the work, for the Tsar might have them flogged when he came, albeit they were innocent.

One Sunday the governor of Epifan came to see Perry.

"Berdan Ramzeich![8] Look what I've brought you! An unheard-of outrage!"

"What is it?" asked Perry.

"Have a look, Berdan Ramzeich! Think the document over in peace and quiet – I'll just sit here for a while. It's damned unhomely here, Berdan Ramzeich! But of course – we have no women here that are suitable for you. I do see this and I'm sorry for you!"

Perry unfolded the note:

To Peter the First, son of Alexey,
Russian Autocrat and Sovereign.

We, your humble servants, Great Sovereign, together with our peasant folk, have been appointed this year to work without respite at your enterprise of canals and locks, and have been absent from our humble homes throughout the time of ploughing, and the time of harvest, and the time of hay-making, and now, after this work and because of this work we have been unable to harvest our winter crop or sow the Spring crop, and there is nothing to be sown and no one to sow it, and there is nothing to ride on since there are no horses, and if any of our fellows or of our serfs are possessed of any old store of milled or unmilled corn, much of that corn has been consumed without recompense by soldiers and labourers making their way, Great Sovereign, in your service to the works at Epifan, and what remains has been eaten, according to the will of God, by mice, and without remainder, and much injury and destruction has been occasioned to us and to our peasants by these soldiers and working people, and they have induced well-nigh all our young girls to break their fast prematurely.

"You see, Berdan Ramzeich?" asked the governor.

"How did you come by this?" Perry asked in surprise.

"Oh, by chance: for two weeks some churls kept begging my clerk to allow them some ink in exchange for a good ham, or else to give them the recipe. But my clerk's a sly rogue – and he's a landowner himself. So he gave them their ink, and he followed them. He found all this out and got hold of the document. Apart from the Governor's chancellery, you see, there's no ink in Epifan, and no one who knows the dyes that go into it!"

"But have we truly caused the people such misery?" asked Perry.

"Come, come, Berdan Ramzeich! Impudent and disobedient – that's our people for you! Do what you like – they just write petitions and bow and scrape their complaints, no matter if they haven't learned letters and don't know how to make ink. But you wait – I'll back them into a tight corner! I'll teach them to hatch their plots and write without let-up to the Tsar! Why, it's a punishment from the Lord! What were they ever taught to speak words for? They can't read, they can't write – we should rid their mouths of words too!"

"Governor, have you received any reports from Lake Ivan? The carts from Epifan, and the columns of workers you sent on foot under guard – are they still complete?"

"What columns? The ones I sent out on Saviour's Day? Come now, Berdan Ramzeich! One of the guards rode back – all of ten days ago – and told me all the men on foot had run off to the Yaik and the Khoper; as for their families, I tell the truth, they're starving in Epifan. The women give me no peace, and all manner of swine are minded to silence me with their denunciations." The governor took out a rag and wiped his elderly face. "I fear our Sovereign, Berdan Ramzeich! If he descends on us, he'll have me flogged just like that. Intercede for me, Berdan Ramzeich, I implore you by the God of the English!"

"Very well, I shall intercede for you," said Perry. "And are the horses and carts at work round Lake Ivan?"

"Berdan Ramzeich! The horses made off before the men on foot: they've scattered all over the steppe, they've run off and hidden in god-forsaken hamlets. Who can track them down? Not that the horses will be any use. They won't plough again – they're done in from the works, many have fallen down dead in the steppe . . . Yes, Berdan Ramzeich, that's how matters stand now!"

"Yes!" exclaimed Perry, and clasped his hands round his hard, thin head that now entertained no consolation. "So what do you intend, governor?" he went on. "I need labouring men! I don't care how, but I need men on foot, and horses and carts. Other - wise the locks will be swept away in the Spring – and there'll be no mercy from the Tsar!"

"As you will, Berdan Ramzeich! Chop off my head – but there are only women left in Epifan. And the rest of the province is overrun by brigands. I can't so much as show myself in my province – how can I find workers there? There's only one path for me – if the people don't chop off my head, the Tsar will!"

"That's no concern of mine! These are your orders, governor, for the week: at Lake Ivan – five hundred men on foot, and one hundred with carts; at the lock by Storozhevaya Dubrovka village – one thousand and five hundred men on foot and four hundred with carts; at the Nyukhovsk lock – two thousand men on foot and seven hundred with carts; at the Lyubovsk canal, between the Shat and the Don – four thousand men on foot and one and a half thousand with carts; and at the Gaevsk lock one hundred men with carts and six hundred on foot. These are your orders, governor! And the entire work-force to be at their posts within seven days! Should you fail, I report to the Tsar!"

"Listen to me, Berdan Ramzeich!"

Perry interrupted: "I've listened enough. You won't win me over with chants and laments – I'm not a young maid. I want workers, not wailing! Go out into your province and make me some living men!"

"At your command, Berdan Ramzeich, at your command, Sir! Only – I swear by my dead mother – nothing will come of this!"

"Out into your province!" said Perry angrily.

"In that case, Berdan Ramzeich, at least let's put off moving the stone until Spring! The peasants are afeared of that stone.

It's a blessed heavy weight, and anyway the Lyutorts quarry will never . . ."

"Very well," answered Perry, understanding that this was no time to embark on new works. What mattered now was to protect from flood what was built already. "But step to it, governor! You're a good talker, but a sly devil when it comes to work!"

"We're grateful for the stone! Goodbye, Berdan Ramzeich! . . ."

The governor uttered a few words in a low voice and went away.

The last words were in the local speech, the dialect of Epifan, and so Perry understood nothing. And had he understood, it would have brought him no cheer.

7

All five German engineers came to Epifan for the winter. Their faces were grown over with beards, and they had aged during the last half year and grown visibly more wild.

Karl Bergen was gnawed by a cruel longing for his German wife, but he had signed an agreement with the Tsar for one year and it was not possible for him to depart earlier: Russian justice in those days was spirited. So the young German trembled with terror and from the longing he felt for his family, and the work fell through his hands.

The other Germans also made blunders, and regretted having travelled to Russia in search of easy roubles.

Perry alone did not give in, and the sadness in his heart for Mary found issue in his raging energy.

In technical conference with the Germans, Perry explained that the condition of the half-finished locks was perilous. The Spring waters could sweep the constructions clean away, especially the locks at Lyutoretsk and Murovlyansk, from which the workers had all run away as long ago as August.

The governor of Epifan had furnished nothing of what Perry had commanded – either from ill-will in the matter or because it truly was impossible to round up more workers.

The engineers proved unable, in their discussions, to contrive a way of protecting the locks from the Spring. Perry knew that Tsar Peter used to order ship-builders in Petersburg to don black burial garments. If the launch of a new ship and her maiden voyage passed successfully, the Tsar gave the engineer a recompense of one hundred roubles or more, according to the capacity of the vessel, and removed the deathly garment from the engineer with his own hands. But if the ship sprang a leak or keeled over for no reason, or worse, sank near the shore, then the Tsar would deliver the ship-builder to immediate execution by beheading.

Perry did not fear the loss of his head but allowed this might happen, though he said nothing to the Germans.

The long Great-Russian winter settled in. Epifan was buried in snow, and the country round about sank into an absolute silence. People here appeared to live in great sorrow and insupportable boredom. But in truth their lives were not so bad. They made visits to one another on the numerous feast days, drank home-made vodka, ate preserved apples and pickled cabbage, and now and again got married.

At Christmas, driven by boredom and solitude, one of the Germans – Peter Forch – married Ksenia Tarasovna Rodionova, the daughter of a rich Epifan boyar and salt merchant. Her father owned a caravan of forty carts which travelled between Astrakhan and Moscow with twenty drivers, supplying the northern provinces with salt. In his youth, Taras Zakharovich Rodionov had himself been a driver. Peter Forch moved in with his father-in-law and soon grew stout from solicitous nourishment and a peaceful life.

Until as late as the European New Year the engineers all worked diligently under Perry's supervision, drawing up detailed plans and estimates for the quantity of materials and the number of hands required, as well as projecting a variety of methods for letting the Spring waters through without damage.

Perry drew up a report for the Tsar, in which he laid out the whole history of the works, pointed to the fatal shortage of workers, and doubted a successful conclusion. Perry also addressed a copy of his report to the English ambassador in Saint Petersburg – as a precaution.

In February a courier from the Tsar arrived in Epifan, bringing Perry a missive.

To Bertrand Perry,
Chief Builder and Engineer of the Epifan sluices and
the canals between the Don and Oka rivers

Report of your incapable work reached me before your petition. From this lack of success I observe that the people there in Epifan are lackeys who do not perceive their own interests, and that you moreover should drive my will upon them and chasten your subordinates so severely that none, be he foreign artificer or unskilled peasant, shall be able to resolve upon disobedience.

Having considered sundry thoughts touching the Epifan sluices, I have settled upon these forestalling measures for the coming summer.

Your governor I have discharged, and I have appointed him a penance: to drag fire ships over the great sandbanks between Azov and Voronezh. As a new governor I send you Grishka Saltykov, a steadfast and expeditious man, known to me in person and spirited in administering justice. He will be your chief assistant in regard to your labourers, both those on foot and those with carts.

And further I declare the province of Epifan under martial law, and the male population I conscribe entire as soldiers. For this purpose I send to you lieutenants and captains of choice quality, who will come to your works with companies of recruits and militia from Epifan. And consider yourself a full general, and assign ranks to your assistants and subordinate artificers as befits them.

In certain neighbouring provinces affected by your works I have also decreed martial law.

Should you this summer go awry with the sluices and canals – beware! That you are British will bring you little joy.

Perry rejoiced at this answer from Peter. After such reforms in Epifan, the success of the works was now secured. As long as Spring played no special tricks and last year's labours were not brought to ruin.

In March Perry received a letter from Newcastle. He read through it as if it were news from the other world – so rusty had his heart grown towards his previous fate.

Bertrand!

My son, my first-born, died on New Year's Day. My whole body aches from the memory of him. Forgive me that I write to you, a man now a stranger, but you used to believe in my sincerity. Do you remember I told you how, for all her life, a woman remembers the man to whom she gave her first kiss? Well, I remember you, and that is why I write about the gift I have lost – my little son. He was dearer to me than my husband, dearer than your memory, dearer than my own self. O how many times dearer than all my most precious treasures! I shall not write of him to you, or I shall begin to weep and not complete even this second letter. I sent you the first a month ago.

My husband has become entirely a stranger to me. He works much, visits the Sailors' Club in the evenings, and I am alone, and so unhappy! My only consolation is in the reading of books, and in letters to you, which I shall write frequently, unless this offends you.

Goodbye, dear Bertrand! You are dear to me as a friend or a distant relative, in you lies my feeling of tender memories. Write letters to me, I shall be very glad to receive them. It is only my love for my husband and my memory of you that hold me to life. But in my dreams my dead boy calls me to share his sufferings and his death with him.

Yet I still live, a shameless and cowardly mother.

Mary.

P.S. It is a warm Spring in Newcastle. As before, on clear days the coast of Europe can be seen across the strait. That coast reminds me always of you, and I grow still more sad.

Do you remember the lines you once sent me in a letter?

> The chance for mournful, arduous passion –
> A sign your soul is loved by God . . .[9]

Who wrote those lines? Do you remember your first letter to me, where you declared your love, ashamed to say to my face the fateful words. It was then I understood your manliness, and the modesty of your nature, and I liked you.

After the letter Perry was seized by a tender sense of peace and humanity. Perhaps he found satisfaction in Mary's unhappiness – their two fates were now in balance.

Having no close friend in Epifan, he began to make visits to Peter Forch; there he would drink tea with cherry jam as he conversed with Forch's wife, Ksenia Tarasovna, about far-off Newcastle, the warm strait and the coast of Europe that can be seen from Newcastle on transparent days. But Bertrand never spoke to anyone about Mary, concealing that she was the source of his humanity and sociability.

It was March. The people of Epifan were fasting; the bells rang mournfully from the Orthodox churches, and on the high ground the fields had already turned black.

Perry's good cheer did not desert him. He did not answer Mary's letter; letters from him would not please her husband, and Perry had no wish to write civil commonplaces.

Perry sent the German engineers out to the most dangerous locks, so they could supervise the work of letting off the Spring waters.

The peasants were now soldiers. The new governor, Grigory Saltykov, raged about the province mercilessly and without respite; the prisons were packed with unruly peasants; and the governor's special place of justice, his whipping-hut, was also at work day after day, inculcating reason into the buttocks of peasants by means of the knout.

There was now no lack of workers, both on foot and with horses, but Perry saw how perilous it all was: mutiny might break out at any moment, and not only would everyone flee the works, but in their fury they would destroy the constructions in one swoop.

The Spring, however, was fitful: small amounts of water would flow during the day, only to freeze solid at night. The water passed through the locks as if through worn buckets; the

Germans and the workers on duty therefore had time enough to plug the cracks in the spillways with thawed-out earth, and no serious damage took place.

Perry was greatly pleased; he paid more frequent visits to Forch's wife, who was now lonely, and he talked with her father about the drivers of salt waggons, the Tartar invasions, and the ancient steppes and their sweet grasses.

Eventually the delightful provincial Spring burst out into the fire of summer, and nature's first youth fell silent. Summer came in ripeness and in rage, and all life on earth felt alarm.

Perry determined to complete all the locks and canals by autumn. He now yearned for the sea, his homeland, and his old father who lived in London.

The father measured his sorrow for his son by the ash from his pipe; out of longing for his son he smoked unremittingly. When they parted, he had said: "Bert! How much tobacco shall I have to burn before I see you again?"

"A great deal, father, a great deal!" Bertrand had answered.

"But no poison will get the better of me, son! Soon, no doubt, I'll start chewing the leaves."

At the beginning of summer, the work began to move at a good pace. Frightened as they were of the Tsar, the peasants laboured diligently. Some of the men, however, ran off and hid in distant Old Believer settlements. And a number of hotheads whispered together and led whole companies to the Urals and the Kalmyk steppes. Men were sent after them, but never to any avail.

In June Perry inspected all the works. He found their progress and speed to be adequate.

Meanwhile Karl Bergen quite delighted him. At the very bottom of Lake Ivan he had discovered a bottomless well-window. So much water flowed from it into the lake that it would provide an additional supply to the canals during years of drought and shallow water. It was necessary only to raise last year's earthen dike round Lake Ivan by one sazhen, so as to collect more of this spring water into the lake, and then, when the need arose, to let off the water into the canals through a special channel.

Perry approved Bergen's invention and ordered him to clean out the well with a sludge-pump, and to insert a large iron pipe with a grating, so the well would not silt up again. Still more water would then flow into the lake, and the waterway would not run dry in a drought.

But fear and doubt stung Perry's pride as he returned to Epifan. The projects drawn up in Petersburg had not taken into account the local conditions, and especially the droughts, which in these parts were not infrequent. It was now becoming apparent that in a dry summer there would be too little water to fill the canals, and the waterway would turn to a dry, sandy track.

On his arrival in Epifan, Perry began to recalculate the technical figures. It was worse still: the project had been drafted according to local data from the year 1682, the summer of which had abounded with moisture.

After talking with local people and with Forch's father-in-law, Perry understood that during years even of average snow and rain the canals would be too shallow for so much as a rowing boat to pass down them. And best not to speak of dry summers: only a sandy dust would rise from the canal bed.

"So it seems I shan't see my father again!" thought Perry. "And I shall not return to Newcastle, nor look at the coast of Europe!"

The one hope that remained was the spring at the bottom of Lake Ivan. Should it furnish much water, then that could feed the canals during years of dry wind.

53

But this discovery of Bergen's still did not return to Bertrand's soul the quiet peace he had enjoyed after the letter from Mary. Secretly he did not believe the well in Lake Ivan would provide an abundance of water, but he concealed his despair behind this small hope.

At present a special raft was being constructed on Lake Ivan, from which they would drill down to deepen the well and insert into it a broad, cast-iron pipe.

8

At the beginning of August Perry received from Karl Bergen an official report. It was brought to him by the governor, Saltykov.

"Here, your Excellency, is a note for you. My lads say those peasant vermin have all gone and left the Tatinka lock without a word. So let me set your mind at rest forthwith: tomorrow I shall find the women, the husbands of whom have fled, and send them straight to Tatinka themselves. As for the fugitives, I shall catch them and turn them over to a field court-martial. Off with their heads – that'll smarten them up! Seems it's the only way!"

"I agree with you, Saltykov," said Perry, benumbed by his cares.

"So, Your Excellency, you will sign me those death warrants? I warn you, you are now the head of the entire work."

"Very well," answered Perry, "I shall sign them."

"And there is one other matter, general. Tomorrow is my daughter's betrothal. A suitor from Moscow, a merchant's son, is taking my Feklusha under his roof in marriage. So come and celebrate with us."

"I'm grateful. Perhaps I shall. Thank you, governor."

Saltykov left. Perry tore open the package from Bergen.

Confidential!

Colleague Perry!

From 20 to 25 June drilling was carried out on the subterranean opening in Lake Ivan – with the aim of
widening, deepening, and cleaning it. The consequence,
according to your assignment, would be a strong influx
of subterranean waters into Lake Ivan.

The drilling was stopped after nine sazhens for reasons
here stated.

At eight o'clock in the evening, on 25 July, the sludge-
pump ceased to bring up viscous clay and was expelling
fine dry sand. I was present in person throughout this
operation.

Casting off from the drilling-raft, to answer a call of
nature on shore, I discovered grass protruding above the
surface of the water, which I had not noticed before. As
I stepped onto dry land, I heard the howls of a dog, one
called Ilyusha that the soldiers feed from their copper.
This troubled me greatly, in spite of my faith in God.

The soldier workers informed me that from noon and
until that moment the water in the lake had been falling.
Water weed had been exposed, and two small islands had
appeared in the middle of the water.

The soldiers were in terrible fear, and said that with the
pipe we had pierced right through the bed of the lake,
and the lake would now waste away.

Yesterday's water level was indeed clearly visible on the
bank, as was today's, and the difference between them
was of half a sazhen.

Returning on board the raft, I ordered the drilling to
be stopped and the outlet plugged up immediately. For

this we lowered a cast-iron trap, one arshin in diameter, onto the well, but this was at once dragged into the underground depths, where it vanished. We then began to block the outlet with a large-bore pipe packed with clay. But the pipe too was sucked into the outlet and dragged away. And this suction continues until now, and the water rushes out of the lake beyond recover.

There is a simple explanation for this. With the bore-pump the artificer pierced through the layer of impermeable clay which held the waters of Lake Ivan.

And beneath this clay lie dry, greedy sands that still suck the water out of the lake and swallow even objects made of iron.

I no longer know what I should do, and so await your orders.

Perry's soul, that had feared no terror, now began to shake and tremble, as befits the nature of man. Bertrand could not endure such a measure of grief and he burst into piteous weeping, leaning his forehead against the desk.

Fate pursued him everywhere: he had lost first his mother-land, then Mary, and now his work had miscarried. He knew he would not escape alive from these dry, spacious plains, that he would never again see Newcastle, or the shore of Europe, or his father with his pipe, or look on Mary for a last time.

The empty, low room resounded from Perry's weeping and frenzied grinding of teeth. He had turned over the table and was thrashing about in the cramped space, howling from this upsurge of anguish and losing all self-command. The element of grief raged inside him, leaving its imprint at random, beyond all supervision on the part of his reason.

After he had calmed down, Bertrand smiled, and felt

ashamed of such shameless despair. He took out a little book from his trunk and began to read:

ARTHUR CHEMSFIELD
The Love of Lady Betty Hugh
A novel in three volumes
and forty chapters

"My lady!
Abounding in love, anguished and groaning, my heart calls to you with an angelic prayer: prefer me to all other men of society or take this heart out of my breast and devour it like a boiled egg!

A sombre whirlwind shakes the vaults of my skull, and my blood flames like liquid pitch! Can you truly refuse me comfort, Madame Betty? Do you not fear your anguish over the grave of a man who is strange to you, but faithful?

Mistress Betty, I know I need only approach your window for Mister Hugh to shoot me with his old gun and his stale gunpowder. May this come to pass! May my fateful destiny be made manifest!

I am an assassin of domestic hearths! But my heart seeks grace under the chemise of my beloved, where her heart beats beneath the hills of her innocent breasts!

I am a homeless vagabond! But I solicit the good will of your respectable husband!

I am tired now of giving my affection to horses and other beasts, and I seek the love of a more tender being – a woman . . ."

Perry sank into a sleep that was unexpected, but was deep and refreshing, and the book fell from his hands – never read, yet of interest . . .

Evening set in; the room turned cold, grew dim, and filled with the sighs of faint rays of light from a hidden and benighted sky.

9

An important year then passed – a long autumn, an interminable winter and a timid, precious Spring.

At last, of a sudden, the lilac blossomed – that rose of the Russian provinces, gift of the modest fences and sign of the inescapable village dream.

The entire complex of works, designated the State Don-Oka Waterway, was now complete.

Answering the requirements of a land-locked country, this would allow free passage for many years to ships both large and small.

Fierce heat set in from the beginning of May. At first the fields were fragrant with the bodies of young plants, but then, in June, they gave off the dusty smell of withering leaves together with the pungency of flowers soured by the deathly heat. There was no rain.

To inspect the sluices and canals, the sovereign sent the French engineer General Trouzesson, accompanied by a special board of three admirals and one Italian engineer.

"Engineer Perry!" Trouzesson declared, "by order of His Majesty the Emperor, I propose to you within one week to bring the entire waterway, from the Don to the Oka, into navigable condition! I am empowered by His Majesty to examine all the watery installations, in order to establish and determine their durability and conformity to the requirements of His Majesty."

"At your service!" Perry replied. "The waterway will be ready at the end of four days."

"That is splendid!" Trouzesson declared with satisfaction. "Do as you have said, engineer, and do not delay our return to Saint Petersburg."

At the end of four days the draw-doors were lowered and the reaches began to fill with water. The head of water, however, was so slight that not even the deep parts filled to a level of more than one arshin. In addition, as soon as the water, blocked by the locks, rose a little in the river, then the underground streams ceased to flow, stifled by the layer of water which lay on top of them.

On the fifth day the water in the reaches of the canals entirely ceased to rise. Moreover, the heat was fierce, there was no rain, and no inflow from the gullies.

A barge, laden with timber, with a draft of little more than one arshin, was launched from the Murovlyansk lock on the Shat river. After covering half a verst, it ran aground in the middle of the channel.

Trouzesson and his inspection commission rode in a troika along the bank of the waterway.

None of the peasants, other than a few necessary workmen, was present at the opening of the waterway. The peasants could not wait for Epifan to be delivered from this calamity, and none of them intended to go out in boats; maybe someone would wade across the water when he was drunk – but even that only rarely: in those days in-laws lived two hundred versts from one another. The womenfolk were not on good terms, so the families of neighbours did not marry.

Trouzesson swore in French and in English, but French and English curses have little power. He was unable to swear in Russian. Consequently not even the workmen on the locks were afraid of the general; they did not understand the spluttering and shouting of this Russian general from foreign parts.

And that there would be little water, and boats would run

aground, had been known for twelve months to every woman in Epifan. Therefore the inhabitants had seen the work as a foreign fancy and a sport of the Tsar's – but none had dared question why these torments should be laid on the people.

Only the women of Epifan felt sorry for the morose Perry: "He's good-looking and well-built – true enough – and he doesn't look old, but when does he have any fun with the girls? Some sorrow gnaws at him, or he's buried his woman, there's no knowing . . . But what a gloom-ridden face – fair makes you shudder . . ."

The following day one hundred peasants were furnished with measuring-rods. The peasants set off through the water. Only when close to the locks and their dikes did they swim a little, but elsewhere they were able to wade. They carried the rods in their hands, and the foremen marked the water level on them with notches, but for the main part the peasants employed their own legs, measuring first to the knee and then counting off spans, though the hand-span of some peasants was nearly nine inches. Palms then were broad and the span of five fingers powerful indeed, and this did not aid the work of measuring.

Within a week all the reaches had been measured. Trouzesson calculated that not even a rowing boat could pass everywhere, and that in certain places the water would not lift a raft.

Yet the Tsar had ordered that the canals be constructed deep enough to allow safe passage to a ten-cannon ship.

Trouzesson and his board drew up a report of their inspection, and read it to Perry and his subordinate Germans.

The report stated that, on account of an insufficiency of water, both the canals and the sections of river with locks were unfit for sailing and navigation. The expenses and labours must be deemed wasted and of no profit to anyone. What additional measures should be undertaken was for the Tsar to determine.

"A fine waterway!" said one of the admirals, a stooge of Trouzesson's. "You've built something that will be laughed at for ever, you've squandered the great labour of the people! You've mocked the Tsar, you've insulted him – why, the whole affair has even given me heartburn. So you look out, you Germans! And as for you, miracle-worker from England, it's the whipping-post for you – and count that a mercy! I'm afeared to submit this report to the Tsar – he'll lash me across the face!"

Perry said nothing. He knew the project had been drawn up in accordance with surveys carried out by this same Trouzesson – but there was no use in trying to save himself now.

The next day, at sunrise, Trouzesson departed with his men.

Perry did not know where to direct his usual capacity for work and walked for entire days in the steppes, while in the evenings he read English novels – but other novels, not *The Love of Lady Betty Hugh*.

The Germans had made off ten days after Trouzesson. Governor Saltykov had sent out search-parties, but these had yet to return.

The only German still remaining in Epifan was the married Forch, a man who loved his spouse.

Governor Saltykov kept Perry and Forch under covert surveillance, but they were both aware of this. Saltykov was waiting for orders from Petersburg, and kept out of Perry's way.

Perry became wild and mute in his heart, and his mind was finally silent. There was no use in beginning any serious endeavour. He knew the justice of the Tsar awaited him. He did, however, write briefly to the British ambassador in Petersburg, begging him to rescue a subject of the British King. But Perry suspected the governor would not dispatch his letter with the next messenger, or else would include it with the official correspondence and direct it to the Secret Service in Petersburg.

Two months later Peter sent an express with a secret missive. The Tsar's messenger rode in a carriage, little boys raced behind, and the dust they threw up shone like a rainbow in the evening sun.

Perry was standing at this moment by the window, and he saw all this rapid movement of his own fate. He understood immediately what the courier had brought, and lay down to sleep, to shorten the useless time.

The next day, at sunrise, there was a knocking at Perry's door. Governor Saltykov came in.

"Berdan Ramzeich Perry, English subject, I declare to you the will of his Imperial Majesty: from this hour you are no more a general but a civil man – and what is more, a criminal. You will be escorted on foot to Moscow, where the Sovereign's justice will be administered. Get yourself ready, Berdan Ramzeich, and vacate these State premises . . ."

10

At noon Perry was walking across the Central Russian continent, contemplating the blades of grass under his feet. On his back was a knapsack, and there were guards beside him.

A long journey lay ahead, and the guards were kind, so as not to expend their souls to no purpose in anger.

The two guards were natives of Epifan. They told Perry that Forch, the remaining German, was to be flogged the next morning in the torture-hut. It appeared the Tsar had appointed him no other punishment; he was merely to be given a good whipping and then sent back to the Germans.

The road to Moscow proved so long that Perry forgot where he was being led; he had grown so tired he just longed for a speedy end to the journey, and death.

In Ryazan the guards from Epifan were changed. The new guards told Perry there might well be war with the kingdom of England.

"But why?" asked Perry.

"Tsar Peter, people say, caught a lover in the Tsaritsa's bed-chamber – and it was the English ambassador! So Tsar Peter chopped off his head and had it sent to the Tsaritsa in a silken bag!"

"Is that true?" exclaimed Perry.

"You don't believe it?" said the guard. "Have you ever seen our Tsar? A giant of a man! They say he tore off that ambassador's head with his bare hands – as if the man were a chicken! I'm not joking . . . Only I've heard the Tsar won't send the people to war over a woman . . ."

Towards the end of the journey Perry no longer sensed his feet. They had swelled up, and he might have been walking in felt boots.

During their last bivouac, one of the guards said without warning to Perry: "And where are we taking you? Could be the torture room! There's nothing about cruelty our Tsar doesn't know! I'd slip away from under our very eyes! Upon my word! And you walk along like a chicken! You're lily-livered, brother – if I were you I'd run berserk. No one's going to flog me – let alone chop off my head!"

II

Perry was led to the Kremlin and delivered to the tower prison. Nothing was said to him, and Perry ceased to question his fate.

Through a narrow window he looked all night at the splendour of nature, the stars, and marvelled at this living fire in the sky, burning at such a height and beyond the law.

This insight filled Perry with joy, and from the deep low

63

floor he laughed carelessly towards the lofty sky which reigned happily in space that took the breath away.

Perry awoke suddenly, not remembering how he had fallen asleep. He awoke not of himself, but because there were people standing above him, talking quietly so as not to disturb the prisoner. But he awoke, sensing them there.

"Bertrand Ramsay Perry," said the scribe, taking out a paper and reading off the name, "by order of His Majesty the Emperor, you are sentenced to be beheaded. More than that I do not know. Goodbye. May you be granted the Kingdom of Heaven. After all, you are a man."

The clerk left and closed the door firmly from outside, working the iron bolt with difficulty.

Another man stayed behind – a huge boor, wearing trousers held up by buttons, but no shirt.

"Off with your trousers!"

Perry began to remove his shirt.

"I said, off with your trousers, thief!"

The executioner's pale blue eyes had turned black and were gleaming with wild feeling, with some kind of turbulent happiness.

"But where's your axe?" asked Perry, losing all sensation except a slight repugnance, as if standing before cold water into which this man was about to throw him.

"Axe!" said the executioner. "I don't need an axe to deal with you!"

An insight struck like a harsh, cutting blade into Perry's brain, an insight alien and terrifying to his nature, as is a bullet to a living heart.

And for Perry this thought replaced the feeling of the axe on his neck: he glimpsed blood in his numb, frozen eyes and collapsed into the embrace of his howling executioner.

An hour later the clerk began to rattle the bolt.

"Finished, Ignaty?" he shouted, leaning against the door and pressing his ear to it.

"Wait outside, vermin!" answered the executioner, breathing heavily and grinding his teeth.

"Satan incarnate!" muttered the clerk. "Never seen such a man. You won't catch me going in – not while he's still raging!"

There was a ringing of bells; early mass was about to start.

The scribe went in to the church, took some communion bread for his first breakfast, and provided himself with a small candle for his solitary evening reading.

* * *

In August, just before the Feast of the Apple Saviour,[10] Saltykov, the governor of Epifan, received a fragrant parcel bearing the stamps of a foreign realm. The writing on it was in a strange language, but three words were in Russian:

To Bertrand Perry

Engineer

Saltykov took fright, not knowing what he should do with this parcel addressed to a dead man. He then put it out of harm's way behind the icon case – to be an eternal home for the spiders.

RUBBISH WIND

Dedicated to comrade Zachow, an unemployed
German, witness at the Leipzig trial,[1] imprisoned
in one of Hitler's concentration camps.

> "Leave my madness
> And summon those
> Who have taken away my mind."
> *The Thousand and One Nights*

OVER THE EARTH, DAWN ROSE IN THE SKY AND A NEW radiant day began: July 16, 1933. Yet by eleven o'clock this day had already aged from the effect of its own excessive energy – from the heat, from the soil's dust-spreading frailty which had eclipsed all space, from the decay of every living breath that had been aroused by the warming light – and the summer's day became turbid, burdensome, and damaging to the sight of eyes.

The element of light penetrated through a large, hot window and lit up a solitary figure asleep on an iron bed, on worn-out sheets that had been disturbed by the movements of sleep. This sleeping man was not old, but his ordinary face had long ago turned grey from the strain of providing himself with life, and a persistent, exhausted despair lay with bony hardness in the expression of his face, like part of the surface of a human body.

It was Sunday. Out of the other room came the sleeping man's swarthy wife, Zelda by name, who had been born in the East, in Russian Asia. With meek solicitude she threw a blanket over her exposed husband and awoke him: "Get up, Albert. The day's begun, I'll find something . . ."

Albert opened his eyes – first one eye, then the other – and everything in the world seemed so undefined and alien that, shaken to the heart, he wrinkled up his face and began to cry – as in the terrifying dream of a child, when suddenly mother is nowhere to be found, and blurred objects rise up and advance menacingly against a small person with screwed-up eyes . . . Zelda stroked Albert's face; he calmed down and his eyes came to a stop – pure eyes that were completely extinguished and that gazed as fixedly as if he were blind. He could not immediately remember that he existed and that it was necessary for him to carry on living, he had forgotten the weight and feeling of his own body. Zelda bent down closer; she was an Afghan who had faded from hunger, though once she had been a dear and magnificent being.

"Get up, Albert . . . I've got two potatoes and some whale fat."

With bitterness Albert Lichtenberg saw that his wife had become an animal: the down on her cheeks had turned into a coat of hair, her eyes had a rabid gleam and her mouth was filled with the saliva of greed and sensuality; she was uttering over his face the cries of her dead madness. Albert shouted at her and drove her away. As he got dressed Lichtenberg saw that Zelda was crying and had lain down on the floor; her leg was bared, it was covered with the rampant sores of an unclean animal; she did not even lick them, she was worse than a monkey – a monkey looks after its organs with painstaking care.

Albert took his stick and wanted to leave. He had gone dark in his thoughts: this former woman had sucked his youth dry, she had nagged him for being poor, for being out of work, for his impotence as a man, and she had sat naked on top of him in the night. Now she was a beast, scum of crazed consciousness, whereas he would always, until the grave, remain a human being, a physicist of the cosmic spaces, and even if hunger were to torment his stomach right up to his heart, it would not reach higher than his throat, and his life would hide away in the cave of his head.

Albert hit Zelda with his stick and went out onto the street, into the southern German province. The bells of the Roman faith were ringing, and white, blessed girls were coming out of a small church on the street, their eyes filled not so much with tears from adoration of Christ as with moisture from love-glands.

Albert looked at the sun and smiled at it as if it were a distant human being. No, it was not the sun, not this universal radiance of energy, nor was it comets or wandering black stars that would finish off humanity on the earth: they were too great for such an insignificant act. People themselves would grind one another down and tear one another to pieces, and the best would fall dead in the struggle while the worst would turn into animals.

ˈA Roman priest came out onto the porch of the Catholic church, excited, damp and red – an ambassador of God in the guise of a man's urinary appendage. Then old women appeared from the church, women in whom once-seething passions now oozed like pus, and in whose wombs the parts of love and motherhood now rotted away in sepulchral darkness. From the porch the priest blessed the hot space and then retired into the cool of his lodgings in the churchyard.

The small bells on the tower still went on ringing, carrying completed prayers up over the church's tormenting Gothic summit and into a dim sky that had been clouded over by the sun's fierce heat. What the eternal bells were saying was the same as what the books and newspapers wrote about, what the music sang about in the night-time cafés: "Waste away, waste away, waste away!"

But Albert Lichtenberg had been hearing the monotonous,

omnipresent sound of "Waste away!" for twenty years, and this call to languor, to the slowing down and destruction of life, was now sounding ever more strongly; only his heart still beat innocently and clearly, as if uncorrupted, as if understanding nothing.

Albert sat down somewhere in the city, amid the currents of heat; the day went on above him with the meticulousness of something trivial, with the precision of a state execution, and with impatience for some unknown mercy. Lichtenberg touched a tree that was growing in front of him. Carefully and tenderly he began to look at this wooden plant that was tormented by the same languor as he was, by the same wish for a cool wind in this dusty, heartfelt existence.

"Who are you?" asked Lichtenberg.

Branches and leaves bent down towards the exhausted man. Albert seized one of the closer branches with that passion and tension of solitary friendliness before which all blissful love on earth is insignificant. Dead butterflies fell from the tree, but a living moth flew away into the dry emptiness.

Lichtenberg gripped his stick in his hand. He walked on further with the fury of his harsh consciousness, he felt the thoughts in his head standing up like stubble, forcing their way through the bone. In the decaying, worn-out air he saw the city square. The large Catholic cathedral, like a sleepy millennium, like suffering organized into stone, stood there silently and with concentration, pushing deep down onto the tombs of its builders. Rubbish was rising from below: a hundred or so National Socialists, in the brown overalls of their *Weltanschauung*, were erecting a monument to Adolf Hitler. The monument had been transported already finished on a truck, it had been cast from high-quality bronze in Essen. Another truck, with a crane on its platform, had unloaded the monument, while four more trucks had brought some tropical plants in sea-blue boxes. The National Socialists laboured without regard for their clothes; their underwear was rotting from sweat, their bones were wearing out, but there was enough clothing and sausage for them, since at that moment millions of machines and sullen people were exerting themselves in Germany, ministering with the friction of metal and of human bones to the fame of a single man and his aides.

From the central street of the city appeared a unanimous crowd, a crowd of several thousand people singing songs from the depths of their guts – Lichtenberg could clearly distinguish the bass voice of the gullet and the tenor of the quivering intestines. The crowd drew near to the monument; the faces of the people signified happiness: the pleasure of power and mind-lessness shone from them, the repose of night and of food was guaranteed for each of them by the dark might of their own numbers. They reached the monument; the vanguard of the crowd proclaimed a greeting in unison – to the man represented in bronze – and then began to help those who were working, and rubbish rose from them with elemental force, so that Lichtenberg felt dandruff even in his soul. Other thousands and millions of people were also now tramping the old, difficult earth of Germany, expressing through their presence alone their joy in the saviour of their ancient motherland and of contemporary humanity. Millions now were in a position not to work, but just to offer their salutes; and in addition there were the hordes and tribes who sat in offices and intellectually, psychically, visually, musically and in writing affirmed the sovereignty of the saviour-genius, themselves remaining silent and anonymous.

Neither those who had been cheering nor those who were silent did enough work even to earn black bread, yet they ate butter, drank wine made from grapes, and each of them fed a faithful wife. Moreover, armed troops were marching in columns across Germany, protecting the glory of the government and the orderliness of the devotion shown to it. These columns of mute, focused people fed every day on ham, and the government encouraged in them the heroic spirit of celibacy yet furnished them with phials to protect them against infection with syphilis by Jewish women (German women, being conscious, did not suffer from syphilis; thanks to the perfect racial composition of their bodies they did not even give off any bad smells).

Lichtenberg did not labour either, he was studying. All the human aggregates he saw were either dying from hunger and madness, or else striding in the ranks of the State Guard. Who fed them with food, clothed them with clothes and furnished them with the luxury of power and idleness? Where did the proletariat live? Or had it died of exhaustion, after expending itself in labour and anonymity? Who, poor, powerful and silent, maintained this world which grew emaciated in horror and frenzied joy rather than in creativity, and which protected itself with a palisade of idols?

Albert Lichtenberg stood in exhaustion on the old Catholic square, viewing with astonishment this kingdom of the imaginary; even he had difficulty in sensing his own existence, he had to struggle after each memory of himself; mostly he kept forgetting himself, perhaps some surplus of suffering consciousness was switching off the life inside him so it should be preserved if only in its sad forgetfulness.

A stranger to all thought, indifferent, as if he did not exist, Lichtenberg walked up to the radiator of the truck. The metal gave off a trembling heat; thousands of men, converted to metal, were resting heavily in the motor, no longer demanding either socialism or truth, sustained by cheap petrol alone. Lichtenberg leaned against the vehicle, pressing his face to it as if to some fallen brotherhood; through the chinks of the radiator he saw the mechanism's tomb-like darkness, in its clefts humanity had lost its way and fallen down dead. Only now and again amid the empty factories could you find mute workers; for every worker there were ten members of the State Guard, and in the course of a day every worker produced a hundred horsepower in order to feed, comfort and arm the guards who ruled over them. One miserable labourer maintained ten triumphant masters, and yet these ten masters were filled not with joy but with anxiety, clutching weapons in their hands against those who were poor and isolated.

Over the radiator of the vehicle hung a golden strip of material bearing an inscription in black letters: "Honour the leader of the Germans – the wise, courageous and great Adolf! Eternal glory to Hitler!" On either side of the inscription lay signs of the swastika, like the tracks of insect feet.

"O splendid nineteenth century, you were wrong!" Lichtenberg said into the dust of the air – and suddenly his thought stopped, transformed into a physical force. He lifted his heavy stick and hit the vehicle in the chest – in the radiator – smashing its honeycombs. The National driver silently got out from behind the wheel and, gripping the torso of the thin physicist, struck his head with equal force against the same radiator. Lichtenberg collapsed into the rubbish on the ground and lay there a while without sensation; this no longer caused him suffering – he had very little sense of himself anyway as a vital body and ego, and his head ached more from the rubbish of reality than from blows against iron.

Above his vision the day shone weak and white, he looked into it without blinking; dust had blocked up his eye sockets, and tears were flowing from them to wash away the tickling dirt. Above him stood the driver; all the animals this man had eaten in the course of his life – cows, rams, sheep, fish and crabs – after being digested inside him, had left on his body and face their expression of frenzy and of deaf savagery. Lichtenberg got to his feet, jabbed his stick into the animal torso of the driver and walked away from the vehicle. Astonished at such an act of heedless courage, the driver forgot to give Lichtenberg a second blow.

In space a wind blew from the south, carrying from France, Italy and Spain the rubbish of everyday life and the smell of cities, traces of agitated noise, the strangled voice of a man . . . Lichtenberg turned his face to meet the wind; he heard the distant complaint of a woman, the melancholy shout of a crowd, the grinding of gear-boxes, the song of moist flowers on the shore of the Mediterranean. He listened closely to this incoherence, to this long, unanswered flow of air that was carrying a howl over the speechlessness of the surrounding bustle.

Lichtenberg went up to the labourers beside the monument. The men's work was already coming to an end. On a cylinder of cast-iron stood the bronze half-body of a human being, topped by a head.

On the statue's face were greedy lips that loved food and kisses, its cheeks had grown fat from universal fame, and on its ordinary, workaday forehead the paid artist had placed a harsh wrinkle, in order to represent the agonized concentration of this half-body on organizing humanity's fate, to make clear its tense spirit of preoccupation. The figure's chest was thrust forward, as if to meet that of a woman; its swollen lips, ready for passion and public speeches, lay in a tender smile – if the lower half of a body had been added to this monument, this man could have been the lover of a young woman, but with only the upper half of a body he could not have been anything except a national leader.

Lichtenberg smiled. One joy still had not left him – inadvertently, out of absent-mindedness, he was able to think.

"O splendid nineteenth century!" Lichtenberg said loudly into the stifling breath of the heat, machines and people that surrounded him. The National Socialists began to listen to his confused speech. Their leader had once compared thought, the word, to a wife: if thought was faithful to the leader alone, as if to a husband, then it was of use; but if it wandered about in the twilight, through houses of despair, seeking its satisfaction in depraved doubt and in fornication with nothing but its own sorrow, then thought was senseless and an organized head should annihilate it – it was more dangerous than Communism and the Treaty of Versailles together.

"O great century!" said Lichtenberg. "At the end of your time you gave birth to Adolf Hitler: the leader of humanity, the most passionate genius of action, the man who has penetrated into the deepest depths of Europe's fate!"

"Bravo! Heil Hitler!" cried out the National Socialist masses who were present there.

"Heil Hitler! You will reign for centuries. You are more enduring than all the imperial dynasties: your dominion will know no end, not until either you begin to laugh or death carries you away into our common home beneath the grass! And what will that matter? After you there will come others, still more frenzied than you are! You were the first to understand that what must be built on the back of the machine, on the poor, sullen hump of precise Science, is not freedom but unyielding despotism! You gather together the unemployed, the lost and the dejected whom the machine has set free, you gather them under your banners into the guard of your glory and protection. Soon you will enrol all the living as your comrades-in-arms, and those few exhausted people who remain by the machines to feed your armies will be unable to destroy you. Emperors have perished because their guards were fed by people – and these people stopped working for them. You will not perish, because your guard will be fed by mechanisms, by an enormous surplus of productive forces! You will not vanish, you will overcome the crisis."

"Heil Hitler!"

"You have invented a new profession in which millions of people will exhaust themselves without ever bringing about an over-production of goods; they will traverse the country, wearing shoes and clothes, they will eliminate the surplus of food, they will glorify your name in joy and in sweat, accumulate years and die. This new industry, this task of inspiring the people to the creation of your glory will put an end to the crisis and will exercise not only the muscles but also the hearts of the population, wearing them out with peace and satiety. You have taken my motherland and given a task to everyone: that of bearing your glory . . ."

Lichtenberg looked round in anguish. The solar centre went on burning with uninterrupted power in the rubbishy emptiness of space; dry insects and assorted trivia made irritated noises in the air, but the people remained silent.

"The earth is beginning to be inhabited by gods, I can find no trace of an ordinary man, I see human beings developing into animals . . . But what is left for me to do? Only this!"

With the power of his body, multiplied by the whole of his reason, Lichtenberg twice struck the head of the statue with his stick, and the stick broke into pieces without harming the metal; the machine-like half-body did not sense the rage of the sad man.

The National Socialists seized Lichtenberg's torso, deprived him of both his ears, destroyed his sexual organ through compression and crushed the rest of his body from every angle by marching across it. Lichtenberg calmly understood his pain and felt no regret for his vanishing organs of life, since they were at the same time the means of his suffering, malicious participants in movement through this universal suffocation. Moreover, he had long ago recognized that the time of the warm, loved, whole human body had passed: it was necessary for each person to become a mutilated cripple. Then he fell asleep from weakness, allowing his blood the possibility of congealing around his wounds. It was night when he came to; there were no stars, and a fine, sharp rain was falling, so fine it seemed dry and nervous, like dandruff.

A nameless person picked Lichtenberg up from the foot of the monument and carried him somewhere. Lichtenberg was astonished that there still existed unknown tender hands which, under cover of night, would silently take an alien cripple to their home. But soon the man carried Lichtenberg into the depths of a back yard, opened the door of a shed over a rubbish pit and threw him down into it.

Lichtenberg sank into the warm moisture of the waste products of everyday life, ate something invisible and soft, and then fell asleep again, warming up amid the decay of cheap substance.

To save labour, the master of the house only occasionally removed the rubbish from the pit, and so Lichtenberg lived for a long time in the kitchen trash, eating without concern whatever can enter the body and be digested there. As a result of the filth and the wounds of his mutilation a dark infection, similar to lupus, had spread over all of his body, while a thick coat of hair had sprouted on top of it and covered everything over. Bushes of hair had also grown on the places where his ears had been torn off, although he had preserved his hearing in the right side of his head. He was no longer able to walk: his legs had been damaged along with his male organ and it was impossible for him to control them. Lichtenberg remembered his wife Zelda only once, without regret and without love, just with a thought in his bony head. Sometimes he muttered various speeches to himself as he lay there in the fish scrapings – crusts of bread appeared very seldom, and potato peelings never. Lichtenberg was surprised they had not removed his tongue; this was an oversight on the part of the State: the most dangerous thing in a man was not his sexual organ – which is always the same, always a submissive reactionary – but his thought. There was a prostitute for you, or worse than a prostitute – invariably wandering where no one needed her and giving herself only to those who paid her nothing. "Great Adolf! You have forgotten Descartes: when he was forbidden to act, fright made him start to think, and he recognized in horror that he existed, that is – once again – that he acted. I too think and exist. And if I live, that means you cannot be! You do not exist!"

"Descartes is a fool!" Lichtenberg said out loud and himself began to listen to the sounds of his wandering thought. "What thinks cannot exist, my thought is a forbidden life, and soon I shall die . . . Hitler doesn't think – he arrests, Alfred Rosenberg thinks only what is meaningless, the Pope has never thought at all, but they exist all the same!

"Let them exist: soon the Bolsheviks will reduce them to a brief digression in their reminiscences."

The Bolsheviks! In the darkened depth of his mind Lichtenberg imagined the pure, normal light of the sun over a moist, cool country covered with corn and flowers, and a serious, thoughtful man walking behind a heavy machine. Lichtenberg felt suddenly ashamed before this distant, almost sad labourer, and in the darkness he covered his pained face with one hand. He now felt sad from grief that his own body had been expended, that his feelings contained no hope, that he would never see the cool plain of rye over which white mountains of clouds were passing, lit by the childlike, sleepy light of the evening sun, and that his feet would never step into the overgrown grass. He would never be a friend to the huge, serious Bolshevik who, in the middle of his spaces, was thinking silently about the whole world; suffocated by the rubbish wind, he himself would die here, in a dry asphyxia of doubt, in the dandruff showering from the head of man onto the earth of Europe.

Every day there was less and less refuse. Lichtenberg had eaten everything that was soft and more or less fit to be eaten. Finally there was nothing left in the rubbish pit but tin and splinters of china.

Lichtenberg fell asleep, his mind in fog, and in his sleep he saw a large woman who was caressing him, but all he could do was cry in her close warmth and look at her pitifully. The woman silently gripped him in such a way that for a moment he felt his legs could run with their own strength – and then he cried out in pain, seizing a strange body. He had caught a rat; it had been gnawing his leg while he slept. The rat was set on living, with a powerful, rational impatience; it was sinking its teeth into Lichtenberg's hand. Lichtenberg strangled it. Then he touched his wound from the rat; the wound was ragged and damp, the rat had drunk a lot of his blood, it had eaten the upper layer of meat, exhausting his life. Lichtenberg's strength was now being preserved in a deceased animal.

Lichtenberg felt a jealous need to safeguard the poor remnant of his existence, he was sorry for the thin body that belonged to him and had been expended in labour and in the anguish of thought, that had been vexed by hunger to the lime of his bones, and had never known pleasure. He reached out to the dead rat and began to eat it, wanting to recover from it the meat and blood that, over thirty years, he had accumulated from the meagre income of poverty. Lichtenberg consumed the small animal right down to its fur, and fell asleep with the satisfaction of having recovered his property.

In the morning a dog came fearfully to the rubbish pit, like a beggar woman. On seeing the dog, Lichtenberg immediately understood that it was a former man who had been reduced by grief and need to the senselessness of an animal, and he did not frighten it any more. But the dog began to tremble with horror as soon as it noticed the man; its eyes moistened over with deathly sorrow; terror sapped its strength and it was only with difficulty that it vanished. Lichtenberg smiled: in the past he had worked on the study of cosmic space, had formulated fantastic hypotheses about possible crystal landscapes on the surface of distant stars, and all this with the secret aim of conquering the Universe through reason; now, however, if this starry Universe were to become accessible, people would run away from one another on the very first day and begin to live in isolation, billions of miles apart, while a paradise of vegetation grew up on the earth, inhabited by birds.

In the afternoon the street police removed Lichtenberg from his refuge and took him, along with other criminal and anonymous persons, to a concentration camp surrounded by a triple barricade of barbed wire. In the middle of the camp were dug-outs, dug in the hope of long life by the people who had been sent there.

Lichtenberg was not asked any questions in the camp office, but only examined – on the assumption that he could hardly be a human being. To cover all eventualities, however, they sentenced him to life imprisonment, writing on his papers: "A possible new species of social animal, developing a layer of hair, extremities debilitated, sexual attributes poorly defined; this subject, now removed from social circulation, cannot be ascribed to a definite gender; judging by superficial characteristics of the head – a cretin; speaks a few words, pronounced with no apparent animation the phrase, 'Supreme half-body Hitler', then stopped. Confined for life."

In the space of the camp grew a single tree. Lichtenberg dug out a small cave beneath the roots of this tree and settled there for an indefinite continuation of his life. At first the other prisoners avoided him, and he kept apart from them, but then one of the Communists took a liking to Lichtenberg. This was a young man whose eyes were black and alert, and whose face was covered with pimples from inactivity and the pressure of his vital strength. He carried Albert in his arms, as a small, concise body, and told him there was no need to feel sorrow: the sun rose and set, branches grew in the forests, historical time flowed into the ocean of Socialism; Fascism would end in universal and gigantic ridicule – the silent, modest masses would smile as they destroyed the domination of both living and bronze idols.

After a while in the camp, Lichtenberg gradually settled down. All he looked forward to were the evenings, when the prisoners came back from work, boiled up some thin broth and talked together. Lichtenberg was not sent out to work, because he could only crawl along the ground. He no longer felt sorrow or fear about anything – neither his past life, nor his love for women, nor his future dark fate; all day he lay in his cave and listened to the noise of the foul dust in the air and the trains passing along the embankment, transporting government officials busy with matters of domination. When he heard voices beyond the barbed wire and the rattle of the guards' rifles, Lichtenberg crawled out to meet people – in the joy of his passionate and light feeling for them.

He was friendly most of all with the Communists: hungry and enslaved as they were, they ran about and played in the evenings like little children, believing more in themselves than in reality, since reality deserved only destruction; and Lichtenberg crawled among them, joining in this shared childish nonsense that concealed a patient courage. Once he asked them, "How can you be so happy?" – and they smiled and took him in their arms. Probably happiness always collects in a man, even if only a few drops at a time, just as seeds of reproduction, being a useless substance, accumulate in a prisoner. Then Lichtenberg would sleep with happiness until morning and get up early to see his comrades off to work. Once, searching through the tall weeds in search of food, he found a scrap of newspaper and read there about the burning of his brochure, "The Universe – a Space without People". The brochure had been published five years ago and had set out to prove that the cosmic world was deserted, filled almost entirely with minerals. The destruction of the booklet confirmed that the earth was itself becoming unpeopled and mineral, but this did not upset Lichtenberg: all he wanted was for every day to have its evening, so he could be happy for one hour among tired, captive people who gave themselves to friendship just as little children, in their games and their imagination, devote them-selves to it in the overgrown yards of their early motherland.

One night like any other, at the end of summer, Lichtenberg woke up unexpectedly. He had been woken by a woman who was standing beside the tree. The woman was wearing a long cloak and a small round hat that did not quite cover her curls, and under her clothes her graceful body was arranged sadly – she was clearly young. Two guards were standing beside her.

Lichtenberg's heart began to beat hard with longing:

deprived of the capacity for love and even for upright movement on his legs, he now tried nevertheless to get up onto his two feet, tormented by shame and fear in the presence of this woman, and with the help of a stick he managed to stand. The woman walked off, and Lichtenberg followed her, once again feeling a hardening strength in his legs. He was unable to ask her anything; his agitation did not pass. As he walked on, falling a little behind her, he could see one cheek of her face; she was looking away from him all the time, into the impending dark of the path.

A tribunal of three officers was waiting for them in the camp office. The woman stopped behind Lichtenberg. The judge announced to Lichtenberg that he was sentenced to be shot – on account of the failure of his body and mind to develop in accordance with the theories of German racism and the level of State philosophy, and with the aim of rigorously cleansing the organism of the people from individuals who had fallen into the condition of an animal, so protecting the race from infection by mongrels.[2]

"You may speak!" the judge said to Lichtenberg.

"I am mute," said Lichtenberg.

"Hedwiga Wotmann!" pronounced the judge. "You are a member of the local Communist organization. Since the time of the National Revolution, a look of mockery towards the supreme leader has never left your face. Since then, while in confinement, you have refused marriage and mutual love to two high-ranking officers of the National Service, insulting their racial dignity. The decision of the tribunal is to have you destroyed as a personal enemy of the tribal genius of the Teutons. Have you anything to say?"

"Yes," answered Lichtenberg's companion with a smile of intelligence and irony. "The two officers were refused my love because I proved to be a woman, whereas they failed to be men."

"What do you mean – failed to be men?" exclaimed the judge in surprise.

"They should be shot for their loss of the capacity for procreation, for the reproduction of the first-class German race. They, Germans, were able to love only in the French manner, not in the Teutonic manner; they are enemies of the nation!"

"Are you a Communist?" asked a member of the tribunal.

"Of course," said Wotmann. "But if you wish to discuss this, I ask you to give me your weapon!"

Her request was refused.

The judge gave the commandant routine instructions with regard to the execution.

"Bring in the next pair of degenerates!" the judge continued.

Lichtenberg and Hedwiga Wotmann were led outside the camp boundary. Four officers escorted them, holding cocked revolvers. Two criminals walked in front, each carrying on his head a plank coffin made with his own hands in the camp.

As before, Hedwiga Wotmann walked gracefully and alertly, as though she were leaving not to die but to be reincarnated. She breathed the same rubbish-filled air as Lichtenberg, she had suffered hunger and the agonies of imprisonment, had waited for Communism, and she was now on her way to die – but she had yielded nothing of her own body and consciousness, neither to sorrow nor to illness, not to fear, nor to pity, nor to repentance; she was leaving life in full possession of all her strengths, which might have gained a difficult victory and a lasting triumph. The gloom-bringing elements of the enemy stopped at her clothes and had not touched even the surface of her cheeks; healthy and silent, she was walking through the night behind her own coffin and feeling no regret for her unrealized life, as if it were a trifle. But why then had she struggled so furiously and so ruinously on behalf of the working class, as if for her own eternal happiness?

Lichtenberg even felt that Hedwiga Wotmann gave off a moist smell of good sense and the sweat of plump, healthy legs; nothing in her had dried up from the hot, turbid wind, and her dignity resided within her own solitary body, which was surrounded by guards.

The coffin-makers went down into a grassy valley and continued along its isolated bottom. Soon they came to the buildings of a long-abandoned ceramics factory, and the two condemned to annihilation were led into a dark, narrow space between the factory walls.

Lichtenberg stayed close to Hedwiga Wotmann and wept from his madness. He thought about this unknown woman with as much grief as if he were nearing the end of the world, but it was only the death of his ephemeral companion that he was regretting. The procession turned the corner of the wall, the coffin-makers disappeared behind some indistinct object. The officer on Lichtenberg's left came to the edge of an abyss that had been dug for some powerful mechanism; carefully and without mishap he began to walk along it, but Lichtenberg suddenly gave him a shove, yielding to a childish wish to push something into an empty space. The officer disappeared and from down below he let out a shout, mingled with the grating of iron and the friction of his snapping bones. The three remaining guards made a movement towards the abyss of the pit, but Hedwiga Wotmann fluttered the edge of her cape and silently, instantaneous as a bird, stole away from the guards and from Albert Lichtenberg for ever. Thinking the prisoner was only a few steps away, the three officers rushed after her, meaning to catch her at once and come straight back.

Lichtenberg remained alone and bewildered. The officer in

the pit had been silent for a long time. The criminals with the coffins on their heads had gone on in front and not come back. Far away, out in the open fields, two shots rang out: Hedwiga Wotmann was disappearing ever further and more irrevocably, it was impossible for anyone to catch up with her. Lichtenberg suddenly wanted her to be caught and brought back; he could no longer do without her, he wanted to look at her once more, even if only for the briefest moment.

No one came back. Lichtenberg lay down on the ground. There was another muffled shot, weak and uncertain, far off in the night. Then a military alarm sounded in the camp. Lichtenberg got up and walked a little way from the place where he should have shared an eternal tomb with the body of Hedwiga; after ten years, when the coffins and the bodies in them had rotted away, when the dust of the earth had been violated, Albert's skeleton would have embraced Hedwiga's skeleton – for long millennia. Lichtenberg now felt sorry this had not happened.

In the morning Lichtenberg came to a small workers' settlement he did not know, where there were six or eight houses. A bright autumn day was beginning, exhausted rubbish was stirring on the empty road between the dwellings, and from far away the sun was climbing towards its supreme emptiness. Albert got as far as the last building without meeting anyone. He came to a well on the outskirts of the village and found there a statue of Hitler: a deserted, bronze half-body; opposite the face of the genius was a bouquet of iron flowers in a stone urn. Lichtenberg looked attentively into the metal face, trying to make out an expression.

He left the statue and entered a house. There was no one inside the house, only a dead boy lying in a bed covered with dust. Lichtenberg began to feel a strange, light strength inside him, he quickly visited two more dwellings and found nothing there, neither people nor animals; the bark had been stripped from the trees in the yards, the trees had withered, and there was no smell from the latrine holes.

In the last house of this little village that had either died or been driven out, Lichtenberg found a woman sitting in a chair; with one hand she was rocking a cradle that hung from the ceiling, while with the other hand she kept wrapping a blanket around a child who was asleep in the cradle. Lichtenberg asked this woman something – she did not answer him. Her eyes did not blink, looking into the cradle with a long, concentrated sorrow that her endurance had already transformed into indifference. Hunger and exhaustion had turned the woman's face the brown colour of a Fascist shirt, the meat beneath the skin had gone to nourish her insides, her flesh all falling from her bones like autumn leaves from a tree, and to sustain her strength even her brain had been sucked out from beneath her skull into her torso, and so the woman now lived with no mind at all – her memory had forgotten the need to blink the lids of her eyes, the dimensions of her body had been reduced to those of a little girl, and only her grief still functioned instinctively. With uninterrupted energy she continued to rock the cheap cradle, protecting the sleeping child, with an inexhaustible, careful tenderness, against a cold that Lichtenberg was unable to sense.

"He's asleep now," said Albert.

"No, they just can't go to sleep," the woman then answered. "I've been rocking them for over a week. They feel cold all the time and they can't get to sleep."

Lichtenberg bent over the cradle and the woman turned down the edge of the blanket for him: in the cradle, on a small shared pillow, with their eyes open and their faces turned towards one another, lay the blackened heads of two dead children; Lichtenberg took the blanket right off and saw a little boy and a little girl, around five or six years old, both covered all over with the blotches of corpses. The boy had placed one hand on his sister, to defend her from the horror of approaching eternity, while the little girl held the palm of one hand trustfully beneath her cheek, like a woman; their feet had not been washed since the last time they played in the yard, and the blue of hoar-frost really was spreading over the delicate skin of both children.

The mother covered the two dead children again with a blanket.

"See how frozen they are," she said. "That's why they can't get to sleep!"

With one finger Lichtenberg closed the lids of the four childish eyes and said to the mother: "Now they've gone to sleep!"

"Yes, they're asleep," said the woman – and stopped rocking the cradle.

Lichtenberg went into the kitchen, lit a fire in the hearth, using pieces of furniture for fuel, and placed a large saucepan of water over the flame. When the water had boiled, he went to the woman and told her he was putting some meat on to cook: she shouldn't go to sleep – soon they would be having a meal together; and if he should happen to fall asleep in the kitchen himself, she should keep an eye on the meat and then eat it on her own, not waiting for him to wake. The woman agreed to wait and then eat on her own, and told Lichtenberg to put a special piece, the very best piece, into the saucepan for her children.

In the kitchen Lichtenberg got the fire as hot as possible, took a chopper and began to cut his left leg, the healthier one, away from his groin, which had now healed over. This was hard work, since the chopper had not been sharpened for a long time and the meat did not yield; Lichtenberg then took a knife and hurriedly sliced off his flesh along the bone, peeling it away in a thick layer right down to the knee; he then successfully chopped this layer into two pieces, one good and one less good, and threw these pieces into the boiling saucepan to cook. After that he crawled out into the fenced yard, and lay face down on the earth. Plentiful life was leaving him in a hot stream, and he could hear his blood soaking into the near dry soil. But he was still thinking; he raised his head and looked at the empty space round about; his gaze came to rest on the distant monument to the saviour of Germany and, following his lifelong habit, he forgot himself.

Within two hours the last of the soup had boiled dry and the meat had cooked in its own fat; the fire had gone out.

That evening a policeman came into the house, accompanied by a young woman with an anxious, oriental face. The policeman was searching with the help of the woman for a State criminal, while the woman, unaware of the policeman's intention, was looking with the help of the State for her poor, insane husband.

The policeman and his companion found a dead woman in the house, her face pressed into a cradle where there were two children, both equally dead. There was no man in the house.

Seeing on the kitchen hearth a saucepan with some nourishing and still warm meat, the tired policeman sat down to eat it for his dinner.

"Have a rest, Frau Zelda Lichtenberg," said the policeman.

But the agitated woman did not listen to him and walked aimlessly out of the house, through the kitchen door into the yard.

Out there Zelda saw an unknown animal that had been killed and left, eyes down. She prodded it with her shoe and thought it might even have been a primitive man who had grown a coat of hair, but that most likely it was a large monkey someone had mutilated and then, as a joke, dressed up in scraps of human clothing.

The policeman followed Zelda out and confirmed her guess that it was a monkey or else some other unscientific animal for which Germany had no use; it had probably been dressed up by some young Nazis or *Stahlhelms*,[3] as a political gesture.

Zelda and the policeman left the empty settlement, where the life of human beings had been lived to the end, with nothing left over.

LOBSKAYA HILL

IN DAYS GONE BY A LABOURER FROM KARELIA WAS ONCE walking along the shore of Lake Onega. All across the face of grey, age-old nature lay stones, dead roots, litter from the rare passers-by, and other dirt, as if the earth were blind here and, never having seen her own face, were unable to tidy herself up.

The labourer looked round in the empty light of the water, the air and the earth. He wanted to settle down somewhere, because he wished to exist until his life ran out. Soon he saw a large mound or a hill, not far from the water's edge. On that hill, like a constellation of impoverished stars, stood a village of four huts; one hut had no chimney, and on the roof of another sat a man, himself about half the size of the hut, who was looking out onto Lake Onega, at some distant place.

The labourer from Karelia came to a stop. He had nowhere to go, the strength lay weak in his body. The clothes on his back, if he sold them in Petrozavodsk on market day, would fetch no more than twenty kopecks. His mother and father had died long ago, away from home, working for a rich Finn. He had gone to Finland then himself, still hoping his life would turn out well, since he was able to work hard and his heart was entirely fit for happiness. In Finland he had been taken on by a farmer who bred dairy cattle and made butter out of their milk. There, on a rich and dreary farm, he had fallen in love with the farmer's daughter, but she had been too afraid of her father and mother to return his love, or anyone else's. Out of fear of her family she lived alone, plain but kind. She was not happy; her father and mother had taught her to love only animals and the goods and chattels they had long hoarded, but it was now time she got to know a stranger. With meekness and terror she would embrace the labourer from Karelia when he was tormented with love beside her, as he often was, and there was no one around outside the house. Soon the owners noticed that their daughter, who lived the life of a labourer in her parents' home, had become pregnant. For the time being they said nothing to her, but they were filled with a secret fury. Probably it upset them that there would suddenly be two new mouths to feed in the household – the daughter's baby and her husband – and that their daughter looked sallow, and had lost her strength, and was unable to do the housework with due diligence, and slept too much. The labourer then worked with all the strength of his heart, so as to vindicate his wife and justify the feeding of a future person. The daughter's parents did not reproach her at all and they did not drive the labourer away, although they did of course guess about the affection and the tender life between them. They stored their anger like misers, as if this anger were a necessary good and it were best not to reveal it to anyone prematurely, so as not to cheapen it.

The child was born suddenly, one country night; it was delivered by the mistress of the house, the baby's grandmother, while the baby's grandfather, the farmer, was in another room, knocking together a little coffin from old boards that had already done long service around the house. The labourer-father stood outside in the darkness of night, where no one could see him. He heard the terrible cry of his child, who had stumbled into life for the first time, and, not being used to life, had immediately fallen ill. The father of the newborn went down onto his knees, pressing his face against the building's stone plinth and trembling with agitation. He heard the steps of the owner's wife and some hammering from a distant room, but he did not understand the meaning of his master's night-time work. The child cried a little and stopped: it had died after living a short while, perhaps two hours; it was as if it had merely half-opened the door into the world, and then not gone in, because it had made a mistake and come to the wrong place. In the morning, weak and out of her mind, the master's daughter went out to her unwedded husband. She told him a boy had been born and had died; he had been suffocated by a pillow that her mother had put on top of his face. She had been asleep herself; blood had been flowing out of her, it still was. In the evening the master carried the baby's body out of the yard in a home-made coffin. The daughter then lived for another two days. She walked round and round the farm, taking stock of grass, objects, buildings and tools, touching and caressing them with her hands. Her father locked the gates, but the daughter did not even try to open them. Weak from giving birth, with blood running down her legs, she now lived without sleep, constantly moving around her parents' farm. But the mother told her daughter not to wander about aimlessly: even if she took only a small light bucket, she could fetch water for the calves. The daughter took a bucket and set off to the well. In the depth of its darkness, in the mirror of the distant water, she saw the light blue sky of spring and the edge of a white cloud, but the wind carried the cloud away and in the mirror of the still water appeared the dead face of her child, a child she had never seen alive; bending towards this distant face was a woman, and in this woman she saw herself. The mother of the dead child kissed her child at the bottom of the well, but suddenly the mother vanished; and again there was only the dead boy. His face was covered by a cloud sailing through the sky; it became invisible. The girl-mother left her small empty bucket beside the well frame and fell down into the well, the sooner to see her child, under the cloud in the sky that had covered his face.

The labourer now felt weary of life; he climbed over the stone wall of the rich, alien farm and left his master without receiving his wages.

Now the labourer was standing on the shore of Lake Onega, where both the land and the water came to an end. He felt he had reached the end of his life; he might go on existing, but nothing new or unknown could happen to him, either in happiness or in sorrow. His heart knew the limits of both.

He climbed the hill and asked the man sitting on the roof, "What is this place?"

"Lobskaya Hill – what else?" said the man on the roof.

"And the village?" asked the labourer.

"The same – Lobskaya Hill. It's the only one in the world, everyone knows it."

"What can you see up there? Why are you sitting on the roof? You'll make a hole in it!"

The man on the roof was advanced in years, but was clean-shaven like a rich man or a scholar.

"I'm looking at the wind on the lake, next I'll go and measure the water," said the man up above with the diligent, scraped face. "We're on the staff of the Imperial Academy of Sciences. We're a post, we measure the water and the storms here."

The labourer too would have been willing to become a post straight away – or anything else, as long as they gave him some food – but who would take him on as one? A post has to shave, to write and make conversation. He chose the poorest, humblest hut and walked up to it, wanting to take shelter there from weariness. The wooden roof of the hut had rotted and was covered with old moss, the lowest rows of beams were now buried in the earth, returning back into the depth of their birthplace, and from them, from the very body of the hut, were growing two new, weak branches which in time would become mighty oaks and eat with their roots the dust of this exhausted dwelling that had been used up by the wind, the rains and the human race. The hut stood on an empty patch of land, which was walled off by stakes, stones taken from the lake shore and thrown down haphazardly, rusty sheets of roof iron that had probably been brought from some distant town by a gale, and other cheap or chance material. But this wall no longer held; the stones were falling down and the stakes had keeled over; they had rotted long ago, worn out in the soil.

Needing to exist, but not sure how to set about pleasing people he did not know, the labourer began to repair this wall, laying the stones in order, straightening the stakes and clearing up bits of old rubbish from the earth. A woman came out onto the porch. She was a full-faced, good-looking woman and she was not yet old; she might have been a widow, or perhaps she was a spinster who had been born to ageing parents.

"Where are you from, chicken-face?" asked the woman. "And what's brought you here to Lobskaya Hill?"

The wanderer put his hand to his face: it was neither very thin, nor spotty – some girls in the past had even said he looked sweet.

"Clear off at once!" said the unknown woman, and went back into her house.

In bewilderment of heart the labourer returned to repairing the wall, even though this task was now pointless. It was getting dark. But there was no sense in grieving, and so he completed the job, to make it beautiful to live in this foreign place. The wooden gates were in a sorry state; planed and painted, however, they would serve a while longer. The labourer regretfully felt the hinges the gates hung on; the old nails had come loose long ago. He knocked them back in with a stone – and there was no more work to be done. He sat down on the ground, resting his back against a stone. The evening darkness intensified the silence; now the water could be heard, moving sadly against the shore of Lake Onega.

The hut door opened; probably the mistress was coming out again, to drive the strange man from her gate. The labourer got up in anticipation, wanting to go away to some empty place and spend the night there.

"Why so sorry for yourself – has someone upset you?" asked the woman. "Come on in!"

The man from far away did as she said and went inside, had some warm cabbage soup, and lay down to sleep on the bench. The mistress lay down on the stove and looked for a long time at the sleeping wanderer, until the wick began to smoulder in the lamp, because the paraffin had burned up.

"He's not a chicken-face!" the mistress said to herself just before she went to sleep. "He's not a bad fellow at all – just skinny and poor!"

Next morning, while the mistress was still asleep, the labourer tidied up the hut, and lit the stove just in case. The woman turned over up above; she had been awake for some time, she was enjoying being lazy. There was no one else there.

"You a widow then?" asked the man.

"Yes I am! I'm a widow!" the mistress answered. "My husband died. So that makes me a widow."

"He died, did he?" said the labourer. "Well, that happens."

They fell silent.

"Pour some water into the pot," said the widow, "and add some buckwheat. Put it in the stove – later on you'll want something to eat!"

The strange man did this, and then asked, "Do you live alone?"

"Yes, I do," said the mistress. "Men come flocking round – I'm buxom. But I'm careful, I don't waste myself – I'm mistress of my own fate now, I don't need a man."

Sorrow passed through the heart of the labourer; if the mistress could do without men, then she had no need of him.

"I won't be a man," he said. "I was a man once, but then I stopped. A woman died."

"You won't?" asked the mistress.

"No," said the labourer. "Don't worry – you take it easy in your hut. I'll cook for you, and guard your home. I'll go and catch fish. And if anything tears, I'll darn it."

The full-faced widow looked searchingly at her unexpected guest. "Well, all right. But it's a bitter life you must lead, to be wanting a widow's bread. Ay, there's no peace from you men – you're a hateful lot!"

"No peace," the labourer agreed. He picked up a stool and took it some way from the house, so as to repair the legs quietly, since the mistress needed peace.

The labourer soon put the property in order and then started to fish in the small lakes close by Lake Onega; he did not have the right tackle for the big lake. He needed fish to feed himself and the mistress. But the mistress soon tired of lenten fare from the lake, and she told him to go to the timber factory; he could earn money there and buy meat, and material for a skirt.

The labourer went to the factory and began to work there from six in the morning to six in the evening. He could only do unskilled work, so his task was to roll the logs by hand up to the sawing-frame. By evening his whole body felt hollow and indifferent from loss of life in long hours of labour; when he came back for the night and sat down by the gate of the widow's plot, he no longer felt any pleasure in being alive. The woman, still a stranger to him, would have prepared supper and would be sitting outside; they would then go into the hut together and eat from the same bowl.

Sometimes, at night, the man suddenly woke up in the dark silence; his heart would be aching but his head would be thoughtless, and he did not want any thought or memory to appear in it. The stirring of the water against the shore was barely audible; probably some distant wind was ruffling Lake Onega, and the water was running from the wind – all the way to the shore. The lodger worked, and he fed the mistress with his earnings, but he was still a little afraid that he might soon be driven out. Maybe the woman would feel cross in the morning, anger might well up in her large body – after all she knew nothing of what might happen inside her, and no one has command of themselves when they are living comfortably, free of grief and fear – and then the strange man would be denied shelter. But the timid, infrequent splashing of the water against the empty shore of Lake Onega brought calm to the soul of the lodger: if you cannot live like a human being, if you must always live in fear, then why try to be a human being? Better to become water, earth or wind. His wife and child had also stopped being people, but they existed somewhere – even if only as wind, water and earth – and they were near by; he could feel them together with him, in the same world as him, in his one heart.

Two months or so after the labourer from Karelia had moved in with the widow, the timber factory was shut down and the workers were all dismissed; there was no more need for boards, or logs, or plywood.

But what are people to do in a nature that is also poor, so poor she barely lives? In Karelia the sun shines slant even during summer, and its warmth flies past the earth into empty air.

THE RIVER POTUDAN

GRASS HAD GROWN AGAIN ON THE TRODDEN-DOWN DIRT
tracks of the civil war, because the war had stopped. With peace
it had become quiet again in the provinces and there were fewer
people: some had died in the fighting, many were being treated
for their wounds and were resting with their families, forgetting
the heavy work of the war in long sleep, while some of the
demobilized men were still making their way home in their old
greatcoats, carrying their kitbags and wearing soft helmets or
sheepskin caps – walking over the thick unfamiliar grass which
there had not been time to see before, or maybe it had just been
trampled down by the campaigns and had not been growing
then. They walked with faint, astonished hearts, recognizing
again the fields and villages along their path. Their souls
had changed in the torment of war, during illnesses and in the
happiness of victory, and they were on their way to live as if for
the first time, dimly remembering themselves as they had been
three or four years ago, for they had turned into quite different
people – they had grown up because they were older; they had
become more intelligent and more patient and had started to
feel inside themselves the great universal hope which had
become the idea of their lives – lives that were small as yet and
which had had no clear aim or purpose before the civil war.

In late summer the last demobilized Red Army soldiers were
returning home. They had been kept back in the labour armies,
where they had worked at various unfamiliar trades and felt
homesick; only now had they been told to go home to their own
lives and to life in general.

A former Red Army soldier, Nikita Firsov, on his way home

to an obscure provincial town, had for more than a day now been walking along a ridge that stretched for some distance beside the river Potudan. Some twenty-five years had passed since this man's birth, and he had a modest face that seemed permanently sorrowing – though this expression may have come not from sadness but from some restrained goodness of character or else from the usual concentration of youth. From under his cap his fair hair, not cut for a long time, hung down onto his ears, and his large grey eyes gazed at the calm and dull features of the monotonous land with a morose tension – as if the man on foot were not from these parts.

At noon Nikita Firsov lay down beside a small stream that flowed from its source along the bottom of a gully and down into the Potudan. And the man on foot dozed off on the earth, under the sun, in September grass that had already tired of growing here ever since the long-ago spring. Life's warmth seemed to go dark in him, and he fell asleep in the quiet of this remote place. Insects flew over him, a spider's web floated above him; a tramp stepped across the sleeping man, neither touching him nor curious about him, and continued on his way. The dust of the summer and of the long drought stood high in the air, making the light of the sky even dimmer and weaker, but still the world's time went on as usual, far in the distance and following the sun. Suddenly Firsov sat up, breathing heavily and in fear, as though he were on fire, winded from some invisible race and struggle. He had had a terrible dream – that a small plump animal was suffocating him with its hot fur, some sort of field creature grown fat from eating pure wheat. Soaking with sweat from its effort and greed, this creature had got into the sleeper's mouth, into his throat, trying to burrow with its tenacious little paws into the very centre of his soul, in order to burn up his breath. Firsov had choked in his sleep and had wanted to cry out and run away, but the small creature had torn itself out of him of its own accord, blind, pitiful, itself terrified and trembling, and had vanished in the darkness of its night.

Firsov washed in the stream and rinsed out his mouth, then quickly walked on; his father's house was not far away now and he could get there by evening.

Just as it got dark Firsov caught sight of his birthplace in the murky beginning of night. It was a slow sloping upland which rose from the banks of the Potudan to some high fields of rye. There was a little town on this upland, now almost invisible because of the darkness. Not a single light was burning there.

The father of Nikita Firsov was asleep; he had gone to bed as soon as he got home from work, before the sun had set. He lived in solitude, his wife was long dead, two sons had disappeared during the imperialist war and the last son, Nikita, was in the civil war. This last son might yet come back, thought the father, the civil war was going on close by, near people's houses, in their yards, and there was less shooting than in the imperialist one. The father slept a lot – from dusk till dawn; otherwise, if he didn't sleep, he started thinking various thoughts and bringing forgotten things to mind, and his heart would ache with longing for his lost sons, and with sorrow for his life that had passed by so dismally. As soon as morning came he went off to the peasant-furniture workshop where for many years now he had worked as a joiner – and there in the midst of work everything became more bearable and he forgot himself. But towards evening his soul felt worse again; returning home to his one room, he would go to sleep quickly, almost in a panic, until the next day; he did not even need any paraffin. But at dawn the flies would start biting his bald patch and the old man would wake and, little by little, would carefully dress himself, put his shoes on, wash and sigh and stamp about, tidy the room, mutter to himself, go outdoors to look at the weather, then come back in – anything to while away the useless time that remained before work began in the furniture workshop.

That night the father of Nikita Firsov was sleeping as usual, from necessity and because he was tired. A cricket had lived for years in the earth ledge outside the house and it used to sing there in the evenings: it was either the same cricket as the summer before last or else its grandson. Nikita went up to the ledge and knocked on his father's small window; the cricket fell silent for a moment as if trying to make out who this could be – a strange man arriving so late. The father got down from the old wooden bed he had slept on with the mother of all his sons; once Nikita himself had been born on that very bed. The thin old man was in his underpants at this moment; they had shrunk and narrowed from years of wear and washing, and now they only reached to his knees. The father leaned right up against the windowpane and looked out at his son. He had already seen him and recognized him, but still he went on looking, wanting to look his fill. Then he ran round through the entrance room and yard, short and skinny as a boy, to open the wicket gate which had been bolted for the night.

Nikita entered the old room, with its sleeping bench, its low ceiling and its one small window onto the street. It still smelt the same here as it had in his childhood, and the same as three years ago when he had left for the war; even the smell of his mother's skirt could still be smelt here – here and nowhere else in the world. Nikita put down his bag and cap, slowly took off his coat, and sat on the bed. All the time his father stood in front of him, barefoot, in his underpants, not yet daring either to greet him properly or to begin talking.

"Well?" he asked after a while. "What's happened to those

bourgeois and Kadets?[1] Are there still a few left, or did you get all of them?"

"Not quite," said his son, "Nearly all of them."

The father pondered this briefly but seriously: they had killed off a whole class – quite an achievement.

"Well, they always were a spineless lot," the old man said of the bourgeois. "What use have they ever been? They've always lived off the backs of others."

Nikita stood up too, in front of his father; he was now a whole head and a half taller than him. Before his son the old man was silent, in the humble bewilderment of his love for him. Nikita laid a hand on his father's head and drew him to his breast. The old man leaned against his son and began to breathe deeply and fast, as if he had reached his resting place.

On one of the streets of that town, which led straight out into a field, stood a wooden house with green shutters. An old widow, a teacher at the town school, had once lived in this house and her children had lived with her – a son about ten years old, and a fifteen-year-old daughter, a fair-haired girl called Lyuba.

A few years ago, Nikita Firsov's father had wanted to marry the widowed schoolteacher, though he had soon given the idea up. Twice, when Nikita was still a boy, his father had taken him along with him to visit the teacher, and Nikita had seen Lyuba there, a thoughtful girl who sat reading books and paying no attention to these strangers who had come as her mother's guests.

The old schoolteacher had treated the joiner to tea and rusks and said something about enlightening the mind of the people and repairing the school stoves. Nikita's father sat silent the whole time; he was embarrassed, he grunted and coughed and smoked home-made cigarettes, then timidly sipped tea from the saucer, not touching the rusks, as if he were already full.

There had been chairs in the schoolteacher's home, in both her two rooms and in the kitchen, and there had been curtains hanging at the windows; in the first room stood a piano and a clothes cupboard, and in the other room, further off, there were beds and two soft armchairs of red velvet, as well as a lot of books on the shelves along the wall – probably a whole collection of works. The father and son had found all this too wealthy and, after visiting the widow only twice, the father had stopped going to see her. He had not even managed to tell her he wanted to marry her. But Nikita had been curious to see the piano again and the thoughtful reading girl, and he had asked his father to propose to the old woman, so they could go on visiting her.

"I can't, Nikit," his father had said, "I'm not educated enough, what would I talk to her about? And I'd be ashamed to ask them to our place: we've got no cups and saucers and our food isn't good enough. Did you see the armchairs they had? Antiques, from Moscow! And the cupboard? Carving and fretwork all over the front – that's something I know about! And as for the daughter! She'll probably go to college."

And now it was some years since the father had seen his old intended bride, though there had been times, perhaps, when he had missed her or at least had thought about her.

The day after he got home from the civil war Nikita went to the Military Commissariat to register for the reserve. Then he walked all round the familiar, beloved town where he had been born, and his heart began to ache to see the small houses grown old, the rotting fences of wood and wattle, and the few apple trees in the yards, many of which were already dead, dried up for ever. In his childhood those apple trees had still been green, and the one-storey houses had seemed large and wealthy, inhabited by mysterious, clever people; the streets had been long, the burdock leaves tall, and the plants growing wild on patches of wasteland, as well as in neglected kitchen plots, had seemed in that time long ago to be sinister copses and thickets. But now Nikita saw that the small houses were low and wretched, in need of paint and repair, that the tall weeds on the wasteland were pathetic, more dejected than terrifying, lived in only by old, patient ants, and that the streets soon came to an end in the earth of the fields and the light space of the sky – the town had shrunk. Nikita thought it must mean he had lived through a lot of his life, if large mysterious objects had now become small and dull.

Slowly he walked past the house with green shutters, where once he had gone visiting with his father. The green paint on the shutters he knew only from memory – nothing but faint traces of it remained, it had faded from the sun, been washed off by showers and downpours, or had flaked off down to the wood; and the iron roof on the house had grown very rusty – rain was probably getting through the roof these days and the ceiling would be damp above the piano. Nikita looked attentively through the windows of the house: there were no curtains at the windows now and on the other side of the panes was somebody else's unfamiliar dark. Nikita sat down on a bench by the wicket gate of this decayed though still familiar house. He thought maybe someone would play the piano inside the house, then he would listen to music. But the house remained silent, giving nothing away. After waiting a little, Nikita looked through a crack in the fence into the yard: old nettles were growing there, an empty path led through great clumps of them into a shed, while three wooden steps went up into the entrance room. The old teacher and her daughter Lyuba must have died long ago and the little boy would have gone to the war as a volunteer . . .

Nikita set off for home. It was getting towards evening; his father would soon be back for the night, and they would need to think together about how he was to live from now on and where he should go for work.

On the main street people were going for their evening stroll; the town had started coming back to life now that the war was over. At present the street was full of office clerks, girl students, soldiers who had been demobilized or who were recovering from their wounds, youngsters, people who worked at home or in their own workshops, and so on; the factory workers came out for a stroll later, when it was quite dark.[2] People were dressed poorly, in old clothes, or in worn-out army uniforms from imperialist times.

Nearly all who passed by, even if they were walking arm in arm and planning to get married, were carrying something for their household. The women carried potatoes in their home-made bags, or sometimes fish, while the men held a ration of bread or half a cow's head under their arm, and some were cupping their hands protectively round pieces of offal to make soup with. But there was hardly anyone who looked miserable, only the occasional exhausted old man. The younger people were mostly laughing, looking closely into each other's faces, animated and trustful, as if on the eve of eternal happiness.

"Hello!" a woman said to Nikita timidly, from one side.

This voice immediately touched and warmed him, as if someone beloved and lost were answering his call for help. Yet it seemed to Nikita that he must be mistaken and that the greeting was for somebody else. Afraid of making a mistake, he took a slow look at the people walking near him. But there were only two of them at that moment and they had already gone past. Nikita looked behind him: a big grown-up Lyuba had stopped and was looking in his direction, giving him a sad, embarrassed smile.

Nikita went up to her and looked at her carefully, for she had been precious to him even in memory: had all of her truly been preserved? Her Austrian shoes, tied up with string, were worn right down, her pale muslin dress reached only to her knees – there had probably not been enough cloth for a longer skirt – and this dress immediately made Nikita feel sorry for Lyuba: he had seen dresses like it on women in their coffins, yet here the muslin covered a body that was alive and full-grown, only very poor. Over the dress was an old jacket – Lyuba's mother must have worn it in her girlhood days – and Lyuba had nothing on her head, just her bare hair, coiled below the nape into a bright firm plait.

"You don't remember me?" asked Lyuba.

"Yes, I do," answered Nikita. "I haven't forgotten you."

"One should never forget," smiled Lyuba.

Her pure eyes, filled with the mystery of her soul, looked tenderly at Nikita as if admiring him. Nikita looked into her face in return, and the mere sight of her eyes, sunk deep from life's privations but illumined by trustful hope, made his heart feel both joy and pain.

Nikita and Lyuba walked back alone to her house – she still lived in the same place. Her mother had died not so long ago, and her younger brother had been fed at a Red Army field kitchen during the famine and had got so used to life there that he had gone off south with the soldiers to fight the enemy.

"He got used to eating kasha there," said Lyuba, "and there wasn't any at home."

Lyuba now lived in one room – it was all she needed. With dazed heart Nikita looked round this room where he had seen Lyuba and the piano and all the costly furnishings for the first time. There was no piano here now, no cupboard with fretwork all over its front; only the two upholstered armchairs remained and a table and a bed, and the room itself was no longer as interesting, as mysterious, as it had been in his early youth – the wallpaper was faded and torn, the floor was worn down, and beside the tiled stove stood a small iron stove which you could heat with a handful of wood shavings so as to warm yourself a little.

Lyuba pulled out a thick notebook from under her blouse, then took off her shoes and stayed barefoot. She was now a student at the district academy of medical science. In those years there were universities and academies everywhere because the people desired to acquire higher knowledge as quickly as possible, the human heart had been tormented too much, not only by hunger and poverty but by the meaninglessness of life, and it was necessary to understand what human existence really was: was it something serious or was it a joke?

"My shoes hurt me," said Lyuba. "Sit there for a while, and I'll lie down and have a sleep. I'm terribly hungry and I don't want to have to think about it."

Without undressing, she slipped underneath the blanket that was on the bed and laid her plait over her eyes.

Nikita sat silently for two or three hours, until Lyuba woke up. It was night by then, and Lyuba got up in the dark.

"I don't suppose my friend will come today," she said sadly.

"Do you need her then?" asked Nikita.

"Yes, very much," said Lyuba. "They're a large family and her father's in the army. If there's any leftovers she brings me supper – first I eat, and then we get down to our studies together."

"Have you got any paraffin?"

"No, I've been given some firewood. We light the little stove – then we sit on the floor. We can see by the flame."

Lyuba smiled helplessly, with shame, as if some cruel, sad thought had entered her mind.

"I expect her elder brother hasn't fallen asleep," she said. "He's just a lad. He doesn't like his sister feeding me, he begrudges it. But it isn't my fault! I'm really not all that fond of eating. It's not me – it's my head. It starts aching and thinking about bread, it stops me from living and thinking about anything else."

"Lyuba!" a youthful voice called out near the window.

"Zhenya!" Lyuba called back.

Lyuba's friend came in. She took four large baked potatoes from her pocket and put them on the iron stove.

"Did you get the Histology?" asked Lyuba.

"Who would I get it from?" answered Zhenya. "They've put my name down for it at the library."

"Never mind, we'll get by," said Lyuba. "I learnt the first two chapters by heart at the academy. I'll say it and you write it down. Will that work?"

"It's worked before!" Zhenya said with a laugh.

Nikita got the stove going so the fire would give them light for their notebooks, then got ready to return to his father's for the night.

"You won't forget me now?" Lyuba asked as she said goodbye.

"No," said Nikita, "I've no one else to remember."

* * *

Nikita rested at home from the war for two days, and then started work at the peasant-furniture workshop where his father was employed. He was taken on as a carpenter, to work on the preparation of materials, and his wage was lower than his father's, almost twice as low. But Nikita knew this was only for the time being, until he got used to the trade; then he would be promoted to joiner and his pay would be better.

Nikita had never lost the habit of work. In the Red Army they had done other things than just fight; during long halts, or while they were held in reserve, they had dug wells, repaired the huts of poor peasants, and planted bushes at the tops of ravines to stop more earth being washed away. For the war would come to an end, but life would remain, and it was necessary to give it some thought in advance.

A week later Nikita went to visit Lyuba again, taking her a present of some boiled fish and bread – the main course of his dinner at the workers' canteen.

Lyuba was at the window, hurrying to get her reading done before the sun was extinguished in the sky, so Nikita sat silently in Lyuba's room for some time, waiting for the darkness of night. But soon the twilight matched the silence of the provincial street, and Lyuba rubbed her eyes and closed her textbook.

"How are you?" Lyuba asked quietly.

"My father and I are all right, we're alive," said Nikita. "I've got something here for you. Please eat it," he begged.

"I will," said Lyuba. "Thank you."

"You won't be going to sleep?" asked Nikita.

"No," answered Lyuba, "I'm having supper now, so I'll be full!"

Nikita brought some kindling from the entrance room and lit the iron stove so there would be light to study by. He sat down on the floor, opened the stove door and put some chips of wood and short thin logs on the fire, trying to make it give more light and less heat. After eating the fish and bread, Lyuba sat down on the floor too, facing Nikita and beside the light from the stove, and began studying medicine from her book.

She read silently, but from time to time she would whisper something, smile, and write down some words in her notebook in small quick handwriting – probably the most important things. And Nikita just made sure the flame burned properly, though from time to time – not too often – he would take a look at Lyuba's face and then stare at the fire again, afraid his look might annoy her. So the time went by, and Nikita thought sorrowfully that soon it would all have gone by and he would have to go home.

At midnight, when the clock chimed from the bell tower, Nikita asked Lyuba why her friend called Zhenya had not come.

"She's got typhus again, she's probably going to die," Lyuba answered – and went back to reading her medicine.

"That's a pity!" said Nikita, but Lyuba did not reply.

Nikita pictured in his mind a sick, feverish Zhenya; no doubt he could sincerely have loved her too if he had known her earlier and if she had been at all kind to him. She too was surely beautiful: it was a shame he couldn't remember her better, that he hadn't been able to make her out more clearly in the dark.

"I want to sleep now," whispered Lyuba, sighing.

"Have you understood everything you've read?" asked Nikita.

"Perfectly! Do you want to hear it?"

"No. Better keep it to yourself, I'll only forget it."

He swept up around the stove with a broom and went off to his father's.

From then on he visited Lyuba nearly every day, though sometimes he let a day or two go by so she would miss him. Whether or not she missed him he did not know, but on those empty evenings Nikita was compelled to walk ten or fifteen versts, several times round the whole of the town, in order to contain himself in his loneliness, to endure without consolation his longing for Lyuba and not go to her.

At her house, his usual occupation was keeping the fire going and waiting for Lyuba to say something to him when she looked up for a moment from her book. He always brought a little food for Lyuba's supper from the canteen at the peasant-furniture workshop; she had a midday meal at the academy, but the portions were too small there, and Lyuba did a lot of thinking and studying, and she was still growing, so she needed more food. The first time he was paid, Nikita bought some cows' feet in a nearby village and boiled them all night on the iron stove to make a meat jelly, while Lyuba studied with her books and notepads until midnight, then mended her clothes and darned her stockings, and at dawn she scrubbed the floors and bathed in the yard in a tub of rainwater, before people woke up.

Nikita's father was unhappy being alone every evening without his son, and Nikita never said where he went. "He's a man in his own right now," the old man said to himself. "He might have been killed or wounded in the war. But he's alive – so of course he wants to go out!"

Once the old man noticed that his son had got hold of two white rolls. But Nikita immediately wrapped them up in a piece of paper and did not offer his father anything. Then he put on his army cap as usual and was off, probably till midnight, taking both the bread-rolls.

"Nikit, take me with you!" the father begged. "I won't say anything. I'll just have a look. It must be interesting there, you must be going somewhere really outstanding!"

"Another time, father," said Nikita, in embarrassment. "It's time you went to bed – tomorrow you've got to work."

That evening Nikita did not find Lyuba, she was not at home. So he sat down on the bench by the gate and began to wait for her. He put the white rolls inside his shirt, to warm them there till Lyuba came back. He sat there patiently until late into the night, watching the stars in the sky and the occasional passers-by hurrying home to their children, listening to the town clock chiming from the bell tower, to dogs barking in the yards, and to various indistinct quiet sounds which do not exist in the daytime. He could probably have gone on living there in expectation until the day he died.

Lyuba appeared soundlessly out of the darkness in front of Nikita. He stood up facing her, but she said: "You'd better go home," and burst into tears. She went into the house; Nikita waited a little longer outside, in bewilderment; then he went in after Lyuba.

"Zhenya has died!" Lyuba told him. "What shall I do now?"

Nikita said nothing. The warm rolls lay inside his shirt; was it best to take them out now, or to do nothing at all? Lyuba lay down fully clothed on her bed, turned her face to the wall and wept there to herself, without a sound and almost without moving.

Nikita stood a long time in the dark room, ashamed to disturb someone else's sad grief. Lyuba paid no attention to him, because sorrow from grief makes people indifferent to all other sufferers. Of his own accord Nikita sat down on the bed at Lyuba's feet and took the rolls out from under his shirt, meaning to put them down somewhere, but as yet unable to find the right place for them.

"Let me stay with you now!" said Nikita.

"But what will you do?" asked Lyuba, in tears.

Nikita thought for a while, afraid of making a mistake or somehow offending her.

"I won't do anything," he replied. "We'll live life as usual, so you won't be unhappy."

"Let's wait, there's no need to hurry," Lyuba pronounced thoughtfully and prudently. "We have to think what to bury Zhenya in – they haven't got a coffin."

"I'll bring one tomorrow," Nikita promised, and put the rolls down on the bed.

Next day Nikita got permission from the foreman and began making a coffin; they were always free to make coffins and the cost was not docked from their wages. Being unskilled, he took a long time over it, but he was especially careful to give a clean finish to the inside, where the dead girl would be resting. He too was upset at the thought of Zhenya being dead, and he let a few tears drop amongst the shavings. His father, passing through the yard, went up to Nikita and noticed his distress.

"What are you sad about? Has your girl died?" he asked.

"No, her friend has," Nikita answered.

"Her friend? Who cares about her! Let me plane off the sides of that coffin for you. You haven't done it right, it looks a mess!"

After work, Nikita took the coffin to Lyuba; he did not know where her dead friend was lying.

There was a long warm autumn that year, and people were glad. "Harvest was poor but we'll save on firewood," said economic folk. Well in advance, Nikita Firsov had ordered a woman's coat for Lyuba to be made from his Red Army great-coat; this coat was now ready, though there was no need for it yet because of the warm weather. As before, Nikita visited Lyuba in her home to help her live and, in return, to receive nourishment for the pleasure of his own heart.

Once he asked her how they would live in the future – together or apart. But she answered that it was not possible for her to feel her happiness until the spring, because she had to finish the medical academy as fast as she could; then they would see. Nikita heard this distant promise, he was not asking for a greater happiness than that which, thanks to Lyuba, was already his, and he did not know whether a better happiness even existed, but his heart was chilled from long endurance and from uncertainty: did Lyuba really need him – a poor, uneducated, demobilized man. Sometimes Lyuba looked smilingly at him with her bright eyes in which there were large, black, enigmatic dots, while around her eyes her face was filled with kindness.

Once, as he was covering Lyuba up for the night before going home, Nikita began to weep, but Lyuba just stroked his head and said: "That's enough of that, you mustn't be so unhappy while I'm still alive."

Nikita hurried to his father's, to hide away there, recover his spirits, and not go to Lyuba's for several days in a row. "I'll read," he resolved, "and start living properly. I'll forget Lyuba, I'll stop remembering her, I won't have anything to do with her. What's so special about her – there are millions and millions of women in the world, some of them even better than she is! She's not good-looking!"

In the morning he did not get up from his place on the floor. As his father left for work, he felt Nikita's head and said: "You're hot: lie on the bed! Be ill for a while, then you'll get better. You weren't wounded anywhere in the war, were you?"

"No," answered Nikita, "nowhere."

Towards evening he lost consciousness. At first all he saw was the ceiling, and on it two belated half-dead flies, sheltering there for warmth to prolong their lives; and then these same objects began to fill him with melancholy and disgust – the ceiling and the flies seemed to have got inside his brain, and he was unable to drive them out of it or stop thinking about them, with thoughts which grew and grew and were already eating away the bones of his head. Nikita shut his eyes, but the flies seethed in his brain; he jumped up from the bed to chase the flies off the ceiling, and fell back against the pillow; the pillow seemed to smell of his mother's breath – she had slept here beside his father; Nikita remembered her, and forgot himself in unconsciousness.

After four days Lyuba found out where Nikita Firsov lived and came to visit him for the first time. It was only the middle of the day, the workers' houses were all empty – the women had gone out to buy provisions, and the children who were not yet at school were roaming about the yards and open spaces. Lyuba sat on Nikita's bed, stroked his forehead, wiped his eyes with the corner of her handkerchief and asked: "Now, how do you feel? Are you hurting anywhere?"

"No," said Nikita, "nowhere."

A high fever was carrying him on its current far away from all people and from the objects around him, and it was difficult for him to see and remember Lyuba; afraid of losing her in the darkness of indifferent reason, he reached out and grasped the pocket of her coat – the coat that had been sewn from his Red Army greatcoat – and clung onto it like an exhausted swimmer clinging to a sheer rock, half drowning, half saved. The illness was continually seeking to draw him away towards an empty, shining horizon, out into the open sea, so he could rest there on its slow, heavy waves.

"You've probably got the flu, I'll cure you," said Lyuba. "Or maybe it's typhus. But don't worry, it's nothing to be afraid of!"

She pulled Nikita up by his shoulders and sat him with his back to the wall. Quickly and determinedly she dressed him in her coat, found his father's scarf and tied it round the sick man's head, and pushed his feet into some felt boots that were lying under the bed waiting for winter. With her arms around him, she told him to put one foot in front of the other and then led him, shivering, out onto the street. A cab was waiting there. Lyuba seated the sick man inside it and they drove off.

"Seems like none of us are long for this world!" said the driver, addressing the horse and constantly urging it with the reins into a gentle provincial trot.

In her own room Lyuba undressed Nikita, put him in the bed and wrapped him up in a blanket, a strip of old carpet, her mother's decrepit shawl – all the warm things she possessed.

"Why lie there at home?" Lyuba said with satisfaction,

tucking the blanket under Nikita's hot body. "What's the point? Your father's at work, you're alone all day long, there's no one to look after you, and you pine for me."

For a long time Nikita tried to work out where Lyuba could have got the money for the cab. Perhaps she had sold her Austrian shoes or her textbook (she would first have learnt it by heart so as not to need it any more), or else she had paid the cab driver her entire monthly stipend.

Nikita lay there during the night in confused consciousness: sometimes he knew where he was and could see Lyuba, who was keeping the stove going and cooking food on it, but then he would see unknown visions of his mind, which was acting independently of his will in the hot, pressured tightness of his head.

His feverish chill kept getting worse. From time to time Lyuba put her palm to his brow and felt the pulse at his wrist. Late in the night she gave him a drink of warm, boiled water; then, taking off her dress, she lay down beside the sick man under the blanket, because Nikita was shivering from the fever and he had to be warmed. Lyuba embraced Nikita and pressed him to herself, while he curled up into a ball against the cold and pressed his face to her breast, to sense more closely someone else's, higher, better life and to forget for a while his own torment, his empty body that was chilled right through. But Nikita felt it would be a pity to die now – not because he cared about himself, but because he wanted to go on touching Lyuba and another life – so he asked Lyuba in a whisper whether he would get better or die: she had studied and so she must know.

Lyuba hugged Nikita's head in her arms and answered him, "You'll soon be better. People die because they are ill and have no one to love them, but now you're with me." Nikita began to feel warm and fell asleep.

* * *

Three weeks later, Nikita had recovered. Snow had now fallen outside, everything had gone suddenly quiet, and Nikita went to his father's for the winter. He did not want to disturb Lyuba until she had finished at the academy: let her mind develop to the full, all of it – she too was one of the poor. The father was pleased to see his son again, although he had visited him every third day, always bringing food for his son and some sort of treat for Lyuba.

In the daytime Nikita began working at the workshop again and in the evenings he visited Lyuba, and the winter passed by uneventfully: he knew that in the spring she would be his wife and a long happy life would then begin. Sometimes Lyuba would touch him, push him about, run away from him round the room, and then – after their game – Nikita would cautiously kiss her cheek. But usually Lyuba did not let him touch her without a reason.

"Otherwise you'll get tired of me, and we've still got our whole lives to live!" she said. "Anyway, I'm not such a tasty morsel. You only think I am!"

On their days off, Lyuba and Nikita went for walks along wintry paths out of town, or else walked a long way downstream, half embracing, along the ice of the sleeping Potudan. Nikita would lie on his stomach and look down through the ice to the quietly flowing water. Lyuba settled down next to him and, their bodies touching, they watched the hidden flow of the water and talked of how lucky the Potudan was, because it went all the way to the sea, and this water under the ice would flow past shores of distant lands where flowers were now growing and birds were singing. After thinking about this for a while, Lyuba would tell Nikita to get up from the ice at once: Nikita now wore his father's old padded jacket, it was too short and not very warm, and he might catch cold.

And so they were friends, patiently, almost all the long winter, tormented by anticipation of their approaching future happiness. The Potudan river also hid under the ice all winter, and the winter crops slumbered beneath the snow. Nikita was calmed and even comforted by these processes of nature: it was not only his heart that lay buried until the spring. In February, when he woke in the morning, he would listen hard to hear whether new flies were buzzing yet; and when he went outside he looked at the sky and at the trees in the next door garden – to see if the first birds were flying in from faraway countries. But the trees, the grasses and the germs of flies were all still asleep in the depth of their strength, in embryo.

In the middle of February Lyuba told Nikita that the final exams would begin on the twentieth, as doctors were greatly needed and the people could not go on waiting for them any longer. And by March the exams would be over: so let the snow lie and the river flow under ice right up to the month of July! Their hearts' happiness would begin before the warmth of nature.

Nikita decided to leave the town until March, to make the time pass more quickly before his shared life with Lyuba began. He volunteered to go with a team of joiners from the peasant-furniture workshop to repair furniture in village soviets and schools.

Around this time, towards the beginning of March, his father unhurriedly fashioned a large wardrobe as a present for the young people, similar to the one that had stood in Lyuba's home when her mother had been, more or less, his intended. The old man was seeing life come full circle for the second or third time. This was something he could understand, but there was little he could do about it, and with a sigh Nikita's father put the wardrobe on a sledge and took it to the home of his son's bride-to-be. The snow had grown warmer and was melting in the sun, but the old man was still strong and he dragged the sledge stubbornly on, even over the black body of the bared earth. Secretly he believed that he himself could perfectly well have married this Lyuba, since he had been too shy with her mother, but he felt somehow ashamed and he had nothing at home with which to attract and pamper a young girl like her. And Nikita's father concluded that life just wasn't normal. His son was scarcely back from the war, and now he was leaving home again, this time for ever. It was clear that he himself, an old man, would have to take someone in, even if it were only a beggarwoman off the street – not so as to have a family life, but so there should be another living being, like a tame hedgehog or rabbit, about the house: never mind if it unsettles your life and spreads dirt everywhere – without it you cease to be human.

As he gave Lyuba the wardrobe, Nikita's father asked her when he would be coming to her wedding. "As soon as Nikita comes back. I'm ready!" said Lyuba.

That night Nikita's father walked twenty versts to the village where Nikita was at work making school desks. Nikita was asleep on the floor in an empty classroom, but his father woke him and told him it was time to go back to the town: he could get married.

"You go. I'll finish the desks for you," said the father.

Nikita put on his cap and at once, without waiting for daybreak, set off on foot for the town. All through the second half of the night he walked alone through empty places; the wind from the fields wandered aimlessly around him, now grazing his face, now blowing against his back, and sometimes withdrawing altogether into the silence of the ravine beside the path. The earth lay dark on the slopes and on the high ploughland, the snow had run off into the hollows, and there was a smell of young water and of the decrepit grass that had lain there since autumn. But autumn was a forgotten and long-ago time – the earth was now poor and free, it was going to give birth to everything all over again and only to those creatures that had never lived before. Nikita was not even in a hurry to get to Lyuba; he liked being in the gloomy light of night on this early earth which had no memory and had forgotten all who had died on it, and which did not know it would be giving birth in the warmth of a new summer.

Towards morning Nikita arrived at Lyuba's house. A light frost lay on the familiar roof and on the brick plinth – Lyuba was probably sound asleep now in her warm bed. Nikita walked past the house in order not to wake his bride, not to make her body cold for the sake of his own comfort.

By the evening Nikita Firsov and Lyuba Kuznetsova had registered their marriage at the district soviet; they then went into Lyuba's room and did not know what to do. Nikita now felt ashamed that complete happiness had arrived for him and that the person he needed most of all in the world wanted to live one life with him, as if some great and precious good lay hidden inside him. He took Lyuba's hand and held it a long time; he enjoyed the warmth of the palm of this hand, through it he felt the distant beating of a heart that loved him, and he thought about an incomprehensible mystery: why, for no reason he knew, was Lyuba smiling at him and loving him? He himself had an exact sense of why Lyuba was dear to him.

"First, let's eat!" said Lyuba and took her hand away from Nikita.

She had done some cooking that day: now that she had graduated from the academy, both her stipend and her rations had been increased.

Shyly Nikita started eating the tasty, varied food his wife had prepared. He could not remember ever having been given food almost as a gift, and he had never had occasion to visit people for his own pleasure, still less to eat his fill with them.

After the meal, Lyuba was first to get up from the table. She opened her arms to embrace Nikita and said: "Well!"

Nikita stood up and timidly embraced her, afraid of harming something in this special, tender body. Lyuba tried to help by clasping him to herself, but Nikita begged, "Wait, my heart hurts", and Lyuba let her husband go.

It was growing dark outside, and Nikita made to kindle a fire for some light, but Lyuba said, "There's no need – I've finished my studies, and today is our wedding day." Nikita then turned down the bed. At the same time Lyuba undressed in front of him, feeling no shame before her husband. But Nikita went behind the wardrobe his father had made and quickly took his clothes off there, then lay down beside Lyuba for the night.

In the morning Nikita got up early. He swept the room, lit the stove to boil the kettle, went to the entrance room for a bucket of water so they could wash, till in the end he could think of nothing more to do while Lyuba slept. He sat down on a chair and hung his head: now Lyuba would probably tell him to go to his father's and stay there, because it turned out one had to know how to enjoy pleasure, whereas Nikita was unable to torment Lyuba for the sake of his own happiness, and all his strength pounded away in his heart, flowing into his throat and staying nowhere else.

Lyuba woke up and watched her husband.

"Don't be downhearted, it's not worth it," she said with a smile. "Everything will work out all right."

"Let me scrub the floor," Nikita begged. "It doesn't look clean."

"All right," she agreed.

"He's so sad and weak – and all because he loves me!" Lyuba thought, in bed. "How I love him, how precious he is to me. So what if I stay a virgin for ever! I can endure that. Or maybe one day he'll love me less, and that'll make him strong." Nikita was working at the floor with a wet rag, scrubbing the dirt from the boards, and Lyuba laughed at him as she lay in the bed.

"So here I am, a married woman," she thought joyfully, slipping out from under the blanket in her nightdress.

After tidying the room, Nikita wiped all the furniture with a damp cloth, then added hot water to the cold water in the pail and pulled out a basin from under the bed for Lyuba to wash in.

Lyuba drank her tea, kissed her husband on the forehead and went off to her work at the hospital, saying she would be back about three o'clock. Nikita put his hand to the place on his forehead where his wife had kissed him, and remained alone. He was not sure why had he not gone to work that day; it felt shameful to go on living now, and perhaps it would be better if he did not – what reason, then, was there for him to earn his daily bread? Still, he made up his mind somehow to live his life through, until he wasted away from shame and misery.

After taking stock of their family possessions, Nikita found some food and prepared a single dish for their meal – millet gruel with some meat. But after this work he lay face down on the bed and began calculating how much time was left before the rivers started to flow again and he could drown himself in the Potudan.

"I'll wait till the ice shifts. It won't be long!" he said out loud to calm himself, and dozed off.

Lyuba brought two pots of winter flowers home from work – a wedding present from the doctors and nurses there. She had behaved importantly and mysteriously with them, like a real woman. The young girls among the sisters and nurses had envied her and one candid woman in the hospital pharmacy had trustingly asked Lyuba whether or not it was true that love was something magical, and that marrying for love was an intoxicating happiness. Lyuba had answered that this was perfectly true – which was why people lived in the world.

In the evening husband and wife had a talk. Lyuba said they might be having children and they must think about this beforehand. Nikita promised to start making children's furniture at the workshop after hours: a little table, a chair and a rocking-cradle.

"The Revolution's here to stay, now's a good time to bear children," said Nikita. "Children will never be unhappy again."

"It's all right for you to talk, but it's me who'll be giving birth to them," said Lyuba, piqued.

"Will it hurt?" asked Nikita. "Don't have any, then. Why make yourself suffer?"

"Oh, I dare say I'll manage!" said Lyuba.

At dusk she made up the bed and, so there would be more room, she brought up two chairs for their feet and said the two of them should lie across the bed. Nikita lay down where she told him to, fell silent, and late in the night began crying in his sleep. Lyuba, though, could not sleep for a long time; she heard Nikita crying and carefully wiped his sleeping face with the edge of the sheet – and when he woke up in the morning he did not remember his night-time sorrow.

From then on their life together went along at its own pace. Lyuba tended people at the hospital, and Nikita made peasant furniture. In his spare time and on Sundays he worked in the house and about the yard, although Lyuba never asked him to. She was no longer quite sure whose house it was. First, it had belonged to her mother, then it had been taken over by the State, but the State had forgotten about it – nobody even once came to collect any rent or to check that the house was intact. None of this mattered to Nikita. He got hold of some green paint through friends of his father's and he gave a fresh coat to the roof and shutters as soon as spring weather had settled in. With the same diligence he gradually repaired the ramshackle shed outside, mended the gates and the fence and prepared to dig a new cellar, since the old one had fallen in.

The Potudan river had begun to stir. Twice Nikita went to its bank, looked at the now flowing water and decided not to die so long as Lyuba could still put up with him; when she stopped putting up with him, he would have time enough to end his life – it would be a while yet before the river froze again. Nikita usually worked slowly on his outside jobs, so as not to sit in the room and vex Lyuba to no purpose. And when he had done everything there was to do, he would scrape up some clay from the old cellar into the flap of his shirt and carry it into their room. He would then sit on the floor and fashion the clay into small human figures and a variety of objects that had no function or likeness to anything – just dead fantasies in the shape of a mountain with an animal head growing out of it, or a huge tree-root, apparently an ordinary root, yet so intricate, impenetrable, with each branch of it biting into the next, gnawing itself and tormenting itself, that looking at this root for any length of time made you want to go to sleep. As he worked at the clay Nikita smiled, unthinkingly and blissfully, and Lyuba sat there beside him on the floor mending clothes, singing little songs she had once heard, and in between her work she would caress Nikita with one hand, stroking his head or tickling him under the arm. Nikita lived through these hours with clenched and gentle heart, and did not know whether he still needed something mightier and more elevated, or whether life really was nothing so very great, nothing more than he already had. But Lyuba looked at him with tired-out eyes that were full of patient kindness, as though goodness and happiness had become a heavy labour for her. Then Nikita would crush his toys, turning them back into clay, and ask his wife if he should stoke up the stove to heat some water for tea, or if there was any errand he should do for her.

"No, no," Lyuba would smile. "I can do everything myself."

And Nikita would realize that life was indeed something great and perhaps beyond his strength, that not all of it was concentrated in his beating heart. It was more interesting still, more powerful, more precious, in another human being whom he could not reach. He took the bucket and went off to the town well, where the water was cleaner than in the tanks on the street. There was nothing, no task, that could wear out his grief and Nikita was afraid, just as in his childhood, of the approaching night. After drawing the water, he called in on his father, carrying the full bucket, and sat in his house for a while.

"Why didn't you have a proper wedding?" asked the father. "You got married on the quiet – Soviet fashion, didn't you?"

"We'll have a wedding yet," his son promised. "Let's make a small table together, and a chair and a cradle. You talk to the foreman tomorrow and get the materials. After all, we'll probably be having children."

"All right, I can do that," the father agreed. "But you won't be having children that soon. It's early days."

Within a week Nikita had made all the children's furniture they needed; he had stayed on late every evening and worked diligently. And his father had given each piece a clean finish and painted it.

Lyuba arranged the furniture in a special corner, adorned the future child's little table with the two pots of flowers, and hung a new embroidered towel over the back of the chair. In gratitude for his loyalty to her and to her unknown children Lyuba hugged Nikita, kissed him on the throat, pressed him against her chest and warmed herself for a long time beside this loving man, knowing this was all she could do. And Nikita, with his arms hanging down, hiding his heart, stood silently before her, not wanting to appear strong when he was helpless.

That night Nikita was unable to sleep long, and he woke soon after midnight. He lay a long while in the silence and listened to the sound of the town clock – half past twelve, one o'clock, half past one: three chimes, one every half hour. In the sky, outside the window, a vague stirring had begun; it was not yet dawn, only a movement of the darkness, a slow baring of empty space, and all the things in the room and the new children's furniture became visible, though they appeared pitiful and exhausted after the dark night they had lived through, as if pleading for help. Lyuba shifted under the blanket and sighed: perhaps she too was not asleep. Just in case, Nikita kept still and listened. But Lyuba did not move any more, she was breathing evenly again and Nikita felt pleased that she was lying beside him, alive, necessary to his soul and not remembering in her sleep that he, her husband, existed. As long as she was whole, and happy! As for himself, the mere consciousness of Lyuba was enough to keep him alive. And Nikita dozed off in peace, drawing comfort from the sleep of this close and loved being. Then he opened his eyes again.

Carefully, almost inaudibly, Lyuba was crying. She had pulled the blanket over her head and was alone there in her distress, choking back her grief so it would die soundlessly. Nikita turned his face towards Lyuba: she had curled up pathetically under the blanket and was breathing fast, in anguish. Nikita did not speak. Not every grief can be comforted; there is a grief which ends only after the heart has been worn away in long oblivion, or in distraction amidst life's everyday concerns.

At dawn Lyuba quietened down. Nikita let some time pass, then lifted the top of the blanket and looked at his wife's face. She was sleeping peacefully, warm and still, her tears now dried up.

Nikita rose, dressed himself without a sound and went outside. A feeble morning was beginning in the world, a passing beggar was walking down the middle of the street with a full bag. Nikita set out after this man, so as to have a reason for going somewhere. The beggar walked on out of the town and set off along the high road to the settlement of Kantemirovka where from time immemorial there had been big markets and a prosperous population: true, they never gave much to beggars there – if you wanted food you had to go to the poorer villages further off; nonetheless Kantemirovka was somewhere lively and interesting and at the market you could live just from watching the throngs of people, as they took your mind off things for a time.

The beggar and Nikita arrived in Kantemirovka towards noon. On the outskirts of the town the beggar man sat down in a shallow ditch, opened his bag and began treating himself and Nikita from it; but in the town they went their different ways, as the beggar had plans of his own, and Nikita had none. Nikita reached the market, sat down in the shade behind a stall and ceased thinking about Lyuba, about life's cares and about himself.

The market watchman had been living at the market for twenty-five years, and had fed lavishly all that time together with his stout, childless old woman. The traders and the people at the co-operative stores had always given him their butcher's waste and bits of reject meat, and they let him have cloth at cost price, as well as such household necessities as thread and soap.

For some time now he had been trading in a small way himself, selling off damaged empty crates and hoarding money at the savings bank. His duties were to sweep the whole market clean of rubbish, to wash the blood from the butcher's slabs, to clean the public latrines, and to keep watch at night over the stalls and storage places. But he gave the hard work to the vagabonds and beggars who spent the night there, and did nothing himself except stroll around at night in a warm sheepskin coat; his wife usually poured out the remains of yesterday's cabbage and meat soup into a slop-pail, so the watchman could always get some poor fellow to clean the latrines in return for food.

His wife was forever telling him not to do the hard work, for just look how grey his beard had grown – he was a supervisor now, not a watchman.

But you cannot get a tramp or a beggar to perform eternal labour in return for food: he will do the work once, eat what he is given, ask for more, then disappear back into the countryside.

Recently, several nights in a row, the watchman had driven one and the same man out of the market. When the watchman gave him a push as he slept, the man would get up and go away without answering back – and then there he was again, sitting or lying somewhere behind a distant stall. Once the watchman chased this homeless man all night long, his very blood leaping from the desire to torment and vanquish an alien and exhausted being. A couple of times the watchman threw a stick at him and hit him on the head, but at dawn the vagabond gave him the slip – he seemed to have left the market place altogether. Then in the morning the watchman found him again; he was in the open air, asleep on the roof of the cesspit, behind the latrines. The watchman called to the sleeping man, who opened his eyes but said nothing; he just looked at him and dozed off again indifferently. The watchman decided the man was dumb.

He poked the point of a stick into the sleeper's stomach and gestured to him to follow.

The watchman took the man to the neat apartment – one room and a separate kitchen – that went with his job. There the watchman offered the dumb man a little cold cabbage soup, with pork-rind, straight from the pot, and then told him to take a broom, a spade, a scraper and a bucket of lime from the entrance room and go and clean up the public latrines. The dumb man looked at the watchman with vague eyes: probably he was deaf too . . . But no, not at all. The dumb man went to the entrance and took all the tools and materials he needed, just as the watchman had told him to – he was evidently able to hear.

Nikita did the work efficiently, and later the watchman came out to check how he had got on. It was not a bad start, so the watchman took Nikita to where the horses were tethered, and entrusted him with the job of collecting the dung and taking it out on a wheelbarrow.

At home the watchman instructed his wife to stop throwing the remains of lunch and supper into the slop pail, and to pour them instead into a separate bowl: let the dumb man finish them up.

"Soon you'll be telling me to make up a bed for him in our room!" said the mistress of the house.

"Nonsense!" stated the watchman. "He's going to sleep outside. He isn't deaf, you know, so let him lie there and listen out for thieves. If he hears anything, he can come and get me. Give him some sacking – he can find himself somewhere to sleep."

Nikita lived a long time at the town market. Having started by losing the habit of speaking, he then began to think less, remember less and suffer less. Only now and then did a weight settle on his heart, but he bore it without reflection, and gradually the feeling of grief inside him wore itself out and went away. He had grown used to living at the market, and the large crowds, the noise of the voices, and the daily goings-on distracted him from the memory of himself and from his own needs – food, rest, and the desire to see his father. Nikita worked constantly: even at night, when he was falling asleep in an empty crate in the middle of the silent market place, the supervisor-watchman would come over to him and order him to doze lightly and to keep listening and not sleep the sleep of the dead. "Anything can happen," the watchman would say. "The other day robbers tore two boards off a stall and ate a whole pood[3] of honey without any bread . . ." By dawn Nikita was already at work, hurrying to clean up the market before the crowds came; during the day there was not even time to eat – there was dung to be shovelled from a heap onto the communal cart, or a new pit needed digging for slops and filth, or else he had to break up the old crates which the watchman got for nothing from the traders and then sold as separate planks to people from the village; or some other task would come up.

In the middle of the summer Nikita was put in prison on suspicion of stealing chandler's goods from the market branch of the agricultural co-operative, but the investigation cleared him – this dumb and extremely worn-out man was too indifferent to the charge against him. The investigator could not find in Nikita's character, or in the humble work he did at the market as watchman's assistant, any sign of greed for life or of desire for pleasure or enjoyment – even in prison he did not eat all his food. The investigator realized that this man did not know the value of either personal or public property, nor was there any clear evidence in the circumstances of the case. "Not worth dirtying a prison with a man like him!" the investigator decided.

Nikita spent only five days in prison, and then went straight back to the market. The watchman-supervisor had got tired out doing the work on his own, so he was glad when the dumb man showed up again by the market stalls. The old man asked Nikita into his apartment and gave him some freshly made hot soup, thus infringing his household regime of thriftiness. "Just one meal – it won't ruin us!" the old watchman-boss reassured himself. "Then it'll be back to yesterday's cold left-overs – when there are any!"

"Go and rake up the rubbish from the grocery stalls," the watchman ordered, when Nikita had finished eating the soup.

Nikita went off to his usual work. By now his sense of his own self was weak and he thought only those thoughts which wandered into his mind at random. By autumn, most likely, he would have quite forgotten what he was, and, when he saw the world going on around him, would no longer have any idea what it meant; he then might seem to everyone else to be living his life in the world, but in fact he would just happen to be there, existing in unconsciousness, in poverty of mind, in absence of feeling, as if in some homely warmth, hiding from mortal grief.

Not long after he had been in prison, when summer was on its way out and the nights were lengthening, Nikita was about to lock the door to the latrines – as was required by the rules – when he heard a voice from inside. "You there, wait a minute, don't lock up yet! There's nothing worth stealing in here, is there?"

Nikita waited for the person to come out. Out of the latrine came his father, with an empty sack under his arm.

"Hello, Nikit," said his father – and suddenly began weeping pitifully, ashamed of his tears and wiping them away with anything so as not to acknowledge their existence. "We thought you were dead and gone long ago. So you're all right?"

Nikita embraced his thin, bowed father, and his heart, that had grown unused to feeling, began to stir.

They went into the empty market place and sheltered in the passage between two stalls.

"I came here for buckwheat, it's cheaper here," his father explained. "But I was late, see, the market's already packed up. So I'll spend the night here, buy some tomorrow, then go back. But what are you doing here?"

Nikita wanted to reply to his father, but his throat had dried up and he had forgotten how to speak. He had a fit of coughing and then managed to whisper, "I'm all right. Is Lyuba alive?"

"She threw herself in the river," said the father. "But some fishermen saw her straight away, they pulled her out and brought her round. She was even in hospital. She got better."

"And she's alive now?" asked Nikita quietly.

"Well, she hasn't died yet," said the father. "Blood often comes from her throat: she must have caught a chill when she was drowning. She chose a bad time – the weather had turned nasty, the water was cold."

The father took some bread from his pocket and gave half to his son and they ate a little of it for their supper. Nikita was silent, and his father spread his sack on the ground, getting ready to settle down for the night.

"Have you got a place yourself?" asked the father. "If not, you lie on the sack and I'll lie on the ground. I won't catch cold, I'm old."

"Why did Lyuba drown herself?" whispered Nikita.

"You got a sore throat or something?" asked his father. "That'll pass. She was unhappy, she was wasting away with grief for you – that's why. For a whole month she walked up and down the bank of the Potudan, she'd walk a hundred versts[4] each way. She thought you'd drowned and would float to the top, and she wanted to see you. And it turns out you were here all the time. That's bad . . ."

Nikita thought of Lyuba, and his heart once more began to fill with grief and strength.

"Sleep here on your own, father," said Nikita, "I'll go and have a look at Lyuba."

"You get going," his father agreed. "It's a good time for walking, it's cool. I'll be along tomorrow, we'll talk then."

Nikita left the town and began running along the deserted highroad. When he felt exhausted, he dropped to a walking pace for a while, and then ran again in the free, weightless air over the dark fields.

Late at night Nikita knocked at Lyuba's window and touched the shutters he had once painted with green paint – in the dark night they looked blue. He pressed his face to the windowpane. A faint light spread through the room from a white sheet that was hanging off the bed, and Nikita could see the children's furniture he and his father had made – it was all still there. Then Nikita knocked loudly on the window frame. But again Lyuba did not answer, she did not come up to the window to see that it was him.

Nikita climbed over the gate, went into the entrance, then into the room. The doors were not locked: whoever lived here did not bother to protect their property from thieves.

Lyuba was lying on the bed, even her head hidden beneath the blanket.

"Lyuba!" Nikita called softly.

"What?" asked Lyuba from under the blanket.

She was not asleep. Perhaps she felt ill and afraid as she lay there on her own, or perhaps she thought that the knock at the window and Nikita's voice were a dream.

Nikita sat down on the edge of the bed.

"Lyuba, it's me, I've come."

Lyuba threw the blanket off her face. "Come to me quickly,"

she begged in her old tender voice, and held her arms out to Nikita.

Lyuba was afraid all this would suddenly vanish; she seized Nikita by the arms and pulled him to her.

Nikita embraced Lyuba with the force that tries to take the other, the beloved, inside one's yearning soul; but he quickly remembered himself and felt ashamed.

"Not hurting, are you?" asked Nikita.

"No! I'm not," answered Lyuba.

He wanted her, all of her, so she would be comforted, and a cruel, pitiful strength came to him. But Nikita's joy from this close love of Lyuba was nothing higher than what he had known ordinarily; he felt only that his heart was now in command of all his body, sharing its blood with a poor but necessary pleasure.

Lyuba asked Nikita if he would light the stove – it would be dark outside for a long time yet. A fire would light up the room, and in any case she didn't want to sleep any more, she would wait for dawn and look at Nikita.

But there was no more firewood in the entrance. So Nikita ripped two boards off the shed in the yard, chopped them into kindling and lit the iron stove. When the fire had got going, Nikita opened the little door to let the light out. Lyuba got down from the bed and sat on the floor where it was light, facing Nikita.

"Will it be all right now, you won't mind living with me?" she asked.

"It'll be all right," answered Nikita. "I've got used to being happy with you now."

"Put more wood on the fire, I'm freezing," said Lyuba.

She was wearing only a threadbare nightdress, and her thin body was chilled to the bone in the cool half-dark of the late time.

THE COW

THE GREY CHERKASSIAN COW FROM THE STEPPE LIVED
alone in a shed; the shed, made of boards and painted on the
outside, stood in the small yard by the house of the level
crossing keeper. In the shed, beside the firewood, the hay, the
millet straw and the household things that had seen better
days – a trunk without a lid, a burnt-out samovar flue, some old
rags, a chair without legs, – there was space for the cow to lie
down in at night, and for her to live in during the long winters.

In the afternoons and evenings, Vasya Rubtsov, her owner's
son, would come and visit her, and stroke the soft hair around
her head. He came this day too.

"Cow, cow," he said, since the cow did not have a name of her
own and he called her what was written in his reading book.
"Yes, you're a cow! Don't fret, your son will get better, my father
will be bringing him back right away."

The cow had a little bull calf; he had choked on something
the day before, and spittle and bile had begun to dribble out of
his mouth. Vasya's father was afraid the calf would die, and he
had taken him along to the station today to see the vet.

The cow looked sideways at the boy and remained silent,
chewing a blade of withered grass that had long ago been worn
out by death. She always recognized the boy, and he loved her. He
liked everything about the cow: her warm kind eyes, framed by
dark circles – as if she were continually exhausted or lost in
thought –, her horns, her brow, and her large, thin body which
was the way it was because, instead of saving her strength for
herself in fat and meat, the cow gave it all away in milk and work.
The boy also looked at her tender, quiet udder with its small

135

shrivelled teats that fed him with milk, and he touched her short, firm dewlap and the strong bones that jutted out in front.

After looking at the boy for a while, the cow lowered her head and took a few blades of grass from the trough with her ungreedy mouth. She could not rest or look around for long, she had to chew without interruption, since she gave birth to her milk without interruption and her food was thin and monotonous; the cow had to labour at it for a long time in order to get enough nourishment.

Vasya went out of the shed. Autumn was in the air outside. Round the crossing-keeper's house stretched level, empty fields which had borne corn and rustled with life during the summer but were now mown flat, sad and deserted.

Twilight was setting in; the sky, wrapped in cool grey fog, was already being closed off by darkness; and the wind, after spending all day rustling stubble and bare bushes that had gone dead in preparation for winter, now itself lay down in the still, low places of the earth, gently creaking the wind-vane on the chimney from time to time as it began the song of autumn.

The single-track railway line passed not far from their home, near the front garden, where by now everything was withered and drooping – grass and flowers alike. Vasya was wary of going inside the fence: the garden now seemed like a cemetery of the plants that he had planted in the spring and brought out into life.

His mother lit a lamp in the house and put the signal lantern out on the bench.

"The 406 will be coming soon," she said to her son. "You signal it by. There's no sign of your father. I hope he's not getting drunk!"

Vasya's father had set off for the station, seven kilometres away, before noon; he had probably left the calf with the vet and was now either at a mechanics lesson or at a Party meeting in the station, or else drinking beer in the canteen. Or there might have been a long queue at the vet's, and his father might still be waiting. Vasya took the lantern and sat down on the wooden beam by the crossing. There was still no sound of the train and the boy felt upset: he did not have time to sit here and see the train past – he had to get up early next morning and he needed to do his homework and then go to bed.

He went to the collective farm elementary school five kilometres away, and he was in the fourth year.

Vasya liked going to school; when he listened to the teacher and read books, he could see in his mind the whole world – a world he did not yet know and which lay a long way away from him. The Nile, Egypt, Spain and the Far East, the great rivers – the Mississippi, the Yenisey, the Quiet Don and the Amazon – the Aral Sea, Moscow, Mount Ararat, Solitude Island in the Arctic Ocean: all this excited Vasya and attracted him. He felt that all these countries and people had been waiting a long time for him to grow up and visit them. But he had not yet had time to go anywhere; he still lived where he had been born, and he had been only to the collective farm where he went to school, and to the station. And so he would gaze with anxious joy at the faces of the people who looked out through the windows of the passenger trains: who were they and what were they thinking? But the trains went by quickly and the people in them were gone before the boy at the crossing could get to know them. And anyway there were not many trains, only two in each direction every twenty-four hours, and three of the trains passed by at night.

Once, thanks to a train going by very slowly, Vasya clearly made out the face of a young, thoughtful man. He was looking through an open window into the steppe, at some place on the horizon he did not know, and smoking a pipe. Seeing a boy standing by a crossing with a raised green flag, he smiled at him, clearly said the words, "Goodbye, mate!" – and then waved farewell. "Goodbye," Vasya answered him to himself. "We'll meet again when I grow up! Stay alive and wait for me, don't die!" And for a long time after that the boy remembered this thoughtful man who had passed by in a carriage on his way to some unknown destination; he was probably a parachutist, an artist, a medal-winner, or something even better, Vasya decided. But soon the memory of the man who had once passed their home was forgotten in the boy's heart, since the boy needed to live on and think and feel other things.

Far away, in the empty night of the autumn fields, the train sang out. Vasya went up close to the line and raised the bright lamp high over his head to signal the "all clear". He listened a little longer to the growing rumble of the approaching train and then looked back towards his home. In the yard the cow began to low mournfully. She was waiting all the time for her son, her calf, but he never came. "Why's father taking so long? Where's he loafing about?" Vasya thought crossly. "Our cow's already crying! It's night, it's dark, and still no father."

The locomotive reached the crossing and, turning its wheels with difficulty, breathing with all the strength of its fire into the darkness, went past the solitary person with a lamp in his hand. The engine driver did not so much as look at the boy – he was leaning way out of the window and watching the engine: steam had burst through the packing in the piston rod gland and was escaping with every stroke of the piston. Vasya had noticed this too. Soon there would be a long climb and it would be difficult for a locomotive with a cylinder defect to pull the train. The boy knew what makes a steam engine work, he had read about it in his physics book and, even if there had not been anything written about it there, he would still have found out. He could not bear to see any object or substance and not understand its workings and how it lived inside itself. And so he was not upset by the engine driver going past without looking at his lantern: the driver was worried about his locomotive – it might stop at night on the long climb, and then he would find it difficult to move the train again. Once the train stopped, the waggons would fall back a little, putting the couplings under tension, and the couplings might break if he started under full steam, while otherwise he would be unable to get going at all.

Some heavy four-axle waggons went past; their springs were compressed, and the boy could tell they were carrying a heavy and precious load. Then came open waggons; on them were motor cars, machines of some kind covered in tarpaulins, mounds of coal, mountains of cabbages, and then some new rails; after that came more closed waggons, carrying livestock. Vasya shone his lantern onto the wheels and axle-boxes, wondering if something was wrong there, but everything seemed to be in order. From one of the livestock waggons came the low of an unknown heifer, and his own cow, yearning for her son, answered from the shed with a long, plaintive cry.

The last waggons went past Vasya very slowly. He could hear the engine struggling, labouring away at the head of the train, but its wheels were spinning and the couplings between the waggons had gone slack. Vasya set off with his lantern towards the engine, since it was in difficulties and he wanted to be near it, as if this would help him to share its lot.

The locomotive was being driven so hard that bits of coal were flying out of the chimney, and the boiler's resonant, breathing insides were clearly audible. The wheels were turning slowly and the engine driver was watching them from the window of his cab. The driver's mate was walking along the track in front of the engine. He was shovelling up sand from the layer of ballast and sprinkling it onto the rails so the wheels would bite. The headlamps lit up a black, exhausted figure who was smeared in engine oil. Vasya put his lantern down on the ground and walked out onto the track towards the engine driver's mate.

"Let me do that," said Vasya. "You go and help the engine. It might come to a stop any moment."

"Can you manage?" asked the driver's mate, looking at the boy with large, bright eyes out of a face that was deep and dark. "All right then, have a go! But be careful – watch out for the engine!"

The spade was too large and heavy for Vasya. He gave it back to the driver's mate.

"I'll use my hands, it's easier that way."

Vasya squatted down, and began clawing up sand and sprinkling it onto the rail in a long stripe.

"And the other rail!" ordered the driver's mate, and ran back to the engine.

Vasya began to sprinkle sand first on one rail, and then on the other. The locomotive followed behind the boy, slowly and heavily, grinding the sand with its steel wheels. Cinders fell on Vasya from above, together with drops of moisture that formed as the steam condensed, but Vasya enjoyed working, he felt he was more important than the locomotive, because the locomotive was going along behind him and it was only thanks to him that its wheels did not slip and bring it to a halt.

If Vasya forgot himself in the zeal of work and let the locomotive come right up to him, the driver gave a short blast on the whistle and shouted down: "Hey, watch out there! And make the sand thicker, more even!"

Vasya got out of the engine's way and worked on in silence.

But then he got angry at being shouted at and ordered around; he jumped off the track and shouted back at the engine driver: "And why did you leave without any sand? Didn't you think?"

"We've run out," answered the engine driver. "We've only got a small sandbox."

"Put in an extra one," ordered Vasya, walking beside the engine. "You can shape one out of scrap iron. Ask a roofer."

The engine driver looked at this boy, but was unable to make him out clearly in the darkness. Vasya was neatly dressed and wearing leather shoes, his face was small and he kept his eyes fixed on the engine. The driver had a little boy at home who was just like him.

"And there's steam in all the wrong places, it's coming out of the cylinder, it's escaping to one side of the boiler," said Vasya. "You waste a lot of power with all those holes."

"A right one you are!" said the driver. "You sit here and look after the train then. I'll walk."

"All right!" Vasya agreed joyfully.

Without moving, the locomotive began spinning all of its wheels at full speed, like a prisoner trying to leap to freedom, and even far down the line the rails beneath it began to thunder. Vasya jumped out again in front of the locomotive and began throwing sand onto the rails underneath the front bogie wheels. "If I didn't have a son of my own, I'd adopt this lad," the engine driver muttered as he brought the spinning wheels under control. "He's still young and he's got everything ahead of him, but he's a real little man already . . . What the hell's going on? Maybe the brakes are sticking somewhere in the rear and the crew have all dozed off as if they're on holiday . . . Well, I'll shake them up a bit on the downhill run." The engine driver gave two long whistles so that, if any of the brakes were still on, the crew would release them.

Vasya looked round and stepped off the track.

"What's up?" shouted the engine driver.

"Nothing," said Vasya. "It won't be so steep now, the engine will be all right on its own, it can manage without me, and then it will be downhill . . ."

"Anything's possible," said the driver from above. "Well then – catch!" And he threw the boy two large apples.

Vasya picked up his present from the ground.

"Wait, don't eat them yet!" said the driver. "On your way back, have a good look under the waggons and listen out in case the brakes are stuck anywhere. Then climb up onto the mound and use your lantern to make a signal. You know how?"

"I know all the signals," said Vasya, and caught hold of the ladder so he could have a ride. Then he bent down and looked underneath the locomotive.

"The brakes are stuck!" he shouted.

"Where?" asked the engine driver.

"Right underneath you! The bogie under the tender! The wheels there are hardly turning, but they're all right on the other bogie!"

The engine driver cursed himself, his mate, and the whole of existence. Vasya jumped down from the ladder and set off home. His lantern was on the ground, shining in the distance. Vasya listened to the working parts of the waggons just in case, but nowhere could he hear brake shoes rubbing or grinding.

The train passed by, and the boy turned towards the place where he had left his lantern. But the beam suddenly rose into the air – someone had picked the lantern up. Vasya ran up and saw it was his father.

"Where's our calf?" the boy asked. "Has he died?"

"No, he got better. I sold him to the slaughterhouse, they gave me a good price. What do we want with a bull calf?"

"He's still little," said Vasya.

"They're worth more when they're little, the meat's more tender," his father explained.

Vasya changed the glass in the lantern, replacing the white pane by a green pane, and made a signal by slowly lifting the lantern above his head several times and then lowering it again, shining it in the direction of the train that had just passed: the wheels were turning smoothly, the brakes were not sticking anywhere – let the train go on its way!

Everything went quiet. The cow in the yard lowed meekly and mournfully. She could not sleep, she was waiting for her son.

"You go back home on your own," said the father. "I'll go and check our section of line."

"What about your tools?" Vasya reminded him.

"It's all right, I just want to look where the spikes are coming out – I won't do any work now," the father said quietly. "My heart aches for the calf – we cared for him a long time, we'd grown used to him . . . If I'd known I'd feel like this, I wouldn't have sold him."

And the father went off down the line with the lantern, turning his head first to the right and then to the left as he checked the track.

The cow gave another long low when Vasya opened the gate into the yard and the cow heard a human being.

Vasya went into the shed and looked closely at the cow, letting his eyes get used to the dark. The cow was not eating anything now; she was breathing slowly and silently, and a heavy, difficult grief languished inside her, one that could have no end and could only grow because, unlike a human being, she was unable to allay this grief inside her with words, consciousness, a friend or any other distraction. Vasya stroked and fondled the cow for a long time, but she remained motionless and indifferent; she only needed one thing – her son, the calf – and nothing could replace him: neither a human being, nor grass, nor the sun. The cow did not understand that it is possible to forget one happiness, to find another and then live again, not suffering any longer. Her dim mind did not have the strength to help her deceive herself; if something had once entered her heart or her feelings, then it could not be suppressed there or forgotten.

And the cow lowed gloomily, because she was entirely obedient to life, to nature and to her need for her son, who was not yet big enough for her to be able to leave him, and she felt hot and aching inside, she was looking into the darkness with large, bloodshot eyes, and she was unable to cry with them, to weaken herself and her grief.

In the morning Vasya went off early to school, while his father began to get the small single-bladed plough ready for work. The father wanted to use the cow to plough some of the land beside the railway line, so he could sow millet there in the spring.

When he came back from school, Vasya saw that his father was ploughing with their cow, but had got very little done. The cow was dragging the plough obediently, lowering her head and drooling spittle onto the ground. Vasya and his father had worked with their cow before, she knew how to plough, and she was patient and used to wearing a yoke.

Towards evening the father unharnessed the cow and let her into the old fields to graze on the stubble. Vasya was sitting at home at the table, he was doing his schoolwork and looking from time to time out of the window. He could see his cow. She was standing in the field nearby; she was not grazing, she was not doing anything.

Evening set in just like the day before, gloomy and empty, and the weather-vane creaked on the roof, as if singing the long song of autumn. Staring into the darkening field, the cow was waiting for her son; now she was no longer lowing for him and calling him, she was enduring and not understanding.

After he had done his schoolwork, Vasya took a slice of bread, sprinkled it with salt and took it out to the cow. The cow did not eat the bread and remained indifferent, just as before. Vasya stood beside her for a while and then put his arms round the cow's neck from underneath, so she would know that he understood and loved her. But the cow abruptly jerked her neck, threw off the boy and, with an uncharacteristic guttural scream, ran away into the field. After running some distance, the cow suddenly turned round and, now jumping, now bending her front legs and pressing her head to the ground, began to approach Vasya, who was waiting for her in the same place.

The cow ran past the boy, past their home, and disappeared in the evening field, and from there Vasya once again heard her strange, guttural voice.

When his mother came back from the collective farm co-operative, she, Vasya and Vasya's father went out into the surrounding fields and walked about until midnight, going in different directions and calling out to their cow, but the cow did not answer them, she was not there. After supper the mother began to cry, because they had lost their worker and their provider, while the father thought about how he'd probably have to write an application to the mutual-aid fund and the railway workers' union, asking for a loan towards the acquisition of a new cow.

Vasya was the first to wake up in the morning, the light in the windows was still grey. He could hear someone near the house, breathing and moving about in the silence. He looked out through the window and saw the cow; she was standing by the gate and waiting to be let back in.

After that, although the cow went on living, and worked when they needed to plough or to go to the collective farm for flour, her milk dried up completely, and she turned sullen and slow-witted. Vasya watered her himself, and cleaned her and fed her, but the cow did not respond to his care, nothing anyone did made any difference to her.

In the daytime they let the cow out into the field, so she could walk about freely for a while and feel better. But the cow did not walk much; she would stand for a long time in one place, walk a little, and then stop again, forgetting to walk on. Once she went out onto the line and began to walk slowly along the sleepers; then Vasya's father saw her, stopped her and led her away. Previously the cow had been timid and sensitive, and had never gone out onto the line. And so Vasya began to fear the cow would be killed by a train or that she would just die, and he thought about her all the time he was at school and then came back home at a run.

And once, when the days were at their shortest and it was already getting dark as he came home from school, Vasya saw that a goods train had stopped opposite their house. Alarmed, he ran up to the engine.

The engine driver – the one whom Vasya had helped not long ago with his train – and Vasya's father were dragging the cow from underneath the tender. She had been killed. Vasya sat down on the ground, numb with the grief of this first close death.

"I'd been whistling at her for ten minutes," the engine driver was saying to Vasya's father. "Was she deaf or stupid or something? I put the emergency brakes on, but there still wasn't time."

"She wasn't deaf, she was crazy," said the father. "She'd probably gone to sleep on the track."

"No, she was running away from the engine, but she was slow and she didn't have the sense to get off the line," said the driver. "I thought she would."

Along with the driver's mate and the fireman, four men together, they dragged the mutilated carcass of the cow out from underneath the tender, and heaved all the beef into a dry ditch beside the track.

"Well, at least it's fresh," said the engine driver. "Are you going to salt the meat for yourselves, or will you sell it?"

"We'll have to sell it," the father decided. "We need to raise the money for another cow, it's difficult to get by without a cow."

"You can't get by without a cow," the engine driver agreed. "You must get the money together and buy one, I'll help out a bit myself. I haven't got much, but I can find something. I'm getting a bonus soon."

"Why do you want to give me money?" Vasya's father asked in surprise. "I'm not family, what do I matter to you? Anyway, I can get by on my own. You know how it is: the trade union, the mutual-aid fund, work, it all adds up . . ."

"Well, I'll chip in a bit too," the engine driver insisted. "Your son helped me, and I'm going to help you. There he is. Hello!" smiled the engine driver.

"Hello," said Vasya.

"I've never run anyone over in my life," said the engine driver, "except once – a dog. It'll be on my conscience if I don't give you anything for the cow."

"What are you getting a bonus for?" asked Vasya. "You drive badly."

"I'm getting a little better now." The driver laughed. "I've been learning. We're short of resources, my boy, you can't even get a spare pound of tow, you can't help driving badly."

"Have you put in another sand-box?" asked Vasya.

"No, but we've swapped the little one for a big one."

"It took you a while to work that out," said Vasya angrily.

At this point the chief guard came up and gave the driver a form he had filled in, about why the train had stopped between stations.

Next day the father sold the whole of the cow's carcass to the district co-operative; someone else's cart came and took it away. Vasya and his father went in the cart too. His father wanted to get the money for the meat, and Vasya was hoping to buy some reading-books from the shop. They stayed the night in the town, spent another half day there, buying this and that, and set off home after lunch.

Their way back took them through the collective farm where Vasya went to school. It was already completely dark when they got there, and Vasya stayed the night with the caretaker instead of going home, so he would not have to come back first thing in the morning and wear himself out to no avail. His father went home on his own.

In school that morning they started their first-term tests. The pupils had to write an essay on the subject: "How I will live and work in order to be of service to our Motherland."

Vasya wrote out his answer in his exercise book: "I do not know how I will live, I have not thought yet. We had a cow. While she lived, my mother, my father and I all ate milk from her. Then she had her son – a calf – and he ate milk from her too, there were three of us and he made four, and there was enough milk for us all. The cow also ploughed and carried loads. Then her son was sold for meat, he was killed and eaten. The cow was very unhappy, but she soon died from a train. And she was eaten too, because she was beef. Now there is nothing. The cow gave us everything, that is her milk, her son, her meat, her skin, her innards and her bones, she was kind.

I remember our cow and I will not forget."

It was twilight when Vasya returned home. His father was already there, he had just come in from the line; he was showing Vasya's mother a hundred roubles – two notes that the driver had thrown down from the engine in a tobacco pouch.

THE SEVENTH MAN

A MAN CROSSED THE FRONT TO OUR LINES. AT FIRST HE wept; then he looked round, ate some food and calmed down.

The man was poorly dressed, in black rags tied to his torso with pieces of string, and his feet were wrapped in straw. There was little soft body left on him, no more than on the corpse of a man who had been dead a long time: nothing had been preserved of him except bones, and his life still clung on around them. Dark blue had begun to cover his face, as if the hoarfrost of death had appeared there, and his face lacked any ordinary expression; only after close scrutiny could one see that on it lay the sorrow of alienation from all people – a sorrow which this man, worn down with suffering, evidently no longer felt or else felt to be his normal condition.

He seemed to live only from habit and not from any desire, since everything he breathed, was nourished by and believed in had been taken from him and estranged. But he was still living and patiently wearing himself out, as if he wanted to fulfil to the end the will of his mother, who had borne him for a happy life, as if he were hoping he had not been deceived by her, that she had not given birth to him only so he would suffer.

His soul – the last desire for life, refusing destruction until the final breath – had already emerged from the dried-up hiding places of his body, and his face and empty eyes were therefore so little animated by any vital need as to have no meaning, and it was impossible to make out this man's character, whether he was good or evil; yet he was still living.

According to his papers he was Osip Yevseevich Gershanovich, a native and resident of the city of Minsk, born in the year 1894, who had worked as a senior planner in the Union of Provincial Light Industries; life, however, had made him into another being, perhaps a holy martyr, a hero of humanity, perhaps a traitor to humanity in the impenetrable protective mask of a martyr. In our time, in time of war, when the enemy has decided to destroy restless, contradictory humanity, sparing only a worn-out, servile remnant of it – in our time evil-doing can appear inspired and righteous, since violence has instilled evil inside man, squeezing out from there his old sacred essence, and man devotes himself to the cause of evil at first in despair, and then with faith and satisfaction, so as not to die of horror. Evil and good can now appear in an equally inspired, touching and attractive form: in this lies the special condition of our time, formerly unknown and impossible; formerly a man might be capable of evil-doing but would feel this as his misfortune, and, escaping it, would once again press himself against the warm, accustomed goodness of life; now, however, man has been forcibly reduced to the capacity to live and warm himself by self-immolation, destroying himself and others.

2

Gershanovich reached us with the help of the partisans, who had been surprised and interested by so rare a man – rare even to them, who had suffered all of their fates – a man able to make room inside him for death and still endure; they led him through the lines, protecting him with their own bodies, carrying him in their arms past fortified enemy positions, so that his heart could recover from suffering, and from the memory of it, and he could begin to live normally.

Gershanovich's speech was like the speech of a man in a dream, as if his main consciousness were engaged in a world we could not see and nothing reached us except a weak light from thoughts that had moved far away. He called himself the seventh man and said that he had not pulled the pin of the hand grenade because the pin was stiff and there had not been time to pull it, and that the pin had been stiff because the work of the quality control department was not good enough, not like in his Provincial Artisans' Union in Minsk.

Then Gershanovich spoke to us more clearly, saying he used to take work home with him in the evening; he had needed money because he had fathered five children and all five had grown up healthy, and they had eaten well, and he had been glad they were eating up his labour and not leaving any over, and he had taught himself to sleep little, so as to have time to do extra work; but now he could sleep for a long time and he could even die; there was no one left for him to feed: all his children, together with his wife and grandmother, were lying in a clay grave near the Borisov concentration camp, and with them lay another five hundred people who had also been killed – all of them were naked, but they were covered over with earth, there would be grass there in summer, and snow in winter, and they wouldn't feel cold there.

"They'll get warm now," said Gershanovich. "Soon I'll join them too, I'm lonely without my family, there's nowhere else for me to go, I want to visit their grave."

"Live with us," one of the soldiers invited him.

"Me live here, while they lie dead there!" exclaimed Gershanovich. "They're in a bad way there, things are hard for them – it's not right. No, I'll try and reach them again by dying. I didn't get there the first time, I must try again."

And he suddenly shuddered from a dark memory: "And again I won't die. I'll kill, but I won't die myself."

"How do you know? That's as may be," said the soldier who was listening to him.

"That's how it will be," said Gershanovich. "The Fascists are careful with death, they're tight-fisted, they make one death do seven men – it was me who thought up that little saving for them – and now they'll try and make it go even further. The Germans have grown poor."

At the time we did not understand what Gershanovich meant. "Let him ramble on," we thought.

Soon afterwards four partisans got through to us. They turned out to have known Gershanovich for a long time, as a member of partisan brigade N, and they told us that Gershanovich was a very wise man and the most skilled partisan in his brigade. His family had indeed been shot near Borisov, and five hundred souls had been shot at the same time, so there would be fewer mouths to feed and fewer Jews.

"And death hasn't once taken him, though he's ready enough," said one of the new partisans. "And you can understand why: Osip Yevseich is no fool, and he needs a death as smart as he is, but the Fascists make a lot of noise when they fight, and they shoot at random. They're no great danger . . . In Minsk, Osip Yevseich got a bullet in the head – and at close range – but it didn't penetrate inside, he stopped it with his mind."

We said this was not possible.

"It is," said the partisan. "It depends how you fight. If you're a skilled fighter, it's possible."

To prove this, he felt the back of Gershanovich's head with his fingers; then we felt the same place ourselves: beneath his hair lay a dent in the skull from a deep wound.

3

After he had lived with us a bit longer, and eaten some good food, Gershanovich became more rational and less strange-looking, and then he once again went off far behind the enemy lines, together with the four partisans. He wanted to pass a second time along the path where death had failed to overcome him, and where he himself had achieved only a partial victory – and then return to us straight away.

Armed, and wearing a Belorussian coat and bast shoes, Gershanovich went off at night into the thick of the enemy, in order to destroy them and to visit his dead children.

After making his way to Minsk along partisan paths, Gershanovich left his companions and again, as on his first journey, came out into the outskirts of the town in the half-light. He walked alone in quiet consciousness, understanding the world around him as a sad fairy-tale or as a dream that might pass him by for ever. He was already used to the absence of people, to the deathly ruins behind the German lines and to the constant chill of a human body that keeps dragging itself along and living.

Gershanovich walked past the camp for Russian prisoners of war. There was no one to be seen now behind the wire fence. After a while a Russian soldier got up in the distance and walked towards the fence. He had no hat and was wearing a scorched greatcoat; one foot was bare, the other wrapped in a rag, and he was walking through snow. As he moved on his difficult, emaciated legs, he muttered something in delirium, the words of his eternal separation from life; then he collapsed onto his hands and lay there face down.

There were a lot of people by the entrance to the camp. "It was just as crowded then," Gershanovich remembered. "There are always people here."

On a bench, beside the sentry box, sat two Fascists, senior Gestapo security officers. They were silently smoking pipes and smiling at what they saw before them.

Two Russian prisoners, who looked well-fed and who were

wearing proper military uniforms, were manhandling two other people out of the camp – also Russian prisoners, but so frail, wasted and apathetic that they seemed already to have died, to be dragging themselves forward with a strength that was not theirs.

The Fascists said something to the Russians, and the two decently uniformed ones gave a push to their two comrades, who fell down submissively, since their weakness made them helpless. Then the two well-nourished Russians forcibly lifted up the enfeebled ones and threw them against the ground. After this the well-fed Russians stopped expectantly, wanting to rest. The Germans shouted out that they must go on working until the last breath of life had left the weak and useless ones. The well-nourished traitors obediently picked up the exhausted soldiers and again flung them down, smashing their heads against frozen hummocks of earth.

The Fascists began to laugh and ordered them to work faster. Gershanovich stood at a distance and watched; he understood that this murder was being carried out in order to economize on cartridges, with which the Germans in the rear were extremely sparing, and that the Fascists found it necessary, moreover, to make murder into something instructive and edifying for the prisoners who were still alive.

Five prisoners walked up to the gates from inside the camp and watched silently as their comrades were tormented to death. The Germans did not chase them away; they watched the Russians with a smile of accustomed, almost indifferent hatred, ordering the traitors not to work so fast now. But by then there was no more point in their work: what they picked up from the ground and threw down again against the hummocks were mere corpses with battered heads and blood that had gone cold and congealed. The men must have died from inner exhaustion when they were smashed against the ground the first time; there was nothing left in them for their breath to hold on to. The Fascists, however, continued this execution of corpses, wishing its educational meaning to be brought out to the maximum benefit of the living.

Gershanovich quietly made his way towards the Germans who were sitting on the bench. The now-exhausted traitors also went up to them and, standing to attention, requested the additional food rations to which their services entitled them.

The Germans grinned without saying anything; then one of them answered that there would be no more extra rations: a supply convoy had been attacked by partisans and they first had to recover the bread from them. "Go and join our punitive corps," said the Germans, "and get the bread back from the partisans, then you'll have enough to eat. There's no bread for you here."

Beneath the skirt of his coat Gershanovich pulled the pin of a grenade and, from close range, hurled the grenade with precision into the middle of the four enemies.

The grenade burst furiously into flame, as if screaming out with a human being's last voice, and the enemies of mankind, after going utterly still for a moment, fell to the ground.

Last time, at the other entrance to this same camp, Gershanovich's grenade had not gone off; he had merely smashed in the head of one enemy with it, as if with a dead piece of metal, but this time he felt glad and he ran off with a satisfied soul.

The sentry in the hut, however, remained alive; he began to shoot at Gershanovich and into the air.

Five armed guards appeared from a pavilion where refreshing drinks had once been sold; with a lot of noise, shouting at one another so as not to feel afraid themselves, they leapt on Gershanovich and disarmed him.

Osip Gershanovich was taken to the District Commandant's Headquarters, where he had already been once before. Down in the cellar men were shot in groups of six – one bullet to each group: it was imperative to save ammunition. The Germans stood the men close behind one another, equalizing their heights by placing thick volumes – somebody or other's collected works – beneath the feet of the shorter men.

Gershanovich was asked at the Commandant's whether he was going to say anything in order to stay alive. He answered that, on the contrary, he was going to say nothing, as he wished to die, and that there was no point in beating him up, not because that would be wrong, but because it would waste the strength of the field police; better to leave intact inside them the mutton and noodles they ate at the State's expense.

Perhaps thinking there was sense in what he had said, the officer ordered Gershanovich to be taken away. But, until he was dead, Gershanovich was alive, and fighting, and hoping to be the victor.

This officer was not the one who had interrogated Gershanovich the first time, and so Gershanovich once again proposed his innovation: one bullet could be used to kill not six men, but seven; the seventh would die later, not straight away, but he would die all the same, and to the State this would represent a saving of fourteen per cent on ammunition.

"The seventh doesn't die," said the officer. "The penetrative force of the bullet is already significantly weaker by the sixth head. It has been reported to me that they tried adding a seventh man on a previous occasion. He survived, and escaped from an unfilled grave, wounded in the back of the head."

"He was a survivor," Gershanovich explained. "He was a man

who knew what was what, but his head still hurt, it had been damaged. And that's the truth!"

"Who was it?" asked the officer.

"How would I know? Could have been anyone. There lived a man, he hadn't lived long, they tried to kill him, he lived again and died anyway, he missed his family . . ."

The officer thought for a moment: "We're trying out a new type of modernized musket. You can be the seventh man, but for the experiment I'll put an eighth there as well."

"By all means!" Gershanovich willingly agreed.

"It'll be interesting to see," said the officer, "whether the bullet lodges in your brain or if it goes out through your forehead and into the eighth man. These muskets keep up a fierce rate of fire, but we don't know their penetrative force."

"It will be interesting. You and I will soon find out," said Gershanovich, thinking the officer was a fool. A guard then took the prisoner away.

5

In the common cell, inhabited by the deceased-to-be, life went on as usual: people were mending clothes, chatting, sleeping and thinking about the way life was and the way it ought to be according to universal justice. The cell had no windows; the small paraffin lamp burned all day and all night. Only a newly arrived prisoner could say what time it was, but they soon all forgot the time again, and argued about it, and nobody knew for sure whether it was day or night in the world, though this was something that interested them all.

Gershanovich found himself a place on the floor and lay down to rest. A thought was now troubling him: who would be the eighth man when they were shot? This eighth man was guaranteed a sure salvation, as long as he didn't turn out to be a coward or a fool. "That's bad," thought Gershanovich. "If it kills me, the bullet won't hit him with much force, it might damage the bone, nothing more – but he'll think he's been killed, and he'll die from fright and consciousness."

Time passed. Gershanovich had not yet got any sleep, but the whole cell was ordered outside. Gershanovich was expecting this; he knew from before that those designated for death were not kept long, since the Germans did not want to have to feed them, or give water to them, or expend their minds to no purpose by giving them any thought at all.

For the second time in his life Gershanovich was going down the dark stone steps to a death in the cellar. Among his comrades, the men who were going with him to destruction, he did not recognize one familiar face, and from their speech he guessed that these people had recently been brought from Poland.

A lance corporal counted off eight men, including Gershanovich, who was the second in line, and left the rest on the staircase.

The cellar was lit by the timid light of a solitary candle, and near the light stood the officer who had interrogated Gershanovich. The officer, a lover of firearms, was inspecting some sort of short-barrelled rifle. "They're always trying to economize," thought Gershanovich. "But we mustn't. If it takes two bullets to kill each German, it'll still be more than worth it!"

The lance corporal began arranging the prisoners so the backs of their heads were in line.

"I'm seventh," Gershanovich reminded him in good time.

"You don't want to be the first to die?" asked the lance corporal. "Want to outsmart us, do you? All right then, die seventh, as a special privilege – but put a brick under your feet, you're not tall enough."

Gershanovich put a brick under his feet and got up onto his place of death. He looked at the eighth and last prisoner: in front of him was the bald patch of an old man, covered with the down of infancy.

"It's going to be death," Osip Gershanovich understood. "But what of it? I've not had a bad life here. If I end up in the next world, I'll get by as best I can there, and things will be all right, and I'll see my children. But if there's nothing there, that means I'll be like my dead children, the same as them, and that'll be fair and just too. Why am I living when my heart's been killed and it's lying in the earth?"

"Ready?" asked the officer. "Breathe deeply!" he ordered, and then promised the prisoners: "Now you'll each sleep the sweet sleep of a child!"

Gershanovich did the opposite. He stopped breathing and listened to the silence that had set in, wanting for his own amusement to hear the shot, but he failed to hear it and fell at once into sweet sleep. His kind mind had of its own accord lost consciousness, thus protecting the man from despair.

On waking, Gershanovich touched his forehead: it was smooth and clean. "The bullet's inside my mind," he decided. Then he touched the back of his head and felt there only the old dent of his previous injury. "I'm still alive, still in this world, it's all just as I thought," the prisoner reflected. "This new gun of theirs is no use at all, the cartridges don't have enough powder, I knew it. So how many have they killed with one bullet? Three or four, probably, but last time the bullet killed the sixth man and got as far as me. The enemy of mankind is growing weak, he's growing weak – I can feel it!"

As he lay there, Gershanovich became used to the dark, which was still illuminated by a mysterious, scarcely breathing light that trembled in the distance. Near him lay the man who had stood in front of him, the bald old man with child-like down on the clean skin of his head. Gershanovich put his hand to the head of the old man; his head had grown cold and the whole man had died, even though he had not been harmed in any way. "It's like I thought – one mustn't be afraid," Gershanovich determined. "The whole world could come to an end from fear, and then what would there be? One mustn't be afraid."

He worked out where he was: this was the cellar where they had been shot, eight of them, and the distant candle had still not burnt down. "It's a shame we're in here," thought Gershanovich. "It's going to be death. But what of it? Before death there's also a little life. Last time they carted me off to a grave, and that didn't stop me living."

An officer bent down towards him. Gershanovich could sense him from his alien breath – a stinking foulness carried out from his innards.

"So what is it you Bolsheviks say?" said the officer. "Didn't work out?! Wanted to live did the Jew, standing seventh in the queue!"

"I'd say it didn't work out for you," answered Gershanovich. "I'm alive!"

"You're dead now!" stated the officer, aiming the barrel of his small personal revolver at Gershanovich's forehead.

Gershanovich looked into the officer's pale eyes, which had been deadened by a secret despair, and said to him, "Fire at me . . . My life is here, but my children are there – I'll be all right wherever I am. We were people here, we were humanity, but there we'll be something higher still, we'll be eternal nature, giving birth to people."

The bullet entered one of Gershanovich's eyes, and he went still; but for a long time his body remained warm, slowly taking leave of life as it returned its warmth to the earth.

6

Long afterwards an elderly partisan came across the front to our lines and recounted the story of Gershanovich's end. This partisan had been the eighth, the last prisoner standing in line to be shot, and Gershanovich had been the seventh. So successfully had this partisan attenuated his breathing and feigned death that he had even been able to make his body go cold, which was how, for the sake of life, he had deceived the German officer and had even, when Gershanovich felt the back of his head, managed to fool him.

The candle in the cellar had gone out, they had not bothered to light another, and this old man, without any proper verification of his death, had been carted off and thrown into a gully together with the truly deceased, and from there he had slipped away. To save manpower, the Fascists do not always dig graves, especially in winter, when the ground is frozen.

NIKITA

EARLY IN THE MORNING THE MOTHER WOULD LEAVE home to go and work in the fields. There was no father in the family; father had gone away long ago to the most important work – the war – and he had not come back. Every day the mother expected the father to come back, but he did not come and he did not come.

Five-year-old Nikita would be left on his own, master of the hut and the whole yard. As she left, his mother would tell him not to burn the hut down, to be sure to collect any eggs the hens laid beneath the fence or in the sheds, not to let any other cocks come into the yard and attack their own cock – and to eat the bread and milk she had put on the table for lunch, and in the evening she would come back and make him a hot supper.

"You haven't got a father, Nikitushka, so don't get up to mischief," his mother would say. "You're a clever boy now, and what's in the hut and yard is all we have."

"I'm clever, it's all we have, and I haven't got a father," Nikita would say. "But come back soon, Mummy, or I get frightened."

"What's there to be frightened of? The sun's shining in the sky, and the fields are full of people. Don't be frightened, you'll be all right on your own."

"But the sun's a long way away," Nikita would say, "and a cloud will cover it up."

When his mother had left, Nikita went round the whole quiet hut – the back room and the other room with its Russian stove – and then went out into the entrance. Big fat flies were buzzing there, a spider was dozing in a corner in the middle of his web, and a sparrow had crossed the threshold on foot and was looking for a grain or two on the earth floor. Nikita knew every one of them: the sparrows, and the spiders, and the flies, and the hens outside; he had had enough of them, they bored him. What he wanted now was to learn something he did not know. So Nikita went on out into the yard and came to the shed, where there was an empty barrel standing in the darkness. Probably someone was living in it, some little man or other; in the daytime he slept, but at night he came out, ate bread, drank water and did some thinking, and then in the morning he would hide inside the barrel again and go to sleep.

"I know you, you live in there," said Nikita. He was standing on tiptoe and speaking down into the dark, resonant barrel. Then he gave it a knock with his fist to make sure. "Get up, you lazybones, and stop sleeping! What are you going to eat in winter? Go and weed the millet, they'll put it down as a work day!"[1]

Nikita listened. It was quiet in the barrel. "Maybe he's died!" Nikita thought. But there was a squeak from the wood, and Nikita got out of harm's way. He realized that whoever lived there must have turned over onto his side, or else was about to get up and chase after him.

But what was he like – this man in the barrel? Nikita pictured him at once in his mind. He was someone small but lively. He had a long beard that reached right down to the ground. Without meaning to, he swept away the litter and straw with his beard when he walked about at night, leaving clean paths on the floor of the shed.

Not long ago his mother had lost her scissors. The little man must have taken them to trim his beard.

"Give us back our scissors!" Nikita said quietly. "When father comes home from the war, he'll take them anyway. He's not afraid of you. Give them back!"

164

The barrel remained silent. In the forest, far beyond the village, someone gave a hoot, and the little man in the barrel answered in a strange black voice: "I'm here!"

Nikita ran out of the shed into the yard. The kind sun was shining in the sky, there were no clouds in the way. Nikita was frightened and he looked at the sun, hoping it would defend him.

"There's someone there – living in a barrel!" said Nikita, looking at the sky.

The kind sun went on shining in the sky, looking back at him in return with its warm face. Nikita saw that the sun was like his dead grandfather; when he was still alive and had looked at Nikita, his grandfather had always smiled and been kind to him. Nikita thought that his grandfather had gone to live on the sun now.

"Grandpa, where are you? Do you live up there?" asked Nikita. "Stay up there then, but I'll stay here, I'll live with Mummy."

Beyond the vegetable plot, in the thickets of burdock and nettles, there was a well. It was a long time since they had taken water from it, because another well had been dug in the collective farm and the water there was better.

Deep down in this abandoned well, in its underground darkness, lay bright water with a clear sky and clouds passing below the sun. Nikita leaned over the well frame and asked: "What are you doing down there?"

Down on the bottom, he thought, lived small water people. He knew what they were like, he had seen them in dreams and wanted to catch them, but they had run away over the grass and into the well, back to their home. They were the size of sparrows, but they were fat and hairless, damp and dangerous. Nikita knew they wanted to drink up his eyes while he was asleep.

"I'll teach you!" Nikita said into the well. "What are you doing living down there?"

The water in the well suddenly went cloudy, and somebody champed their jaws. Nikita opened his mouth to scream, but nothing came out, he had lost his voice from fear; his heart just trembled and missed a beat.

"A giant and his children live here too!" Nikita realized. "Grandpa!" he shouted out loud, looking at the sun. "Are you there, Grandpa?" And Nikita ran back to his home.

Beside the shed he came to his senses. Beneath its wattle wall were two burrows in the earth. They too had their secret inhabitants. But who were they? They might be snakes. They would creep out at night, they would steal into the hut and bite his mother while she was asleep, and his mother would die.

Nikita ran quickly back inside, took two bits of bread from the table and carried them out. He put one piece by each burrow and said to the snakes: "Eat up the bread, snakes, and don't bother us at night."

Nikita looked round. There was an old tree stump in the vegetable plot. When he looked at it, Nikita saw it was the head of a man. The stump had eyes, a nose and a mouth, and the stump was quietly smiling at Nikita.

"Do you live here too?" the boy asked. "Come out and join us in the village. You can plough the earth."

The stump quacked out an answer, and its face turned angry.

"All right then, don't come out!" said Nikita, taking fright. "Stay where you are!"

It had gone quiet everywhere in the village, there was no sound of anyone. His mother was far away in the fields, he would never reach her in time. Nikita left the angry tree stump and went back into the entrance of the hut. He didn't feel frightened in there, his mother had been there not long ago. It was hot in the hut now. Nikita wanted to drink the milk his mother had left him, but when he looked at the table he noticed the table was a person too, only it had four legs and no arms.

Nikita went back out onto the porch. Far beyond the vegetable plot and the well stood the old bath hut. It was black inside from the chimney being blocked, and his mother said that his grandfather had liked to wash there when he was still alive.

The bath hut was old and covered in moss; it was a miserable little building.

"It's our grandmother, she didn't die, she turned into a bath hut!" Nikita thought in terror. "She's alive, she's alive: That's her head – it's not a chimney, it's a head: And that's her gap-toothed mouth. She's pretending to be a bath hut, but really she's still a woman. I can tell!"

Someone else's cockerel came in off the street. Its face was like the face of the thin shepherd with the short beard who had been drowned that spring in the river; he had tried to swim across the flood waters so he could go and have fun at a wedding in another village.

Nikita decided that the shepherd had not liked being dead and had become a cock; so this cock was a man – a secret man. There were people everywhere, only they seemed not to be people.

Nikita bent down over a yellow flower. Who was it? Gazing into the flower, Nikita saw that its small round face was little by little taking on a human expression, and then he could see tiny eyes, a nose and a moist open mouth that smelt of living breath.

"And I thought you really were a flower!" said Nikita. "Let me have a look inside you. Do you have insides?"

Nikita snapped the stem – the body of the flower – and saw some milk in it.

"You were a baby, you were sucking your mother!" said Nikita in surprise.

He went to the old bath hut.

"Grandma!" Nikita said to her quietly. But Grandma's pock-marked face bared its teeth at him furiously, as if he were a stranger.

"You're not Grandma, you're someone else!" thought Nikita.

The stakes looked out at Nikita from the fence like the faces of crowds of people he did not know. And every face was unfamiliar and did not love him: one was smirking angrily, another was thinking something spiteful about him, while a third stake was pushing against the fence with the withered branches that were its arms, about to climb right out of the fence to chase Nikita.

"What are you doing here?" asked Nikita. "This is our yard!"

But on every side there were strange, angry faces, looking fixedly and piercingly at Nikita. He looked at the burdocks – surely they would be kind? But now even the burdocks were sullenly shaking their big heads and not loving him.

Nikita lay down on the earth and pressed his face to it. Inside the earth were humming voices, there must be many people living there in the cramped darkness, Nikita could hear them scrabbling with their hands to climb out into the light of day. Nikita got up in terror; people were living everywhere, strange eyes were looking at him from everywhere; and if there was anyone who could not see him, they wanted to climb out after him from under the earth, from out of a burrow, from under the black eaves of the shed. He turned to the hut. The hut was looking at him like an old woman passing through on her way from some far-off village; it was whispering to him: "Oo-ooh, you useless children, there are too many of you in the world – eating good wheaten bread for free."

"Come home, Mummy!" Nikita begged his far-away mother. "Let them just put you down for half a work day. Strange people have come into our yard. They're living here. Make them go away!"

The mother did not hear her son. Nikita went behind the shed, he wanted to see if the tree-stump-head was climbing out of the earth. The tree stump had a big mouth, it would eat all the cabbages on their plot – how would his mother be able to make cabbage soup in the winter?

Keeping his distance, Nikita looked timidly at the tree stump in the vegetable plot. A gloomy, unfriendly face, grown over with wrinkly bark, looked back at Nikita with unblinking eyes.

And from far away, from the forest on the other side of the village, someone shouted loudly: "Maxim, where are you?"

"In the earth!" the tree-stump-head answered in a muffled voice.

Nikita turned round, to run to his mother in the field, but he fell over. He went numb with fear. His legs were like strange people now and they would not listen to him. Then he crept along on his stomach as if he were still little and could not walk.

"Grandpa!" Nikita whispered, and looked at the kind sun in the sky.

Then a cloud blocked out the light, and the sun could no longer be seen.

"Grandpa, come and live with us again!"

Grandpa-sun appeared from behind the cloud, as if he had immediately removed the dark shadow from his face so he could see his enfeebled grandson creeping along the earth. Grandpa was looking at him now; knowing his grandfather could see him, Nikita got up onto his feet and ran towards his mother.

He ran for a long time. He ran all the way through the village along the empty, dusty road; then he felt tired out and sat down in the shade of an outlying barn.

Nikita did not mean to sit down for long. He laid his head on the ground, however, and fell asleep, and did not wake up until evening. The new shepherd was driving the collective-farm sheep. Nikita would have gone on further, to look for his mother in the field, but the shepherd told him it was late now and his mother had long ago left the field and gone home.

When he got home, Nikita saw his mother. She was sitting at the table and gazing at an old soldier who was eating bread and drinking milk.

The soldier looked at Nikita, then got up from the bench and took him in his arms. The soldier smelt warm, he smelt of something good and peaceful, of bread and earth. Nikita felt shy and said nothing.

"Hello, Nikita," said the soldier. "You forgot me a long time ago, you were just a baby when I kissed you and went off to the war. But I remember you. I didn't forget you even when I was close to death."

"It's your father, Nikitushka, he's come home," said the mother, wiping the tears from her face with her apron.

Nikita took a good look at his father − at his face, his hands, the medal on his chest − and touched the bright buttons on his shirt.

"And you won't go away again?"

"No," said the father. "I'm going to stay with you for ever. We've destroyed the enemy, now it's time to think about you and your mother."

In the morning Nikita went out into the yard and said out loud to everyone who lived there − to the burdocks, to the shed, to the stakes in the fence, to the tree-stump-head in the vegetable plot, and to grandfather's bath hut: "Father's come home. He's going to stay with us for ever."

Everyone in the yard was silent − Nikita could see they were all afraid of a father who was a soldier − and it was quiet underground too: no one was scrabbling to get out into the light.

"Come here, Nikita. Who are you talking to out there?"

His father was in the shed. He was having a look at the tools and running his hands over them: axes, spades, a saw, a plane, a vice, a bench and all the other things he owned.

When he had finished, the father took Nikita by the hand and went round the yard with him, working out what was where, what was in good shape and what had rotted, what was needed and what was not.

Just as he had the day before, Nikita looked into the face of every creature in the yard, but now he could not see a hidden person in any of them; not one of them had eyes, a nose, a mouth or a spiteful life of its own. The fencing stakes were thick, dried-up sticks, blind and dead, and grandfather's bath hut was a tiny little house that had rotted and was slipping away into the earth from being so old. Now Nikita even felt sorry for the bath hut: it was dying, soon it would be quite gone.

His father went into the shed for an axe and began chopping up the old tree stump in the vegetable plot to make firewood. The stump began to fall apart at once, it had rotted all the way through, and from underneath his father's axe its dry dust rose into the air like smoke.

When there was nothing left of the tree-stump-head, Nikita said to his father: "But when you weren't here, he said words, he was alive. He's got legs under the ground, and a belly."

The father led his son back into the hut.

"No," he said, "it died a long time ago. It's you – you want to make everything alive because you've got a kind heart. Even a stone seems alive to you, and old grandma's living again on the moon."

"And grandpa's living on the sun!" said Nikita.

In the afternoon the father was planing boards in the shed,

to make a new floor for the hut, and he gave Nikita some work too – straightening the crooked nails with a little hammer.

Nikita eagerly got down to work, just like a grown-up. When he had straightened the first nail, he saw a kind little man in it, smiling at him from underneath his little iron hat. He showed it to his father and said to him: "Why were all the others so cross? The burdock was cross, and the tree stump, and the water people, but this man is kind."

The father stroked his son's fair hair and answered, "They were all people you thought up, Nikita. They're not there, they're not solid, that's what makes them cross. But you made the little nail-man by your own labour – that's why he's kind."

Nikita began to think.

"Let's make everything by our own labour. Then everything will come alive."

"Yes, let's!" agreed the father.

He was sure Nikita would remain a kind person all his life long.

THE RETURN

ALEXEY ALEXEEVICH IVANOV, A GUARDS CAPTAIN, HAD been demobilized and was leaving the army. His unit, in which he had served all through the war, gave him a send-off, as was fitting, with regret, love and respect, with music and with wine. His close friends and comrades accompanied him to the railway station and, after saying their final goodbyes, left him there on his own. But the train had been delayed for hours; and, after those long hours had passed, it went on being even more delayed. A cold autumn night was already beginning; the station building had been destroyed in the war and there was nowhere to spend the night, so Ivanov got a lift from a car going his way and returned to his unit. The following day Ivanov's fellow servicemen gave him another send-off; once again they sang songs and embraced the departing man to show their eternal friendship, but this time they expended their feelings more briefly and the party was just a group of close friends.

Then Ivanov set out for the station a second time; at the station he learned that yesterday's train had still not arrived, so he could indeed have gone back to his unit for one more night. But it would have been awkward to be seen off a third time and cause his comrades more trouble, and Ivanov stayed, ready for a long wait on the deserted asphalt of the platform.

Near the points just beyond the station stood a pointsman's hut which had survived the war. A woman in a padded jacket and a warm headscarf was sitting on a bench beside the hut; she had been there with her luggage the day before, and she was still sitting there, waiting for the train. The day before, as he left to spend the night with his unit, Ivanov had wondered whether to invite this lone woman back with him: she could sleep in the warm with the nurses; why leave her to freeze all night? – there was no knowing if she would ever get warm in the pointsman's hut. But while he was wondering, the car had begun to move and Ivanov had forgotten about the woman.

Now the woman was still there, still motionless and in the same place as before. Such constancy and patience showed the loyalty and immutability of a woman's heart – at least in relation to her possessions and her home, to which the woman was most likely returning. Ivanov went up to her: maybe she too would find it less dull to have company than to be on her own.

The woman turned her face towards Ivanov and he recognized her. It was a young woman they had called "Masha the bath-house-attendant's daughter" because this was what she had once called herself – she really was the daughter of someone who had worked in a bathhouse. Ivanov had come across her now and then during the war, on his visits to an Airfield Service Battalion where this bathhouse Masha worked as a civilian assistant to the canteen cook.

The autumn countryside around them felt gloomy and forlorn at this hour. The train which was to take both Masha and Ivanov to their homes was somewhere far off in grey space. There was nothing to divert or comfort a human heart except another human heart.

Ivanov got into conversation with Masha and began to feel better. Masha was a straightforward and good-looking girl, and there was a kindness in her large worker's hands and her healthy young body. She too was returning home and wondering what it would be like to start living a new civilian life; she had got used to the airforce women, and to the pilots who loved her like an elder sister, gave her chocolate and called her "Big Masha" because of her height and the way she had room in her heart for all her brothers at once, like a real sister, and not just for one of them in particular. It was unaccustomed and strange, and even frightening, to be going home to relatives she was no longer used to.

Ivanov and Masha felt orphaned now without the army, but Ivanov could never stay sad or despondent for long; if he did, he would feel as if someone were laughing at him from a distance and being happy instead of him, while all he did was scowl like a half-wit. So he would always turn back quickly to the business of living; he would find something to be interested in or consoled by, some simple makeshift pleasure, as he put it himself, and would thus escape his depression.

He moved up closer to Masha and asked her to let him give her a comradely kiss on the cheek. "Just a tiny one," he said, "because the train's late and it's so boring waiting for it."

"Only because the train's late?" asked Masha, looking intently at Ivanov's face.

The ex-captain looked about thirty-five; the skin of his face was brown, wind-beaten and sunburnt; his grey eyes looked at Masha modestly, even shyly, and his speech, though direct, was tactful and courteous. Masha liked the hoarse, husky voice of this older man, his rough dark face and the expression it had of strength and defencelessness. Ivanov put out his pipe with a thumb that was inured to the smouldering heat, and sighed as he waited for permission. Masha drew away from Ivanov. He smelt strongly of tobacco and dry toast, and a little wine – pure substances that come from fire or else can give birth to fire. It was as if Ivanov fed solely on tobacco, rusks, beer and wine.

He repeated his request. "I'll be careful, Masha, just a surface kiss . . . Imagine I'm your uncle."

"I already have. Only not my uncle – my father."

"Splendid. So you'll let me?"

"Fathers don't ask for permission," Masha laughed.

Ivanov was to say to himself later that Masha's hair smelt of autumn leaves fallen in the forest, and he was never able to forget it . . . He walked away from the railway line and lit a small fire to fry some eggs for his and Masha's supper.

In the night the train arrived and carried Ivanov and Masha away, towards their homes. They travelled together for two days, and on the third day they reached the town where Masha had been born twenty years before. She collected her things together in the carriage and asked Ivanov to settle the bag more comfortably on her back, but Ivanov took her bag on his own shoulders and followed Masha out of the carriage, even though he had more than a day's journey still ahead of him.

Masha was surprised and touched by Ivanov's considerateness. She was afraid of finding herself suddenly alone in the town she had been born in, and had lived in, but which was now almost a foreign country to her. Her mother and father had been deported by the Germans and had died in some unknown place; now Masha had only a cousin and two aunts in her home town, people to whom she felt no real attachment.

Ivanov arranged with the station commandant to break his journey, and stayed with Masha. Really he should have hurried on to his own home, where his wife and two children, whom he had not seen for four years, were waiting for him. But Ivanov was putting off the joyful and anxious moment of reunion with his family. He was not sure why he was doing this – perhaps he wanted to enjoy his freedom a little longer.

Masha did not know Ivanov's family circumstances, and girlish shyness prevented her from asking. She trusted herself to him in the goodness of her heart, with no thought beyond the moment.

Two days later Ivanov resumed his journey home. Masha

saw him off at the station. He kissed her in a habitual way and promised courteously to remember her image for ever.

Masha smiled in reply and said, "Why remember me for ever? There's no need – and anyway you won't . . . I'm not asking you for anything. Forget me."

"My dear Masha! Where were you before? Why didn't I meet you long, long ago?"

"Before the war I was at school, and long long ago I didn't exist at all."

The train arrived and they said goodbye. Ivanov departed and did not see how Masha, left on her own, began to cry because she could not forget any friend or comrade, or anyone at all whose path had even once crossed hers.

Ivanov looked out of the carriage window at the small houses of the little town they were passing and which he was unlikely ever to see again in his life, and reflected that in a house just like one of these, though in another town, his wife Lyuba lived with their children, Petya and Nastya, and that they were expecting him; he had sent his wife a telegram when he was still with his unit, saying he was coming home without delay and that he longed to embrace her and the children as soon as he possibly could.

For the last three days Lyubov Vasilyevna, Ivanov's wife, had been to meet all the trains coming from the west. She took time off work, failed to fulfil her norm, and was unable to sleep at night for joy, listening instead to the slow indifferent movement of the pendulum of the wall clock. On the fourth day Lyubov Vasilyevna sent Petya and Nastya to the station – to meet their father if he came during the day – but once again went to meet the night train herself.

Ivanov arrived on the sixth day. He was met by his son Petya. Petya was now getting on for twelve, and the father did not immediately recognize his son in this serious lad who seemed older than his years. The father saw that Petya was a thin, under-sized little boy, but with a large head, a broad forehead and a calm face that seemed already accustomed to life's cares, while his small brown eyes looked at the world around him morosely and disapprovingly, as if all they saw everywhere was disorder. Petya was neatly dressed and shod: his boots were worn but still had some use in them, his trousers and jacket were old, cut down from his father's civilian clothing, but there were no holes in them, they had been darned and patched where necessary; all in all, Petya was like a little peasant who had no money to spare but who took care of his clothes. His father was surprised, and he sighed.

"So you're my father, are you?" asked Petya, when Ivanov lifted him up and hugged and kissed him. "You must be!"

"Yes, I am. Hello, Pyotr Alexeevich!"

"Hello. Why have you been so long? We've been waiting and waiting."

"It was the train, Petya. It was very slow. How are your mother and Nastya? Alive and well?"

"They're fine," said Petya. "How many decorations have you got?"

"Two, Petya, and three medals."

"And mother and I thought your chest would be covered with them. Mother has two medals as well. She got them for good service . . . Why haven't you got any more luggage – just a bag?"

"I don't need any more."

"I suppose a travelling trunk gets in the way when you're fighting?" asked the son.

"Yes," the father agreed. "It's easier with just a bag. No one there uses a trunk."

"And I thought you all did. I'd keep my things in a trunk – in a bag things get crumpled and broken."

Petya took the bag and carried it home while his father walked along behind him.

The mother met them on the porch; she had asked for time off work again, as if she had sensed in her heart that her husband would arrive that day. She had gone straight home from the factory, meaning to go on from there to the station. She was afraid Semyon Yevseevich might have turned up at the house. He liked to drop in sometimes during the day; turning up in the afternoon and sitting with Petya and five-year-old Nastya had become a habit of his. True, Semyon Yevseevich never came empty-handed, he always brought something for the children – sweets or sugar, a small loaf of white bread or a coupon for shoes and clothing. Lyubov Vasilyevna had never had anything to reproach Semyon Yevseevich for; all these two years they had known each other he had been good to her, and he had been like a father to the children, kinder, in fact, than many a father. But Lyubov Vasilyevna did not want her husband to see Semyon Yevseevich today; she tidied up the kitchen and the living room, wanting the house to be clean, with nothing that did not belong there. Later, tomorrow, or the next day, she herself would tell her husband everything, all that had happened. Fortunately, Semyon Yevseevich had not come that day.

Ivanov went up to his wife, put his arms round her and stood there with her, not moving away, feeling the forgotten and familiar warmth of someone he loved.

Little Nastya came out of the house and, after looking at the father she did not remember, started pushing at his leg, trying to separate him from her mother; then she burst out crying. Petya stood silently beside his father and mother, with his father's bag on his back; after waiting a while, he said: "That's enough, you two – Nastya's crying, she doesn't understand."

The father moved away from the mother and picked Nastya up. She was crying from fear.

"Nastya!" Petya called to her. "Calm down, I tell you! This is our father, he's one of the family."

Once inside the house, the father had a wash and sat down at the table. He stretched out his legs, closed his eyes and felt a quiet joy in his heart, a peaceful satisfaction. The war was over. During it his feet had walked thousands of versts.[1] Lines of tiredness lay on his face, and his eyes felt a stabbing pain beneath their closed lids – they wanted to rest now in twilight or darkness.

While he sat there, the whole family bustled about in the living room and in the kitchen, preparing a celebration meal. Ivanov examined, one after another, all the objects around the house – the clock, the crockery cupboard, the wall thermometer, the chairs, the flowers on the window sills, the Russian kitchen stove. They had lived here a long time without him, and they had missed him. Now he had come back and he was looking at them, getting to know each one of them again, as if they were relatives whose lives had been poor and lonely without him. He breathed in the familiar, unchanging smell of the house – smouldering wood, warmth from his children's bodies, a burning smell from the grate. This smell had been just the same four years ago, it had not dispersed or changed in his absence. Nowhere else had Ivanov ever smelt this smell, although in the course of the war he had been in several countries and hundreds of homes; the smells there had been different, always lacking the special quality of his own home. Ivanov also recalled the smell of Masha, the scent of her hair; but that had been a smell of leaves in a forest, of some overgrown path he did not know, a smell not of home but once again of unsettled life. What was she doing now and how was she coping with civilian life,

Masha the bathhouse-attendant's daughter? God be with her . . .

Ivanov could see that the busiest person around the house was Petya. Not only did he work hard himself, but he also told his mother and Nastya what to do and what not to do, and how to do everything properly. Nastya was obeying Petya meekly and was no longer afraid of her stranger-father; she had the alert and attentive face of a child who did everything in life seriously and truthfully, and she surely had a kind heart too, since she did not mind Petya.

"Nastya, empty the potato peelings out of the mug, I need it."

Nastya obediently emptied the mug and washed it. Meanwhile their mother was quickly making a spur-of-the-moment pie, without yeast, to put in the stove; Petya had already got the fire going.

"Come on, Mother, get a move on!" Petya commanded. "You can see I've got the stove ready. You're not much of a Stakhanovite,[2] you're a dawdler!"

"Just a minute, Petya, I'm nearly there," said his mother obediently. "I'll just put some raisins in and it'll be done. It must be a long time since your father had raisins. I've been saving them for ages."

"He's had raisins all right," said Petya. "Our troops get raisins. Just look at their fat faces – they get enough food all right. Nastya, why are you sitting down – think you're a guest here? Go on, peel some potatoes, we're going to fry some for supper. You can't feed a whole family on nothing but pie!"

While his mother was making the pie, Petya took the large oven-fork and put a cast-iron pot of cabbage soup in the oven, so the heat would not go to waste; as he did this, he even admonished the fire: "Why are you burning so messily, jumping about all over the place? Just burn evenly, and stay under the food – what do you think the trees in the forest grew up to make firewood for? And you, Nastya, why have you shoved the kindling into the stove just any old how? You should have laid it the way I taught you. And you're peeling too much off the potatoes again, you should peel them thinly and not dig out the flesh – that's how our food gets wasted! How many times do I have to tell you? This is the last time – do it again and you'll get a clout round the head!"

"Petya, why keep getting at Nastya?" their mother said gently. "Just think for a moment! How can she peel so many potatoes, and do them all just as you want them, like a barber never nicking the flesh? Father's come home, and all you can do is find fault!"

"I'm not finding fault, I'm talking sense. Father needs feeding, he's just back from the war, and you two are wasting good food. Think how much we've wasted in potato peelings in a whole year! If we'd had a sow, we could have fed her all year on potato peelings alone, then taken her to the show and been given a medal. Just imagine it! But you don't understand."

Ivanov had not known that his son had turned out like this; he sat and marvelled at his cleverness. But he preferred gentle little Nastya, who was also working away at household tasks. Her little hands were quick and deft – they must have had a lot of practice.

"Lyuba," Ivanov said to his wife, "why aren't you saying anything to me? Tell me how you've got on without me. How's your health been? And what work do you do?"

Lyubov Vasilyevna felt shy of her husband now, like a young bride; she was not used to him any more. She even blushed when he spoke to her and, just as in her youth, her face took on the timid, scared expression which Ivanov found so attractive.

"We've been all right, Alyosha. The children haven't been ill too often. I've taken care of them. The bad thing is that I've only been here with them at night. I work at the brick factory, at the press. It's a long way on foot."

"Where do you work?" said Ivanov, not understanding.

"At the brick factory, at the press. I had no qualifications, of course, so at first I just did odd jobs outside. Then they gave me some training and put me on the press. It's been good to be working – only the children have been alone all the time. You can see how they've turned out. They know how to do everything themselves, they're like grown-ups," Lyubov Vasilyevna said quietly. "Whether that's a good thing, Alyosha, I just don't know."

"We shall see, Lyuba . . . We'll all be living together now. There'll be time enough to work out what's good and what's bad."

"Everything will be better now you're here. When I'm on my own I don't know what's right and what's wrong, and I've been afraid. Now it's for you to think about how to bring up the children."

Ivanov stood up and paced about the room.

"So, all in all, you've kept in good spirits, have you?"

"It's been all right, Alyosha, and it's over now, we've stuck it out. Only we missed you dreadfully and we were afraid you'd never come back to us. We were afraid you'd die there, like others have . . ."

She began to cry over the pie, which she had already placed in its iron mould, and her tears dropped onto the dough. She had just smeared the top of the pie with beaten egg and was still smoothing it with her palm, now smearing the festive pie with her tears.

Nastya gripped her mother's leg in her arms, pressed her face into her skirt and stared up at her father sternly from beneath her brows.

Her father bent down to her. "What's the matter, Nastya, what's wrong? Are you cross with me?"

He gathered her up in his arms and stroked her head. "What's the matter, little daughter? You've completely forgotten me, haven't you? You were tiny when I went away to the war."

Nastya laid her head on her father's shoulder and she too began to cry.

"What is it, little Nastenka?"

"Mummy's crying, so I'm crying too."

Petya, who was standing in front of the stove, was bewildered and annoyed.

"What's the matter with you all? While you're all having moods, the heat's going to waste. Do you want the stove heated up all over again? Who'll give us coupons for more wood? We've used up the last lot, there's just a tiny bit left in the shed – about ten logs, and it's only aspen. Give me the dough, mother, before the heat all gets lost."

Petya took out the big iron pot of cabbage soup and raked the embers on the floor of the stove, and Lyubov Vasilyevna, as if trying to please Petya, hurriedly put the two pies in, forgetting to brush the second one with egg.

Ivanov was finding his own home strange and rather hard to understand. His wife was the same, with her sweet, shy, though now deeply exhausted face, and the children were the same ones that had been born to him, except that they had grown older during the war, as was to be expected. But something was stopping Ivanov from feeling whole-hearted joy at being back home – no doubt he was simply not used to family life any more and so was unable to understand even those nearest and dearest to him. Looking at Petya, his firstborn, now so grown-up, listening as Petya gave commands and instructions to his mother and little sister, watching his worried, serious face, Ivanov confessed to himself with a sense of shame that he did not feel fatherly enough towards this boy, that he did not feel drawn to his own son. Ivanov was all the more ashamed of this lack of fatherly feeling because he was aware that Petya needed love and care more than the others did, for it was painful to look at him. Ivanov did not know in any detail how his family had lived while he was away, and he could not yet grasp at all clearly why Petya had come to be like this.

Sitting at the table, amongst his family, Ivanov realized what he had to do. He must get to work as soon as he could – he had to find a job and earn money, and help his wife bring up the children properly; then everything would gradually get better, and Petya would start running about with other children, or sitting with a book, not standing at the stove with an oven-fork in his hands and giving orders.

During the meal Petya ate less than anyone else, but he scooped up all the crumbs and tipped them into his mouth.

"What are you doing, Petya?" his father asked him. "Why are you eating crumbs when you haven't finished your pie? Eat it up and your mother will cut you another piece."

"I could eat it all up," Petya said with a frown. "But I've had enough."

"He's afraid that if he starts eating a lot, then Nastya will copy him and eat a lot too," Lyubov Vasilyevna explained straight-forwardly. "And that worries him."

"You're not worried about anything," said Petya unemotion-ally. "I just want there to be more for you."

Father and mother glanced at each other and shivered at their son's words.

"Well, and why aren't you eating?" the father asked little Nastya. "Are you copying Petya? Eat up, or you won't grow up to be a big girl."

"I am a big girl," said Nastya.

She ate a small piece of pie, but pushed away another, bigger piece and covered it with a napkin.

"What are you doing?" her mother asked. "Shall I put some butter on it for you?"

"No, I'm full up."

"Well eat it like that then. Why've you pushed it away?"

"Because Uncle Semyon might come. I'm leaving it for him. It's not your pie, it's my pie I'm not eating. I'm putting it under my pillow so it doesn't get cold."

Nastya got down from her chair; she took the pie wrapped up in a napkin over to her bed, and put it under the pillow.

Her mother remembered how she herself had once laid pillows over a pie she had baked for May Day, to keep it warm for Semyon Yevseevich.

"Who is this Uncle Semyon?" Ivanov asked his wife.

Lyubov Vasilyevna did not know what to say. "I don't know who he is," she said. "He comes on his own to see the children. His wife and his own children were killed by the Germans, he's grown fond of our two and he comes here to play with them."

"To play with them?" said Ivanov in surprise. "What kind of games do they play when he comes? How old is he?"

Petya looked quickly at his mother, then at his father; his mother did not answer his father's question, she only looked at Nastya with sad eyes. The father smiled unpleasantly, got up from his chair, lit a cigarette and then asked Petya, "Where are the toys you and this Uncle Semyon play with?"

Nastya got down from her chair, climbed up onto another chair by the chest of drawers, took out some books and brought them to her father. "They're book toys," she said. "Uncle Semyon reads them out loud to me. Look what a funny teddy bear, he's a toy and he's a book too . . ."

Ivanov took the book toys his daughter handed him:

about Misha the Bear, and a toy cannon, and the little house where Granny Domna lived, spinning flax with her grand-daughter . . .

Petya remembered it was time to close the damper in the stove-pipe, so the warmth would not escape from the house. After closing the damper, he said to his father, "Semyon Yevseevich is older than you . . . He helps us out, leave him in peace."

Glancing out of the window just in case, Petya noticed that the clouds in the sky were not the right kind of clouds for September. "Look at those clouds," he said. "They're the colour of lead – they must be full of snow. Don't say winter's going to set in tomorrow! What will we do? We haven't dug up the potatoes yet, we haven't stocked up on food. What a situation to be in!"

Ivanov looked at his son, listened to him talking and realized he felt shy of him. He would have liked to ask his wife more about this Semyon Yevseevich who had been coming to visit for the last two years, and whether it was Nastya this man came to see or his good-looking wife, but Petya distracted Lyubov Vasilyevna by talking about household matters: "Mother, give me tomorrow's bread coupons and the registration cards, and give me the paraffin coupons as well – tomorrow's the last day and we must get our charcoal, oh but you've lost the sack, they won't give us any charcoal without one, you must have a good look for the sack right now, or else sew a new one out of rags, how can we manage without a sack? And tell Nastya not to let anyone into our yard tomorrow for water – they take too much from the well; with winter coming the water will drop and our rope's not long enough to let the bucket down lower, and we don't want to have to eat snow, anyway we'd need firewood to thaw it out."

As he said all this, Petya swept up around the stove and

sorted out the kitchen utensils. Then he took the pot of soup out of the oven.

"We've had some pie and now we're having some cabbage-and-meat soup, with bread," Petya announced. "And you, father, must go first thing tomorrow to the District Soviet and the Military Commissariat. Then you'll be put on the list straight away and we'll get ration cards for you more quickly."

"All right," said the father obediently.

"Yes, and mind you don't oversleep and forget."

"I won't," the father promised.

Their first shared meal after the war – soup with meat – was eaten by the family in silence, with even Petya sitting there calmly; it was as if father and mother and children were afraid of destroying, through some chance word, the quiet happiness of a family sitting together.

Then Ivanov asked his wife, "How have you managed for clothes, Lyuba? Is everything worn out?"

"We've been wearing all old things, but now we can buy something new," Lyubov Vasilyevna smiled. "I had to mend the children's clothes while they stood up in them. Then I cut down your suit, your two pairs of trousers and all your underclothes. There was no money to spare, you see, and the children had to wear something."

"You did right," said Ivanov. "Children shouldn't have to go without."

"They haven't had to. I even sold the coat you bought me. Now I wear my padded jacket."

"Her jacket's too short. She could catch cold in it," commented Petya. "I'll go and work as a stoker at the bathhouse. I'll earn some money and get her a coat. People bring clothes to sell at the market, I've had a look and checked the prices. Some of the coats are all right."

"We can get by without you and your wages," said the father.

After dinner Nastya put a large pair of glasses on her nose and sat by the window to darn the little knitted mittens her mother now wore at the factory inside her work mittens. It was already autumn; the weather had turned cold.

Petya glanced across at his sister and began to scold her: "What are you up to now? Why have you got Uncle Semyon's glasses on?"

"I'm not looking through them, I'm looking over them."

"Oh really! I can see what you're doing! You'll ruin your eyesight and go blind, then you'll be on a pension and be a burden for the rest of your life. Take the glasses off this minute, I tell you, and stop darning those mittens, mother will darn them, or I'll do them myself as soon as I have a moment. Get out your exercise book and practise your writing – goodness knows when you last did any!"

"Does Nastya go to school then?" asked the father.

Their mother replied that Nastya was not yet big enough for school, but that Petya made her do lessons every day; he had bought her an exercise book, and she practised drawing the strokes for letters. Petya was also teaching his sister to do sums, adding and subtracting pumpkin seeds in front of her, while Lyubov Vasilyevna was herself teaching Nastya to read.

Nastya put down the mitten and took an exercise book and a pen and nib out of the chest of drawers, while Petya, satisfied that everything was being done properly, put on his mother's padded jacket and went outside to chop wood for the next day; he usually brought the firewood into the house at night and laid it behind the stove to dry out, so it would give out more heat and be more efficient.

In the evening Lyubov Vasilyevna got supper ready early. She wanted the children to go to sleep in good time so that she and her husband could sit together and talk. But the children did not fall asleep until long after supper; Nastya, lying on the wooden couch, kept watching her father from under the blanket, while Petya, who had lain down on the Russian stove he always slept on, winter and summer alike, tossed and turned, grunting and whispering something, and it was quite some time before he quietened down. But the night wore on, and Nastya closed her eyes that were tired from looking, while Petya started to snore on the stove.

Petya always slept lightly and on his guard: he was afraid something might happen in the night and he would not hear – a fire, or robbers breaking in, or his mother might forget to latch the door and it would come open during the night and all the warmth would escape. This time it was the troubled voices of his parents that woke him; they were talking in the room next to the kitchen. What time it was – midnight or nearly morning – he did not know, but his father and mother were not asleep.

"Alyosha, don't make so much noise, the children will wake up," his mother was saying quietly. "You mustn't say bad things about him, he's a good man, and he's loved your children."

"We don't need his love," said the father. "I love my children myself. Loving other people's children – I like that! I sent you certificates regularly and you had your job – what did you need this Semyon Yevseevich for? Still hot-blooded, are you? Oh Lyuba, Lyuba! You're not the woman I thought you were . . . You've made a fool of me."

The father fell silent, then struck a match to light his pipe.

"What are you saying, Alyosha? How can you?" the mother burst out. "When I've brought up the children and they've hardly ever been ill and they've got plenty of flesh on them."

"So what?" said the father. "Some women were left with four children, but they managed all right, and their kids are no worse than ours. And as for Petya and the way you've brought him up – he carries on like an old man, but it wouldn't surprise me if he's forgotten how to read."

From his place on the stove Petya sighed and then pretended to snore, so he could go on listening. "All right," he thought, "maybe I am an old man, but it was all very well for you – you didn't have to worry where your next meal was coming from!"

"Yes, but he's learnt some of life's hardest lessons!" said the mother. "And he doesn't fall behind in his schoolwork."

"Who is this Semyon of yours?" said the father angrily. "Stop leading me up the garden path."

"He's a good man."

"You love him, do you?"

"Alyosha, I'm the mother of your children."

"Go on, give me a straight answer."

"I love you, Alyosha. I'm a mother. It's a long time since I was a woman, and that was only ever with you. I can't even remember when it was."

The father said nothing, smoking his pipe in the darkness.

"I've missed you, Alyosha. Of course I had the children, but that's not the same as having you. I was waiting for you all the time, all those long terrible years. Often I was afraid to wake up in the morning."

"What's his job, where does he work?"

"He works at our factory, in the supplies section."

"I see, a swindler."

"He isn't a swindler. I don't know . . . His whole family were killed in Mogilyov. There were three children, the daughter was already grown up."

"Doesn't matter. He found himself another family, ready-made, and a woman who's still quite young, and good-looking – he's got things nice and cosy again."

The mother did not reply. There was a silence, but soon Petya could hear his mother crying.

"He talked to the children about you, Alyosha," she began, and Petya could tell that big tears were hovering in her eyes. "He told the children how you were fighting for us and how you were suffering. They'd ask why, and he'd say because you're a good man."

The father gave a laugh and knocked the ash out of his pipe.

"So that's the kind of man he is, your Semyon Yevseevich! Never even seen me, yet he sings my praises. Quite a character!"

"No, he's never seen you. He made things up, so the children would go on loving you, so they wouldn't lose touch with their father."

"But why? Why was he doing it? Because he wanted you and he was in a hurry? Go on, tell me, what was he after?"

"Maybe he just has a kind heart, Alyosha, maybe that's why. Why shouldn't it be?"

"I'm sorry, Lyuba, but you're a fool. No one does things for nothing!"

"But Semyon Yevseevich often brought things for the children. He always brings something – sweets, white flour, sugar. Not long ago he brought Nastya some felt boots, only they were no good, they were too small. And he's never asked for anything from us. We didn't need anything either, Alyosha, we could have managed without his presents, we'd got used to the way we were living, but Semyon Yevseevich says he feels better when he's doing something for other people, it stops him missing his dead family so badly. It really isn't what you think – you'll see when you meet him."

"You're talking nonsense!" said the father. "Stop trying to trick me ... I'm fed up with you, Lyuba. And I still want to enjoy life."

"Enjoy life with us, Alyosha."

"While you're carrying on with Semyon Yevseevich?"

"I won't, Alyosha. He'll never come here again. I'll tell him to stop coming."

"So something has been happening, if it's going to stop? Oh Lyuba, how could you? You women are all the same."

"And what about you men?" the mother said in a hurt voice. "What do you mean – we're all the same? I'm not the same. I've been working day and night, we've been making linings for locomotive fireboxes. I've grown thin in the face and horrible-looking, no one recognizes me, beggars don't even ask me for money. I've had a hard time too, and the children were alone at home. I'd get back from work – and there was the stove to light, the supper to cook, it was dark, and the children were miserable. They couldn't help round the house like they do now, even Petya was still little. And it was then that Semyon Yevseevich started calling on us. He'd come round – and just sit with the children. He lives all on his own, you see. 'Can I come and visit you sometimes,' he asked, 'so I can warm up a bit?' I told him our house was cold too, and the firewood was damp, but he said, 'It's my soul that's chilled to the marrow. Just let me sit near your children, you don't need to heat up the stove for me.' 'All right,' I said, 'come round then. With you here the children won't be so frightened.' Then I got used to his visits too. We all began to feel better when he came. I'd look at him and think of you, I'd remember we had you . . . It was so sad without you, it was awful. Why not let someone come round? I thought. Time will pass quicker, we won't be so miserable. What use is time to us when you're not here?"

"Well go on, what happened after that?" said the father impatiently.

"Nothing happened after that. Now you're back, Alyosha."

"Well, all right then, if that's the truth," said the father. "It's time to get some sleep."

"Stay up a bit longer," the mother begged. "Let's talk, I'm so happy to be with you."

"Will they never quieten down?" thought Petya, lying on the stove. "They've made it up – what more do they want? Mother's got to get up early for work, but she's still wide awake. A fine time she's chosen to cheer up and stop crying!"

"And did this Semyon love you?" asked the father.

"Wait a minute. I'll go and tuck Nastya in, she gets uncovered in her sleep and she'll be cold."

The mother covered Nastya up with the blanket, went into the kitchen and paused by the stove to check whether Petya was asleep. Petya knew what she was up to and started to snore. Then she went back and he heard her voice again.

"I dare say he did love me. I saw him looking at me affectionately – and I'm not much to look at now, am I? Life's been hard on him, Alyosha, and he had to love somebody."

"You might at least have given him a kiss then, if that's the way things were," said the father in a nice voice.

"Don't be silly! He did kiss me, twice, but I didn't want him to."

"Why did he do it then, if you didn't want him to?"

"I don't know. He said he just lost his head, and that he was thinking of his wife, and I look a bit like her."

"And does he look like me?"

"No, he doesn't. No one's like you, Alyosha, you're the only one who's like you."

"The only one? Counting starts with one: first one, then two."

"He only kissed me on the cheek, not on the lips."

"Makes no difference where."

"Alyosha, it does make a difference. And what do you know about how things have been for us?"

"What do you mean? I've fought through the whole war, I've been closer to death than I am to you at this moment."

"While you were fighting, I was dying of worry. My hands were shaking from grief, but I had to keep working cheerfully. I had to feed the children and help our State against the Fascist enemy."

She was talking calmly, but her heart was heavy, and Petya was sorry for his mother; he knew that she had learnt to mend shoes for all three of them, not to have to pay a lot of money to the cobbler, and that she had repaired electric cooking rings for their neighbours in return for potatoes.

"I couldn't go on like that, longing for you," said the mother. "And if I had, it would have been the end of me, I know it would, and there were the children to think of. I needed to feel something else, Alyosha, some sort of happiness, just to get some rest. There was a man who said he loved me, and he was gentle to me, like you used to be long ago."

"You mean this Semyon Yevsey of yours?"

"No, someone else. He works as an instructor for our trade union district committee, he's an evacuee."

"To hell with who the man is! So what happened? Did he console you?"

Petya knew nothing about this instructor, and this surprised him. "So our mother's been naughty too," he whispered to himself. "Fancy that!"

"I got nothing from him, no joy at all," the mother replied. "Afterwards I felt even worse. My soul had been drawn to him because it was dying, but when he was close to me, really close, I felt nothing. All I thought about was household things, and I wished I hadn't let him be close. I realized I could only be calm and happy with you and that I'd only rest when you were close to me again. I'm lost without you, I can't even keep myself going for the children. Stay with us, Alyosha, we'll have a good life."

Petya heard his father get up from the bed without speaking, light his pipe and sit down on the stool.

"How many times did you meet him and be really close?" asked the father.

"Only once," said the mother. "It never happened again. How many times should I have?"

"As many times as you like, that's your business," declared the father. "So why say you're the mother of our children, and that you've only been a woman with me, a long time ago?"

"It's the truth, Alyosha."

"How can it be? What kind of truth? You were a woman with him too, weren't you?"

"No, I wasn't a woman with him, I wanted to be, but I couldn't. I felt I couldn't go on without you. I just needed someone to be with me, I was so worn out, my heart had gone all dark, I couldn't love my children any more, and you know I'd go through anything for them, I'd give the very bones from my body!"

"Just a minute," said the father. "You say you made a mistake with this second Semyon of yours. You didn't get any happiness from him – and yet here you are, you're still in one piece."

"Yes", whispered the mother. "I'm still alive."

"So you're lying to me again! So much for your truth!"

"I don't know," whispered the mother. "I don't know very much at all."

"All right, but I know a lot, I've been through more than you have," said the father. "You're a whore, that's what you are."

The mother was silent. The father's breathing was fast and laboured.

"So here I am, home at last," he said. "The war's over, and now you've wounded me in the heart . . . All right, you go and live with your Semyons. You've made a fool of me, you've turned me into a laughing-stock. But I'm not a plaything, I'm a human being."

In the dark the father began putting on his clothes and his shoes. Then he lit the paraffin lamp, sat down at the table, and wound up his watch.

"Four o'clock," he said to himself. "Still dark. It's true what they say: women a-plenty, but not a wife to be found."

It grew quiet in the house. Nastya was breathing evenly, asleep on the wooden couch. Up on the warm stove, Petya pressed his face into the pillow and forgot he was meant to be snoring.

"Alyosha," said the mother in a gentle voice. "Alyosha, forgive me."

Petya heard his father groan, and then heard the sound of breaking glass; through a gap in the curtain he could see it had got darker in the other room, though a light was still burning. "He's crushed the glass," Petya guessed. "And there's no lamp glass to be got anywhere."

"You've cut your hand," said the mother. "You're bleeding. Take a towel from the chest of drawers."

"Shut up!" the father shouted at her. "I can't stand the sound of your voice. Wake the children! Wake them up this very minute! Wake them, do you hear? I'll tell them what sort of mother they've got! I want them to know."

Nastya cried out in fear and woke up.

"Mummy!" she called out. "Can I get into bed with you?"

Nastya liked getting into bed with her mother in the night, to lie under the blanket with her and get warm.

Petya sat up on the stove, swung his legs over the edge, and said to everyone: "Go to sleep! Why have you woken me up? It's not day yet, it's still dark outside! Why are you making such a noise? Why is the lamp burning?"

"Go to sleep, Nastya, go back to sleep, it's still early, I'll come to you in a minute," the mother answered. "And you lie down, Petya, and don't talk any more."

"Why are you talking then?" said Petya. "And what does father want?"

"What's that to do with you?" the father replied. "A right sergeant-major you are!"

"And why have you smashed the lamp glass? Why are you frightening mother? She's thin enough as it is. She eats her potatoes without any butter, she gives all the butter to Nastya."

"And do you know what your mother's been up to here, do you know what she's been playing at?" the father cried plaintively, like a little boy.

"Alyosha!" Lyubov Vasilyevna said softly to her husband.

"Yes, I do, I know everything!" said Petya. "Mother's been crying for you, she's been waiting for you, and now you've come back home – and she's still crying! You're the one who doesn't know!"

"You don't understand anything yet!" said the father furiously. "A fine son we've produced!"

"I understand everything perfectly," Petya answered from the stove. "It's you who don't understand. There's work to do, we have to go on living, and you two are quarrelling like stupid fools."

Petya stopped. He lay down on his pillow; and silently, without meaning to, he began to cry.

"You've had things too much your own way in this house," said the father. "But it's all the same now. You can carry on being the boss."

Petya wiped away his tears and answered: "Some father you are, saying things like that, and you a grown-up who's been through the war! You should go to the war invalids' co-op tomorrow – you'll find Uncle Khariton there, behind the counter, he cuts the bread and he never cheats anyone. He's been in the war too and come back. Go and ask him – he tells everyone, he laughs about it, I've heard him myself. He's got a wife, Anyuta, she learnt to drive and now she delivers the bread, and she's a good woman, she doesn't steal any of it. Anyuta had a friend too, and she used to visit him and they'd have a drink and something to eat. This friend of hers has a decoration, he's lost an arm and he's in charge of the shop where you take your coupons to get clothes."

"Stop talking nonsense and go to sleep," said his mother. "It'll soon be light."

"Well, you two are stopping me sleeping . . . And it won't soon be light . . . This man with no arm made friends with Anyuta, life got better for them, but Khariton still lived at the war . . . Then Khariton comes back and starts cursing Anyuta. He curses her all day long and at night he has some vodka and something to eat, but Anyuta just cries and doesn't eat at all. He curses and curses, till he's tired out, then he stops tormenting Anyuta and says, 'You fool of a woman, having only one man – and a man with only one arm at that! When I was away on my own I had Glashka and I had Aproska, and then there was Maruska and Anyushka your namesake, and then I had Magdalinka into the bargain!' And he laughs. And Anyuta laughs too. And she starts boasting about her Khariton: what a fine man he is, no better man anywhere, he killed Fascists and he had so many women after him he couldn't ward them off . . . Uncle Khariton tells us all this in the shop, he's taking in the loaves of bread one by one . . . And now they're quite peaceful, they have a good life . . . And Uncle Khariton laughs again and says, 'But I deceived my Anyuta – I hadn't had any-one. No Glashka, no Nyushka, no Aproska, and no Magdalinka into the bargain. A soldier's the son of the Fatherland, he's got no time to fool around, his heart is levelled against the enemy. I just made all that up to give Anyuta a scare.' Go to bed, father, put the light out – without the glass it just smokes!"

Ivanov listened in amazement to this story told by his son. "What a devil!" he said to himself. "I kept thinking he'd start talking about my Masha."

Petya was exhausted and he began snoring; this time he really was asleep.

When he woke up it was broad daylight, and he was frightened to find he had slept so long and not yet done anything in the house.

No one was at home except Nastya. She was sitting on the floor turning the pages of a picture book her mother had bought her a long time ago. She looked through this book every day, because she had no other books, and traced the words with her finger, as if she were reading.

"Why are you messing up your book already?" Petya said to his sister. "Put it away. Where's mother? Has she gone to work?"

"Yes," answered Nastya quietly, closing the book.

"And where's father got to?" Petya looked round the house, in the kitchen and in the living room. "Has he taken his bag?"

"Yes, he has," said Nastya.

"What did he say to you?"

"Nothing. He kissed my mouth and my eyes."

"Did he?" said Petya, and began to think.

"Get up off the floor," he ordered his sister. "I'll give you a proper wash and get you dressed, we're going out."

At that moment their father was sitting in the station. He had already drunk a large glass of vodka and had got himself a hot meal with his travel voucher. In the night he had made up his mind once and for all to take the train to the town where he had left Masha and to meet up with her there again, perhaps never to part from her. A pity he was so much older than this bathhouse-attendant's daughter whose hair smelt of the countryside. But you can never tell – there's no knowing the future. All the same Ivanov hoped Masha would be at least a little bit glad to see him again; that would be enough, it would mean he too had a new and close friend, one, moreover, who was beautiful and cheerful and kind. You never can tell!

Soon the train arrived, going in the direction Ivanov had come from only yesterday. He took his kitbag and went onto the platform. "Masha isn't expecting me," he thought. "She told me I'd forget her, whatever I said, and that we'd never meet again; yet here I am, on my way to her for ever."

He got into a carriage and stood at the end of it, so that when the train pulled out he could look for a last time at the little town where he had lived before the war and where his children had been born. He wanted to look one more time at the house he had left; it could be seen from the train – the street it stood on led to the level crossing, and the train had to go over the crossing.

The train started, and went slowly over the points and out into the empty autumn fields. Ivanov took hold of the handrail and looked out from the carriage at what had been his home town – at the little houses, the bigger buildings, the sheds, the lookout tower of the fire station . . . In the distance he recognized two tall chimneys: one was the soap factory, the other was the brick factory – Lyuba would be working there now at the press. Let her live her own life now, and he would live his. Maybe he could forgive her, but what difference would that make? His heart had hardened against her now and there was no forgiveness in it for a woman who had kissed another man and lived with him just so that the war, and separation from her husband, would not make her so lonely and miserable. And the fact that it was the hardness of her life, and the torment of need and yearning, that had driven Lyuba to her Semyon or her Yevsey was no excuse; it was simply proof of her feelings. All love comes from need and yearning; if human beings never felt need or yearning, they would never love.

Ivanov was about to enter a compartment, to lie down and sleep; he no longer wanted a last look at the house where he had lived and where his children still did live: why torment oneself to no purpose? He looked out to see how far it was to the crossing – and there it was in front of him. It was here the railway crossed the track that led into the town; on this track lay wisps of straw and hay that had fallen off carts, and willow twigs and horse dung. There was rarely anyone on the track, except on the two market days of the week; just occasionally there would be a peasant on his way to the town with a full cart of hay, or on the way back to his village. That was how it was now: the track was deserted. All he could see, in the distance, running down the street that led into the track, were two children. One of them was bigger and one smaller, and the big one had taken the smaller one by the hand and was hurrying it along, but the small one, no matter how fast it tried to move its little legs, could not keep up with the bigger one. Then the bigger one began to drag the smaller one. They stopped at the last house of the town and looked towards the station, evidently wondering whether or not to go that way. Then they looked at the passenger train going over the crossing and began to run down the cart track, straight towards the train, as if suddenly wanting to reach it before it passed by.

Ivanov's carriage had passed the crossing. Ivanov picked up his bag, meaning to go through into the carriage and lie down for a sleep on the upper bunk where other passengers would not disturb him. But what about those two children? Had they managed to reach the train before the last carriage went by? Ivanov leaned out and looked back.

The two children, hand in hand, were still running along the track towards the crossing. They both fell down together, got up and ran on. The bigger one raised his one free hand and, turning his face towards Ivanov as the train passed by, began to beckon to someone, as if calling them to come back to him. Then they both fell down again. Ivanov could see that the bigger child had a felt boot on one foot and a rubber galosh on the other, which was why he kept falling.

Ivanov closed his eyes, not wanting to see and feel the pain of the exhausted children now lying on the ground, and then felt a kind of heat in his chest, as if the heart imprisoned and pining within him had been beating long and in vain all his life and had only now beaten its way to freedom, filling his entire being with warmth and awe. He suddenly recognized everything he had ever known before, but much more precisely and more truthfully. Previously, he had sensed the life of others through a barrier of pride and self-interest, but now, all of a sudden, he had touched another life with his naked heart.

Once more, from the carriage steps, he looked down the train towards the distant children. He knew now that they were his own children, Petya and Nastya. They must have seen him when the train was going over the crossing, and Petya had beckoned him home to their mother, but he had paid no attention, he had been thinking of something else and had not recognized his own children.

Now Petya and Nastya were a long way behind, running along the sandy path beside the rails; Petya was still holding little Nastya by the hand and dragging her along behind him when she was unable to move her legs quickly enough.

Ivanov threw his kitbag out of the carriage onto the ground, and then climbed down to the bottom step and got off the train, onto the sandy path along which his children were running after him.

TWO CRUMBS

ONCE THERE WERE TWO CRUMBS. THEY WERE BOTH small, and both black, but they had different fathers: one Crumb had been born to Bread, the other to Gunpowder. They lived in a beard, and the beard grew on the face of a hunter, and the hunter was asleep in a forest, lying on the grass while his dog dozed beside him.

It had all begun when the hunter ate some bread, loaded his gun, and then put his hand to his beard to straighten it; the two Crumbs had jumped off his palm and settled down in his beard.

So the two Crumbs lived side by side. They had no work to do, nothing to keep them busy, and so they started to boast.

"I," said the Crumb that had been born to Gunpowder, "am strong and terrifying. I am fire, I can set fire to the whole earth! And you?"

"I," answered the Bread Crumb, "can feed a man!"

"Feed him then!" said the Gunpowder Crumb. "But just see what I can do – I'll make him go up in flames!"

"Oh no you won't!" said the Bread Crumb. "A man can get mind from Bread, and with mind he can overcome fire! And I'm the daughter of Bread – so I must be stronger than you are!"

The Gunpowder Crumb got cross. "So you're stronger," she said, "but I'm more wicked!"

"You may be more wicked," replied the Bread Crumb, "but I'm more kind."

"We can see who's the stronger," said the Gunpowder Crumb. "If I explode now, I'll burn both you and the man right up. Then who'll be stronger?"

"You'll get the better of me," said the Bread Crumb, "but you won't overcome the man!"

"The man's asleep now," said the other Crumb. "I can get the better of him. You watch – I'm going to explode!"

"Wait a moment," said the Bread Crumb. "First it's my turn to try my strength."

"No," shouted the Gunpowder Crumb. "First it's my turn!"

"No – it's mine!"

"I'll set you on fire and burn you up!"

"I'll wake the man!"

"I'll set him on fire!"

"Oh no you won't! He's stronger than you are!"

The Gunpowder Crumb crawled up to the Bread Crumb, so she could get close and burn her better. But the Bread Crumb crawled out of the way. She crawled to the eye of the sleeping hunter. She saw an eyelid that had been closed over the eye, crawled up onto it and sat where everyone could see her. "What shall I do now?" she thought. She caught sight of a sparrow. The sparrow was sitting on a branch and looking at the Bread Crumb. He wanted to peck her up, but he was afraid of the Man.

"Eat me! I'm soft," said the Bread Crumb. "What's the use of going up in flames?" she was thinking. "I'd do better to feed a sparrow!"

But the Gunpowder Crumb had crept up right next to her. She was about to explode from rage.

The sparrow plucked up her courage, flew down from the branch and perched on the hunter's forehead. This woke the hunter. He opened his eyes, picked the Bread Crumb off his eyelid, looked at it, dropped it into his mouth and chewed it: why let good food go to waste? The sparrow quickly pecked up the Gunpowder Crumb, thinking it was a bread crumb, and shot up into the sky in fear.

The Bread Crumb then went right inside the man, turned into the man's blood, and became man herself. But the Gunpowder Crumb exploded immediately, inside the sparrow. The sparrow was roasted in the fire and fell to earth.

The hunter saw the roast sparrow drop onto the grass beside him and gave it to his dog. The dog ate the sparrow and looked up: perhaps another roast bird would fall from the sky?

The Bread Crumb, now a part of the man's life, smiled and pronounced: "She wanted to set fire to the whole earth, but all she could do was roast a sparrow!"

So ended the quarrel between two Crumbs in the beard of a sleeping man.

A NOTE ON TRANSLATING PLATONOV

Certain words recur with haunting frequency in Platonov's writing. We were not always able to use the same English word for each repetition. The important recurrence of words for "forget", "remember", "memory", in "The River Potudan", went into English unproblematically, as did some of the words that seem to be central in "The Locks of Epifan": "powerful", "abundant", "secret" and – a word I will dwell on – "wild" (*dikii*) with its verb "to go wild" (*odichat*).

"Wild" often has the same meaning in Russian as in English, but not always. We were able to follow Platonov's use of this word in such sentences as: "The Russes are wild and gloomy in their ignorance" (Ch. 1) or: "Tsar Peter is a most powerful man, although ... his understanding is the image of his country: secretly abundant, but of a wildness made manifest by its beasts and forests" (Ch. 1). (It is noteworthy that all four central words are applied to Peter here: powerful, secret, abundant, wild.) We could use the same word, too, when he writes of Perry's wish to work with the Tsar in civilizing "this wild and mysterious country".

But some occurrences of "wild" posed problems. "For four years I have lived as a wild man" seemed better when altered to ". . . as a savage" (Ch. 1). In this case, it was a matter of choosing an English word that would be as normal in its context as the Russian word was in its own, even if the choice meant under-emphasizing a leitmotif. But then there were two cases, towards the end of the story, where "wild", so often used until then of Russia and the Russians, began to be used – in its verb form *odichat* – of the English Perry and the German engineers, marking something of a climax in narrative and theme. Here we had to work hard to retain the key word.

The "five German engineers . . . had gone visibly wild". This would not do, nor would "gone native"(!), nor – though we pondered it for a long time – "had let themselves go". Finally we hit on "grown more wild" (Ch. 7); only when qualified by "grown" and "more" could the word "wild" be well used here. Later, Perry, at the height of catastrophe and facing certain death, "became wild in his heart, and in his thought he finally fell silent". This is again a literal translation which would not do. "Went wild" suggests "raged with anger", while what was meant was something like "lost touch with civilized ways of being", or (perhaps) "became like wild flowers – free and unconscious", or "like a wild animal – quiet, withdrawn, prowling". A good deal of thought and of experiment with paraphrases took place before we had the idea of combining "wild" with a notion taken from the second part of the same phrase: "mute". This removed the suggestion of rage yet preserved the surprising concept "wild". "Perry became wild and mute in his heart, and his mind was finally silent" (Ch. 9).

Every story had its difficulties, some simple, some complex. A simple problem, fundamental to all translating, arises when an otherwise satisfactory version turns out to contain an ambiguity. In "The River Potudan", Nikita "ran through the light air over the dark fields", but "light" has two meanings in English, and "not-dark" got in the way of the required meaning, "weightless" – which is what we finally put. But there were far more complex problems than this, sometimes because the Russian had no English equivalent, sometimes because Platonov used an ordinary phrase in some oddly changed way of his own. Sometimes both these things happened at once, as when Nikita enters Lyuba's room, which he has not seen for many years, *s zamershim chuvstvom*. *Zamershim* comes from a verb English does not have. The dictionary offers "to stand still, to freeze, to be rooted to the spot", yet it is often used with "heart" and may then be translated as "to sink" ("my heart sank") – not, however, in dismay or dread, as it always does sink in English, but in expectation of something unimaginable. Moreover, Platonov is using this verb, not about "heart", as would be conventional, but about "feeling" (chuvstvo), so that the phrase strikes a Russian reader as somehow weird. At first we translated it as "With stunned feeling". This, however, came to seem too close to "feeling stunned": it is Nikita's whole capacity for feeling that has been stunned. We finally translated the phrase as "With dazed heart", thus restoring "heart" while preserving the tinge of weirdness by giving it an unexpected adjective.

All Platonov's writing is different, not only from any standard or norm of Russian prose, but also from the ways in which other modernist writers have differed from that standard. There is no self-conscious inventiveness, exuberance of word play, astonishing alliteration or allusion. His style is indeed inventive and astonishing, with allusive and etymological subtleties, but all this usually in a subdued, melancholy, or apparently whimsical way that makes it seem so unlike that of any other prose that Joseph Brodsky once said Platonov had "no forebears in Russian literature".

The degree of strangeness varies from one story to another. We have tried to capture it in each of them by seeking equivalent English oddities and, above all, by keeping as close as we could, without sounding un-English, to the words and the word order of the originals.

A. L.

A NOTE ON THE PEASANT HUT

Most instances of the word "hut" (and some instances of the word "house") correspond to the Russian word *izba*. As *izba* and some of the words connected with it have different connotations from the corresponding English words, a note on some features of the traditional Russian rural dwelling may be useful.

In Northern and Central Russia, where wood was plentiful, the *izba* was built of logs (in the South it was of brick). Usually it was one storey high, with its floor raised two or three feet above ground level; this formed a cellar space beneath the house. On the outside, this part of the building was often surrounded by an earth ledge (*zavalinka*) – heaped earth held in by boards – which stopped cold air getting under the house and served as a bench in the summer. (A wealthier *izba* might be much larger than this, with several rooms and possibly an upper storey.)

Between the outer door or porch and the habitable room or rooms was an unheated entrance room (*seni*). This provided further insulation from the cold and could be used for storing tools and firewood or for housing animals.

In the long cold winter of Russia the question of heating has always been all-important. Platonov's stories frequently mention the stove (*pech*), sometimes calling it, more specifically, "the Russian stove". A Russian stove was a very large brick or clay structure taking up between one fifth and one quarter of the room it stood in. It was used for heating the house, for heating water, for baking bread and for all the cooking, for drying linen and foodstuffs, for conserving grain and plants, for protecting small farm animals (holes were made in its walls for them), and sometimes for taking a steam bath: when the fire had burnt out a person could climb right inside the stove's mouth.

Loaves or pies to be baked were placed deep inside the stove after the fuel had burnt out or had been raked to the side; they were handled by means of an oven-fork (*rogach* or *ukhvat*) – a long iron stick with two prongs, heavy enough to need two hands to lift it. Soup was cooked in a large cast-iron pot.

Beds as such were rare, but several sleeping places were arranged in relation to the stove. A sleeping bench (*lezhanka*) might be attached to one side of it to share its warmth; a wide shelf (*polati*) extended under the ceiling above it and could be slept on; and people often slept directly on the warm brick surface of the stove itself; this might be a few feet above the ground or as high as a person.

A very poor *izba* would have no chimney, the smoke going out through the door and window and inevitably blackening the inner walls. This was known as a "black izba" or hut "heated without a chimney". The bathhouse (*banya*) was also usually "black"; it was a small building separate from the house, with a wooden bench, a rough stove and cauldron of water, and with hot stones onto which water was splashed to raise steam.

A. L.

NOTES

INTRODUCTION

1. For this quotation, and for much of the biographical information in this introduction, I am indebted to the excellent commentaries by Natalya Kornienko in *Vzyskanie pogibshikh*, a selection of Platonov's work published in Moscow in 1995 by Shkola Press.

2. This date is uncertain. See Thomas Langerak, *Andrei Platonov*, Amsterdam, Pegasus, 1995, pp. 94–95. Even if the story was indeed written only in the mid-thirties, it remains Platonov's most vivid evocation of his youth.

3. First published in *Novyi mir*, 1991, No. 1.

4. This sentence casts an interesting light on the first page of "The Locks of Epifan".

5. Kornienko, p. 640.

6. Thomas Seifrid, *Andrei Platonov*, Cambridge, Cambridge University Press, 1992, p. 7.

7. Quoted in Kornienko, p. 638.

8. This connection is reinforced by Platonov's choice of vocabulary. He uses the diminutive *trubka* to refer both to the pipe Perry bites, and – surprisingly – to the *large* pipe that pierces through the lake-bed. See Geoffrey Smith, *Andrei Platonov, Constant Idealist of a Fickle Revolution*, M.Phil thesis, London, SSEES, pp. 96-97.

9. The historical Perry's first name was John.

10. For most of the following paragraph, as well as for the point about the importance of Perry's names, I am indebted to Eric Naiman, one of Platonov's most perceptive critics. See his forthcoming article, to be published in *Novoe literaturnoe Obozrenie*, "V zhopu proprubit okno: Seksualnaya patologiya kak ideologichesky kalambur u Andreya Platonova".

11. Platonov's own phrase.

12. Kornienko, op. cit., p. 662.

13. Platonov was a member of the Party only from 1920 to 1921. It seems likely that he was expelled; a record exists of his having

been regarded as "an unstable element". See Thomas Langerak, op. cit., p. 26.

14. Mikhail Heller, *Andrei Platonov v poiskakh schastya*, Paris, YMCA Press, 1982, p. 175.

15. Joseph Brodsky, *Less than One*, London, Penguin, 1987, p. 290

16. Heller, op. cit., p. 363.

17. Ibid., p. 362.

18. Most of what I have said about word play in "The Potudan River" is drawn from another article by Eric Naiman: "Andrei Platonov and the Inadmissibility of Desire", *Russian Literature XXIII*, 1988, pp. 319–66.

19. Quoted in Shentalinsky, *The KGB's Literary Archive*, London, Harvill, 1995, p. 211.

20. Thomas Seifrid has written that Platonov's story "For Future Use" purportedly inspired Stalin to write in its margins, "Talented, but a bastard". *Andrei Platonov: Uncertainties of Spirit*, Cambridge, Cambridge University Press, 1992, p. 137.

21. Quoted by Kornienko, op. cit., p. 633.

22. According to Kornienko, in conversation, no pages of Platonov's manuscripts bear the trace of such painstaking revision as those devoted to descriptions of steam engines.

23. The story must have been written in the late thirties or early forties, but the exact date is not known.

24. See John and Carol Garrard, *The Bones of Berdichev*, New York, The Free Press, 1996. *The Black Book* has still to be published within Russia.

25. Natalya Kornienko has recently unearthed an original version of the story "The Demand of the Dead", published in an army newspaper, which she considers to be greatly superior to the text she herself published in the volume *Vzyskanie pogibshikh* (private conversation).

THE MOTHERLAND OF ELECTRICITY

1. A pood is an old measure of weight, the equivalent of 40 lb.

2. Compare this with the following passage from Orlando Figes's account of the 1905 Revolution: "Some villagers even took the

paintings and statues, the Bohemian crystal and the English porcelain, the satin dresses and the powdered wigs, which they then divided among themselves, along with the livestock, the grain and the tools. In one village the peasants broke up a grand piano, which they had hauled away from the manor, and shared out the ivory keys." From *A People's Tragedy*, London, Cape, 1996, p. 182.

3. The Soviet regime classified peasants as either "poor peasants" (*bednyaki*), who had no property of their own, "middle peasants" (*srednaki*), who owned property but did not employ hired labour, or "rich peasants" (*kulaki*), who owned property and employed hired labour.

THE EPIFAN LOCKS

1. Present-day Theodosia, in the Crimea (tr.)
2. Platonov's geographical error, to be repeated later, may be indicative of how little was available to him in the way of source material. He wrote this story in Tambov, in conditions of extreme isolation.
3. A verst is slightly more than a kilometre.
4. A sazhen is slightly longer than a metre.
5. An arshin is about 3/4 of a metre.
6. Mine-master.
7. Peat-master.
8. As well as having difficulty with English pronunciation, the governor has created a Russian-style patronymic out of Perry's second name – Ramsay.
9. From a mediocre poem by Turgenev.
10. The second of the summer festivals in honour of the Saviour, held on August 6.

RUBBISH WIND

1. Where the Communists accused of burning down the Reichstag (February 23, 1933) were sentenced. In reality, the Nazis had started the fire themselves – in order to justify their initial persecutions of Communists, Jews, etc.

2. The death penalty by axe and executioner was introduced later [author's note].

3. The *Stahlhelms* or Steel Helmets were the youth wing of the *Deutsch-Nationale Volkspartei*, a far-right Party that competed unsuccessfully with the Nazis and was eventually absorbed by them. They can best be seen as an equivalent to the Brown Shirts.

THE RIVER POTUDAN

1. I.e. members of the Constitutional Democratic Party, a middle-class liberal party outlawed by the Bolsheviks in late 1917.

2. This and the following paragraph help to establish the politico-social background to the story. In 1921 Lenin, faced with industrial collapse and a peasantry that had been alienated by the forced requisitioning of grain, introduced the New Economic Policy or NEP. This allowed a considerable measure of private trade and manufacturing and was therefore seen by more radical Communists, including the young Platonov, as a betrayal of their ideals. A central theme of the story is the trauma caused by peace, the difficulty of adapting to a life without overt, heroic struggle.

3. See note 1 to "The Motherland of Electricity".

4. See note 3 to "The Epifan Locks".

NIKITA

1. Effectively a unit of payment on a collective farm. Workers were paid according to how many "work days" they completed. By working hard, it was possible to complete more than one "work day" during a day.

THE RETURN

1. See note 3 to "Epifan Locks".

2. Alexey Stakhanov : a coal-miner whose improbably vast output of coal led to his being held up as a model for workers and to the establishment of the "Stakhanovite Movement".

THE RETURN
and Other Stories

ANDREY PLATONOVITCH PLATONOV (1899–1951), the son of a railway-worker, was born near Voronzeh. He fought in the Red Army during the civil war, and then became an electrical engineer and land-reclamation specialist. From 1918 he published articles, verse and essays, passing from the optimistic vision of the pamphlet *Electrification* (1921), through a science-fiction trilogy, to the stories that began to appear, from 1926 on, in the "thick" Moscow journals. His talent was spotted early by Maxim Gorky, but after initial success, tales such as "Doubting Makar" (1929) and "For Future Use" (1931) were strongly criticized. Stalin is reputed to have written "scum" in the margin of the latter, and to have said to Fadeev (later to be Secretary of the Writes' Union) "Give him a good belting – 'for future use'". During the Great Patriotic War (1941–5) Palatonov worked as a war correspondent and once more began to receive some measure of official recognition. However, like Akhmatova and Zoshchenko, he came under attack again in the post-war clamp-down, and died of consumption caught from his teenage son whom he had nursed on his return from the Gulag in 1946. Although Platonov's stories began to be republished in the late 1950s, his major writings of the late 1920s and early '30s, including his two great novels, *The Foundation Pit* and *Chevengur*, remained unpublished in Russia until the late 1980s. When the KGB's "literary archive" was partially opened in the early 1990s, the draft of a previously unknown Platonov work, *The Technical Novel*, was discovered in his file.

ROBERT CHANDLER has translated a number of books from Russian, including Platonov's *The Foundation Pit* (co-translated with Geoffrey Smith), and Vasily Grossman's epic novel, *Life and Fate*.

ELIZABETH CHANDLER has over the years made an increasing contribution to her husband's translations.

ANGELA LIVINGSTONE has been a professor of Russian Literature at the University of Essex since 1992. She has published books on Pasternak and Lou Andreas-Salomé, and is the translator of Marina Tsvetaeva's essays on poetry.